PUFFIN BOOKS

# DIARY OF A WIMPY KID
# Do-It-Yourself Book

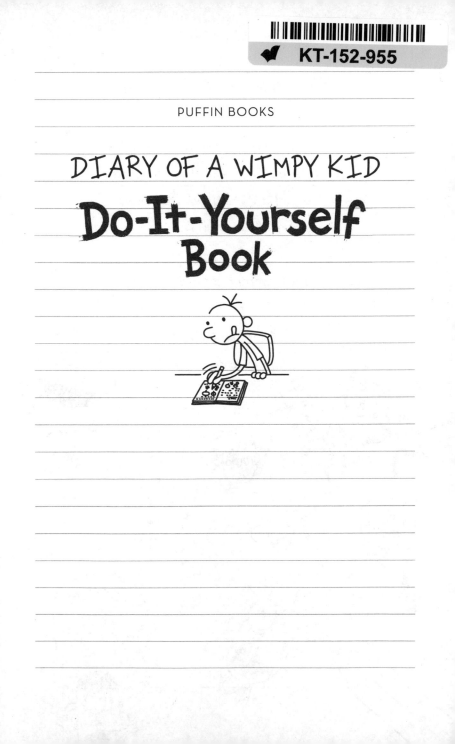

**OTHER BOOKS BY JEFF KINNEY**

*Diary of a Wimpy Kid*

*Diary of a Wimpy Kid: Rodrick Rules*

*Diary of a Wimpy Kid: The Last Straw*

*Diary of a Wimpy Kid: Dog Days*

*Diary of a Wimpy Kid: The Ugly Truth*

*The Wimpy Kid Movie Diary*

COMING SOON

*Diary of a Wimpy Kid 6*

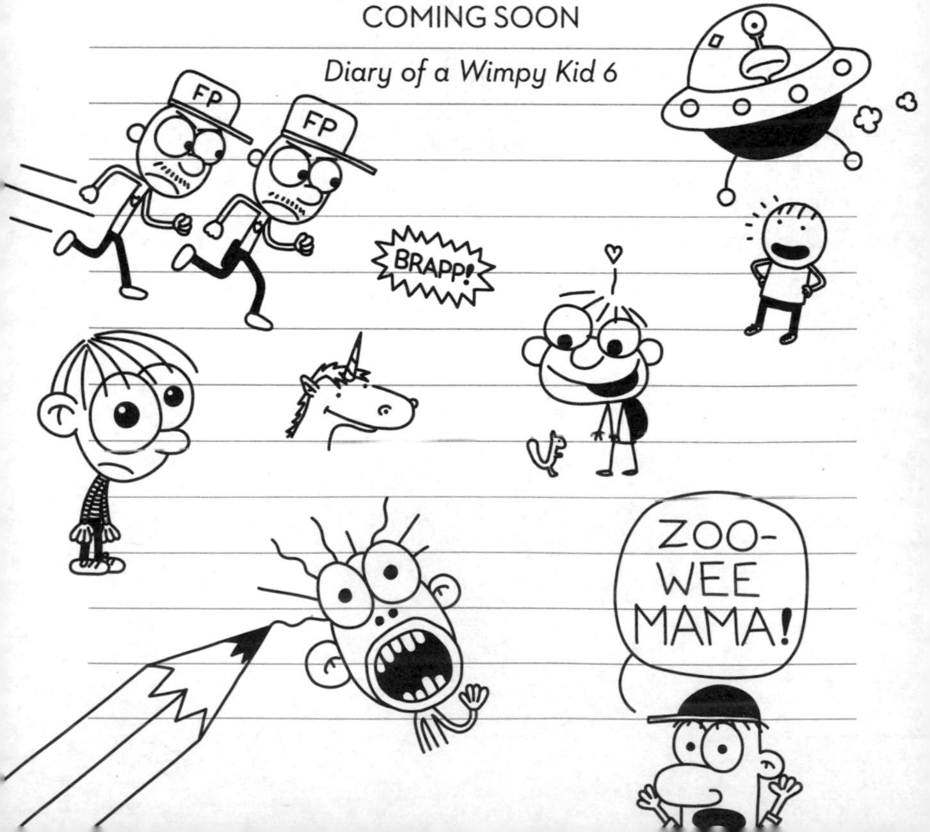
FP
FP
BRAPP!
ZOO-WEE MAMA!

# DIARY of a Wimpy Kid

# Do-It-Yourself Book

by Jeff Kinney

YOUR
PICTURE
HERE
↓

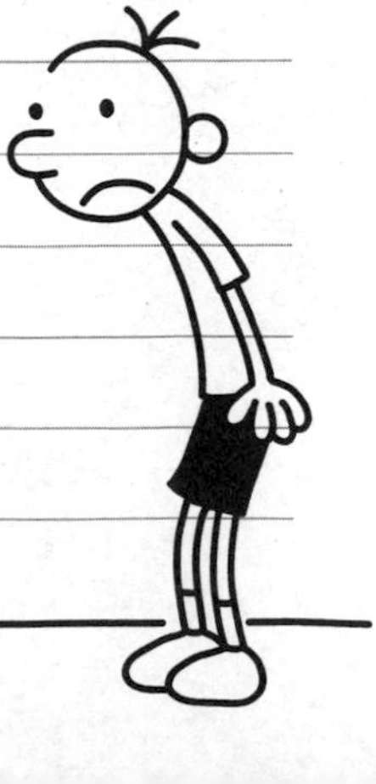

PUFFIN

PUFFIN BOOKS

Published by the Penguin Group
Penguin Books Ltd, 80 Strand, London WC2R ORL, England
Penguin Group (USA) Inc., 375 Hudson Street, New York, New York 10014, USA
Penguin Group (Canada), 90 Eglinton Avenue East, Suite 700, Toronto, Ontario, Canada M4P 2Y3
(a division of Pearson Penguin Canada Inc.)
Penguin Ireland, 25 St Stephen's Green, Dublin 2, Ireland (a division of Penguin Books Ltd)
Penguin Group (Australia), 250 Camberwell Road, Camberwell, Victoria 3124, Australia
(a division of Pearson Australia Group Pty Ltd)
Penguin Books India Pvt Ltd, 11 Community Centre, Panchsheel Park, New Delhi – 110 017, India
Penguin Group (NZ), 67 Apollo Drive, Rosedale, Auckland 0632, New Zealand
(a division of Pearson New Zealand Ltd)
Penguin Books (South Africa) (Pty) Ltd, 24 Sturdee Avenue, Rosebank,
Johannesburg 2196, South Africa

Penguin Books Ltd, Registered Offices: 80 Strand, London WC2R ORL, England

puffinbooks.com

First published in the English language in 2008 by Harry N. Abrams, Incorporated, New York
(All rights reserved in all countries by Harry N. Abrams, Inc.)
This extended edition first published in the USA by Amulet Books,
an imprint of Harry N. Abrams, Inc., 2011
Published in Great Britain in Puffin Books 2011

047

Wimpy Kid text and illustrations copyright © 2008, 2011 Wimpy Kid, Inc.
DIARY OF A WIMPY KID and Greg Heffley cover image are trademarks of Wimpy Kid, Inc.

Book design by Jeff Kinney
Cover design by Jeff Kinney and Chad W. Beckerman
Cover photograph by Geoff Spear
Colouring on last sixteen colour comics by Nate Greenwall
All rights reserved

The moral right of the author/illustrator has been asserted

Printed in Great Britain by Clays Ltd, St Ives plc

British Library Cataloguing in Publication Data
A CIP catalogue record for this book is available from the British Library

ISBN: 978-0-141-33966-5

www.greenpenguin.co.uk

MIX
Paper from
responsible sources
FSC
www.fsc.org   FSC™ C018179

Penguin Books is committed to a sustainable
future for our business, our readers and our planet.
This book is made from Forest Stewardship
Council™ certified paper.

## THIS BOOK BELONGS TO:

_Oliver Hobern_

## IF FOUND, PLEASE RETURN
## TO THIS ADDRESS:

_Esmonde Gardens Elgin door 13_

### (NO REWARD)

# What're you gonna do with this thing?

OK, this is your book now, so technically you can do whatever you want with it.

BONK
HEY!

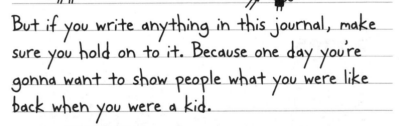

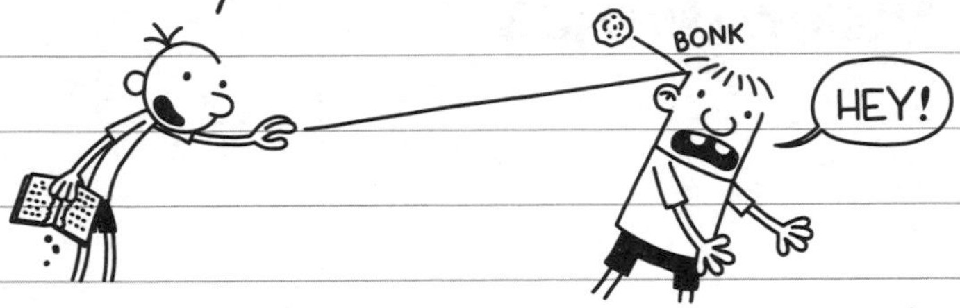

But if you write anything in this journal, make sure you hold on to it. Because one day you're gonna want to show people what you were like back when you were a kid.

WOW, HE WAS INCREDIBLY SMART AND WITTY EVEN THEN!
IT'S TRUE!

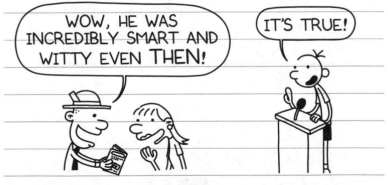

Whatever you do, just make sure you don't write down your "feelings" in here. Because one thing's for sure: this is NOT a diary.

# Your DESERT

If you were gonna be marooned for the rest of your life, what would you want to have with you?

## Video games

1.
2.
3.

## Songs

1.
2.
3.

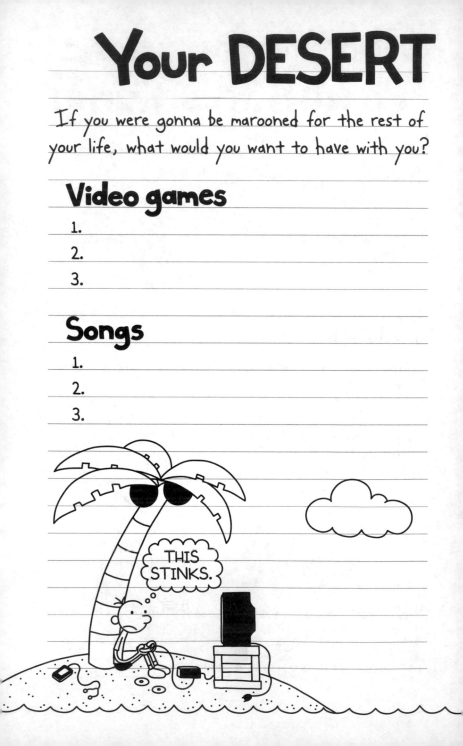

# ISLAND picks

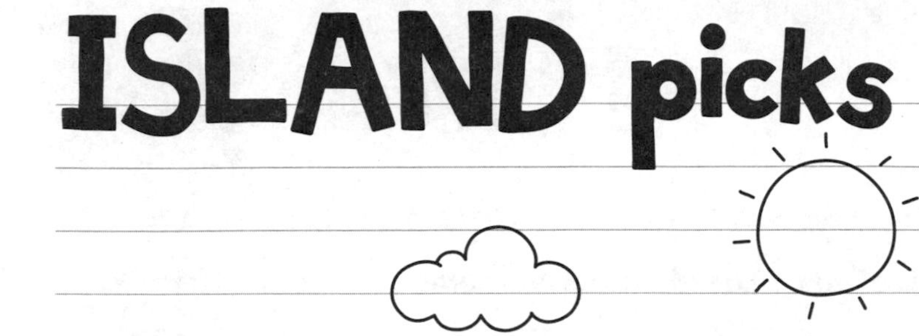

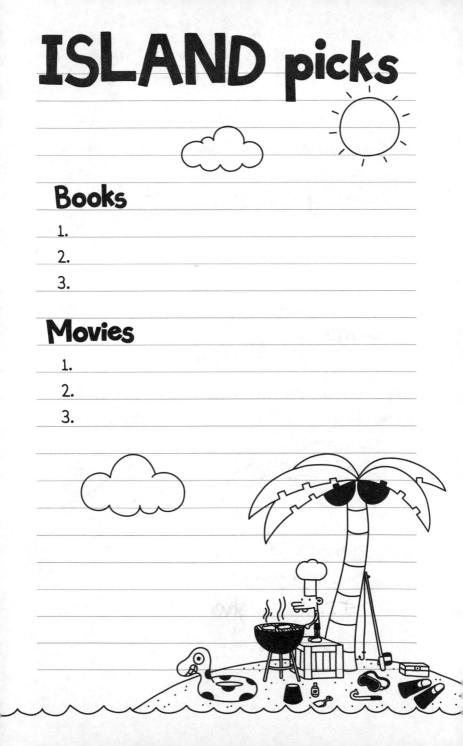

## Books

1.
2.
3.

## Movies

1.
2.
3.

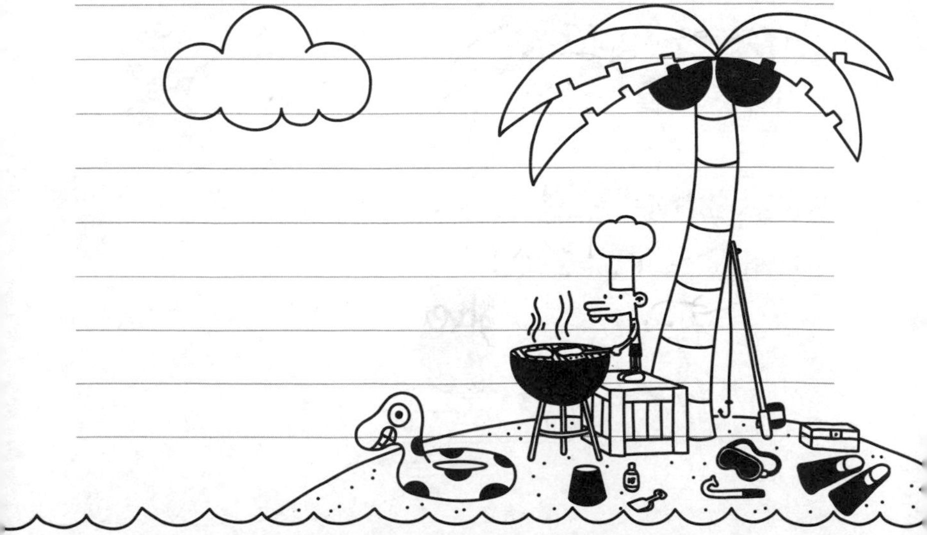

# Have you

Have you ever got a haircut that was so bad you needed to stay home from school?

YES ☐ NO ☑

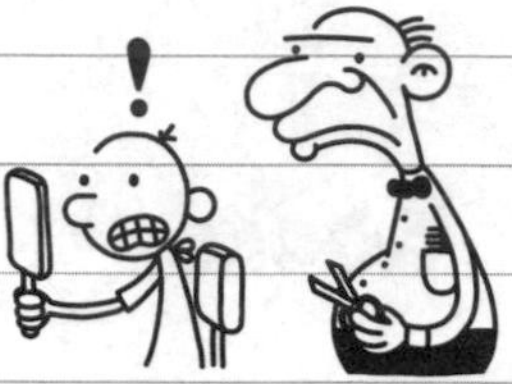

Have you ever had to put suntan lotion on a grown-up?

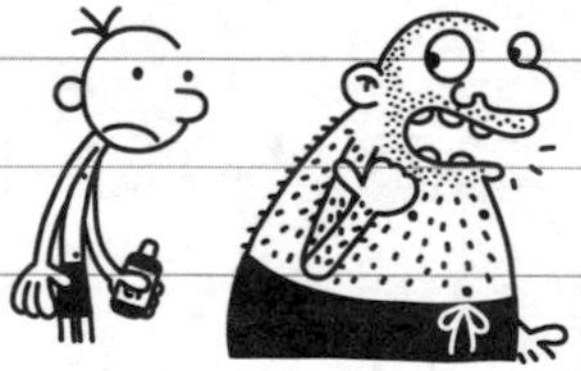

YES ☑ NO ☐

Have you ever been bitten by an animal?

YES ☑
NO ☐

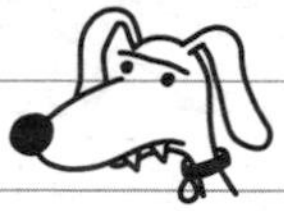

Have you ever been bitten by a person?

YES ☐
NO ☑

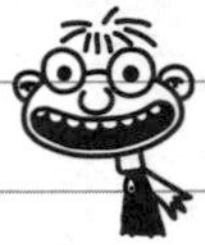

Have you ever tried to blow a bubble with a mouthful of raisins?

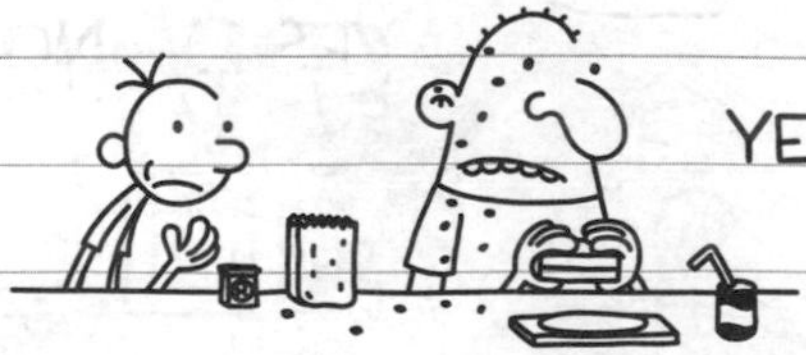

YES ☐ NO ☑

# EVER...

Have you ever peed in a swimming pool?

YES ☐ NO ☒

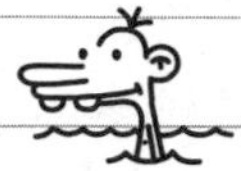

Have you ever been kissed full on the lips by a relative who's older than seventy?

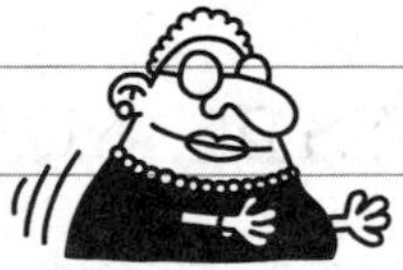

YES ☐ NO ☒

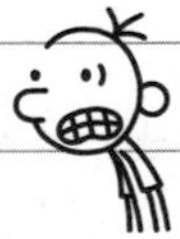

Have you ever been sent home early by one of your friends' parents?

YES ☐ NO ☒

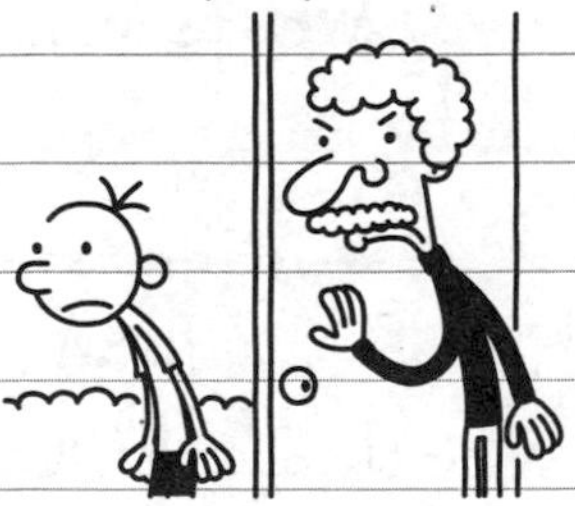

Have you ever had to change a diaper?

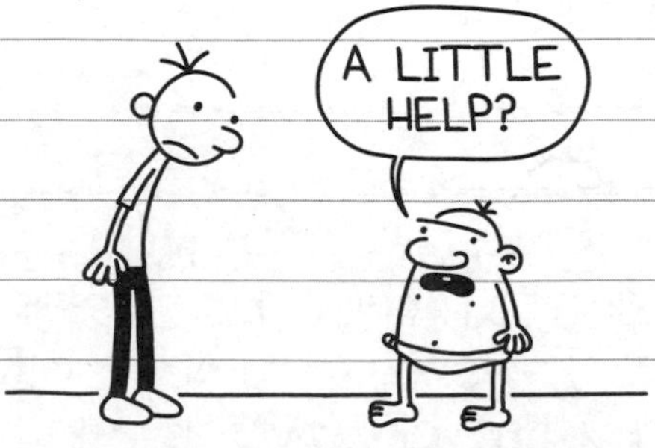
A LITTLE HELP?

YES ☐ NO ☒

# PERSONALITY

What's your favourite ANIMAL?

a snake

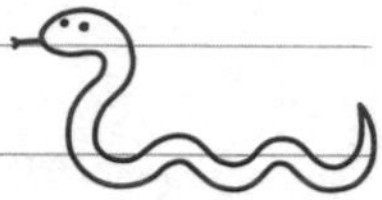

Write down FOUR ADJECTIVES that describe why you like that animal:

(EXAMPLE: FRIENDLY, COOL, ETC.)

cool slithers

some are Friendly cool colours

What's your favourite COLOUR?

blue

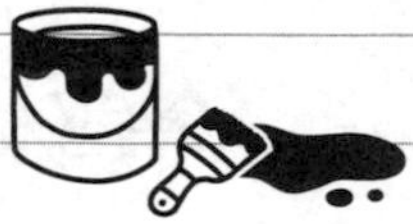

Write down FOUR ADJECTIVES that describe why you like that colour:

it looks good its cool

Its a good colour

- - - - - - - - - - - - - - - - - - - - - - - - - - - - - - - -

The adjectives you wrote down for your favourite ANIMAL describe HOW YOU THINK OF YOURSELF.

The adjectives you wrote down for your favourite COLOUR describe HOW OTHER PEOPLE THINK OF YOU.

# TEST

ANSWER THESE QUESTIONS AND THEN FLIP THE BOOK UPSIDE DOWN TO FIND OUT THINGS YOU NEVER KNEW ABOUT YOURSELF.

What's the title of the last BOOK you read?

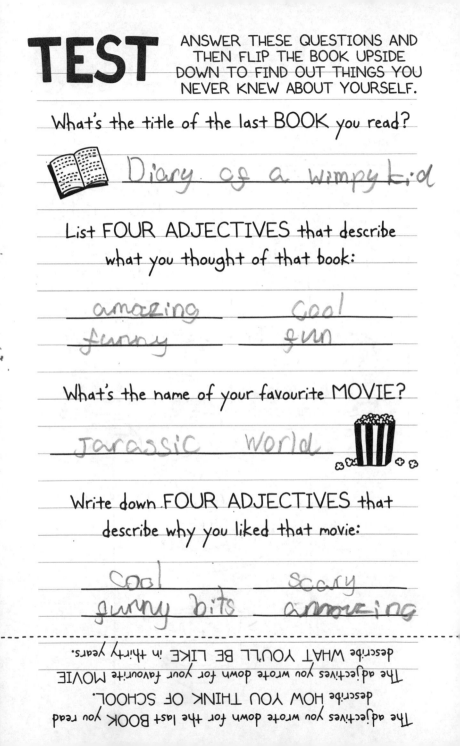

Diary of a wimpy kid

List FOUR ADJECTIVES that describe what you thought of that book:

amazing          cool

funny            fun

What's the name of your favourite MOVIE?

Jurassic World

Write down FOUR ADJECTIVES that describe why you liked that movie:

cool             scary

funny bits       amazing

---

The adjectives you wrote down for the last BOOK you read describe HOW YOU THINK OF SCHOOL.
The adjectives you wrote down for your favourite MOVIE describe WHAT YOU'LL BE LIKE in thirty years.

# Unfinished

## Zoo-Wee Mama!

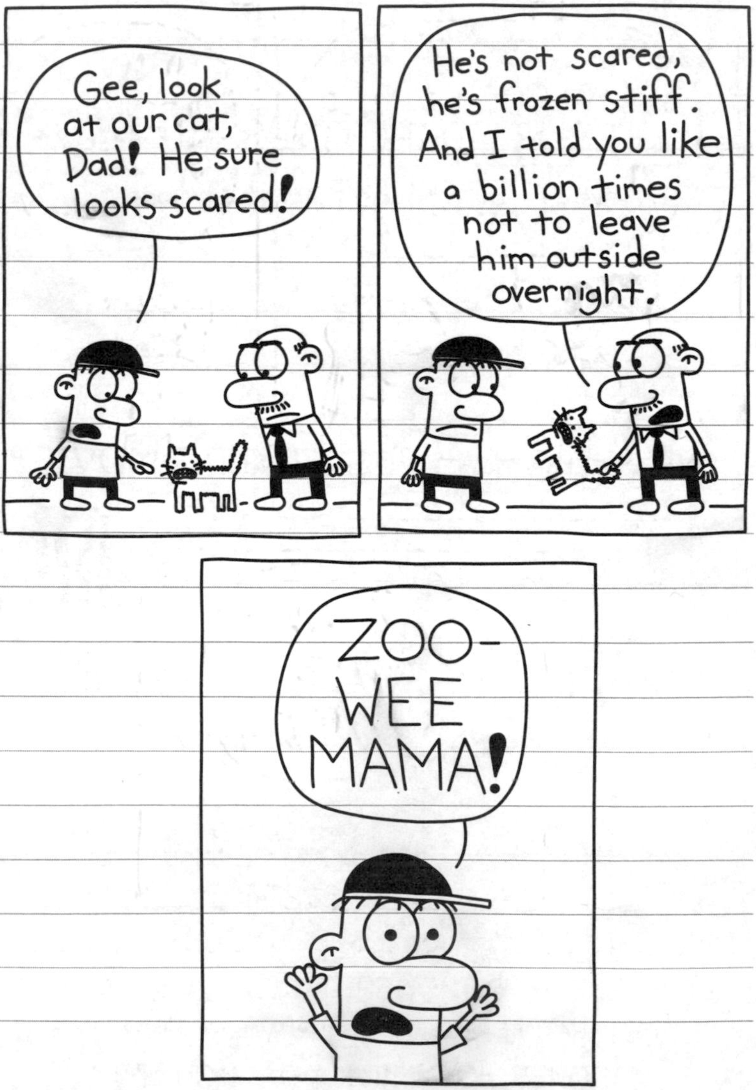

Gee, look at our cat, Dad! He sure looks scared!
He's not scared, he's frozen stiff. And I told you like a billion times not to leave him outside overnight.
ZOO-WEE MAMA!

# COMICS

## Zoo-Wee Mama!

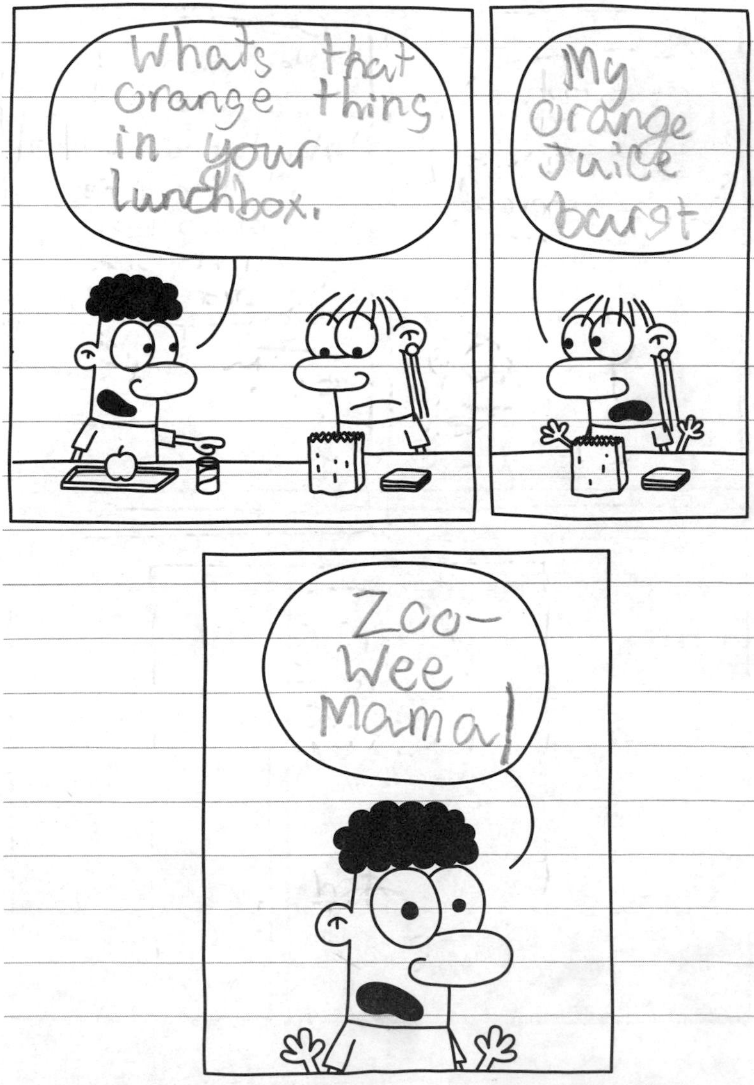
Whats that orange thing in your lunchbox.
My orange Juice burst
Zoo-Wee Mama!

# Make your

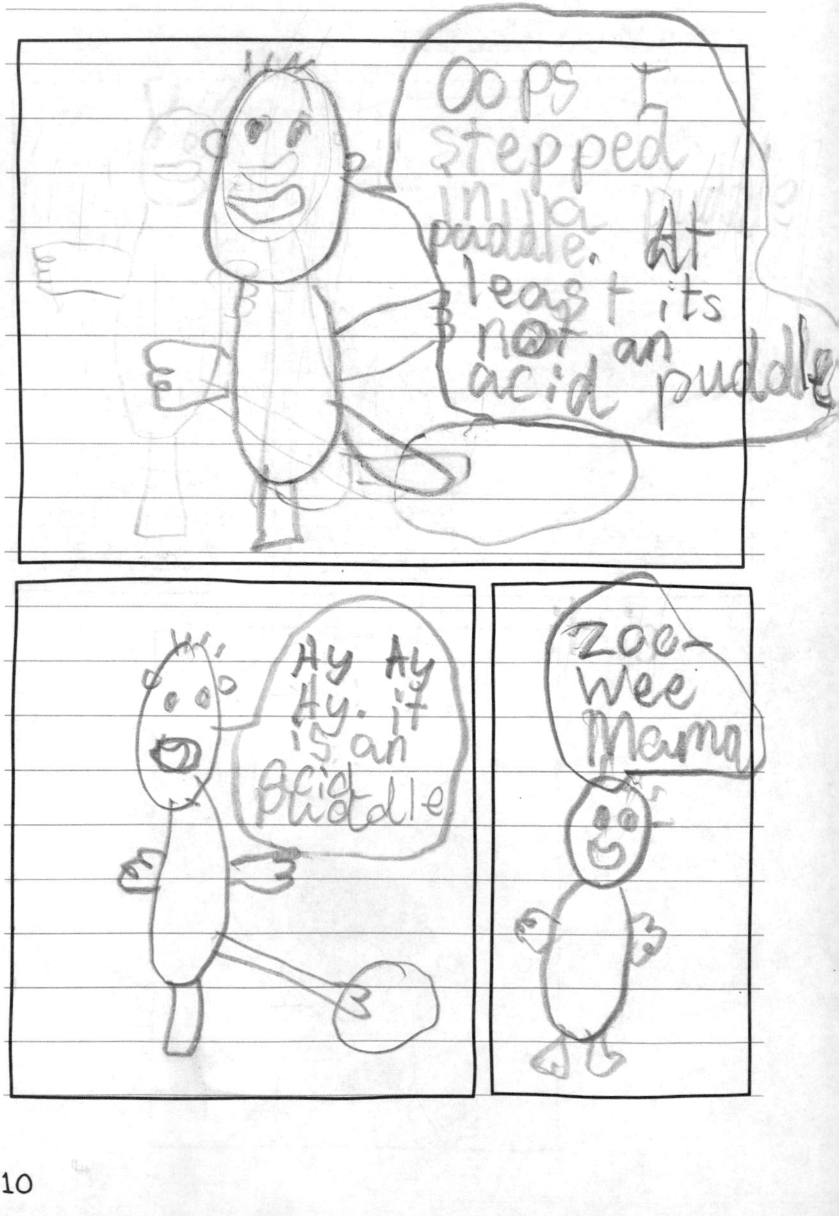
Oops I stepped in a puddle. At least its not an acid puddle
Ay Ay Ay. it is an acid Puddle
Zoo-Wee Mama

# OWN comics

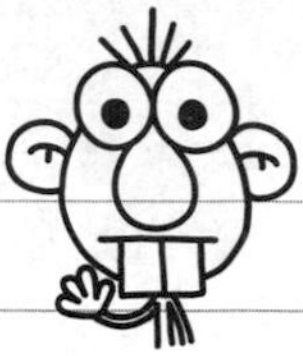

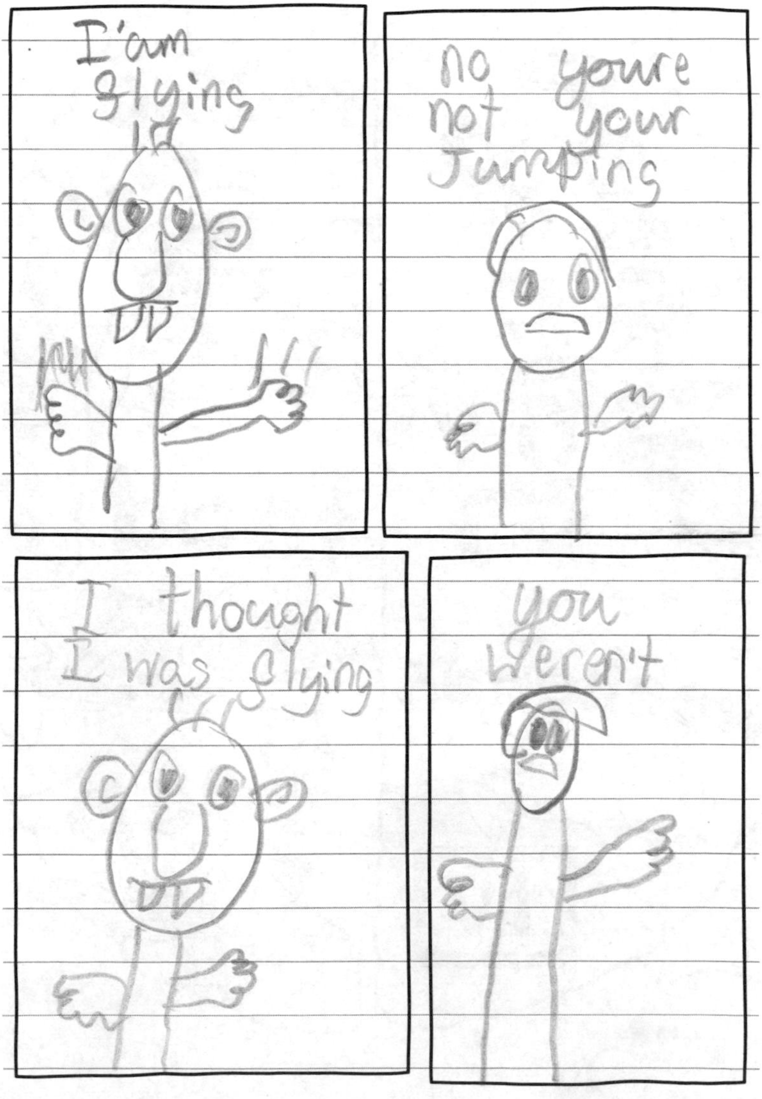
I'am flying
no youre not your Jumping
I thought I was flying
you weren't

# What's in your

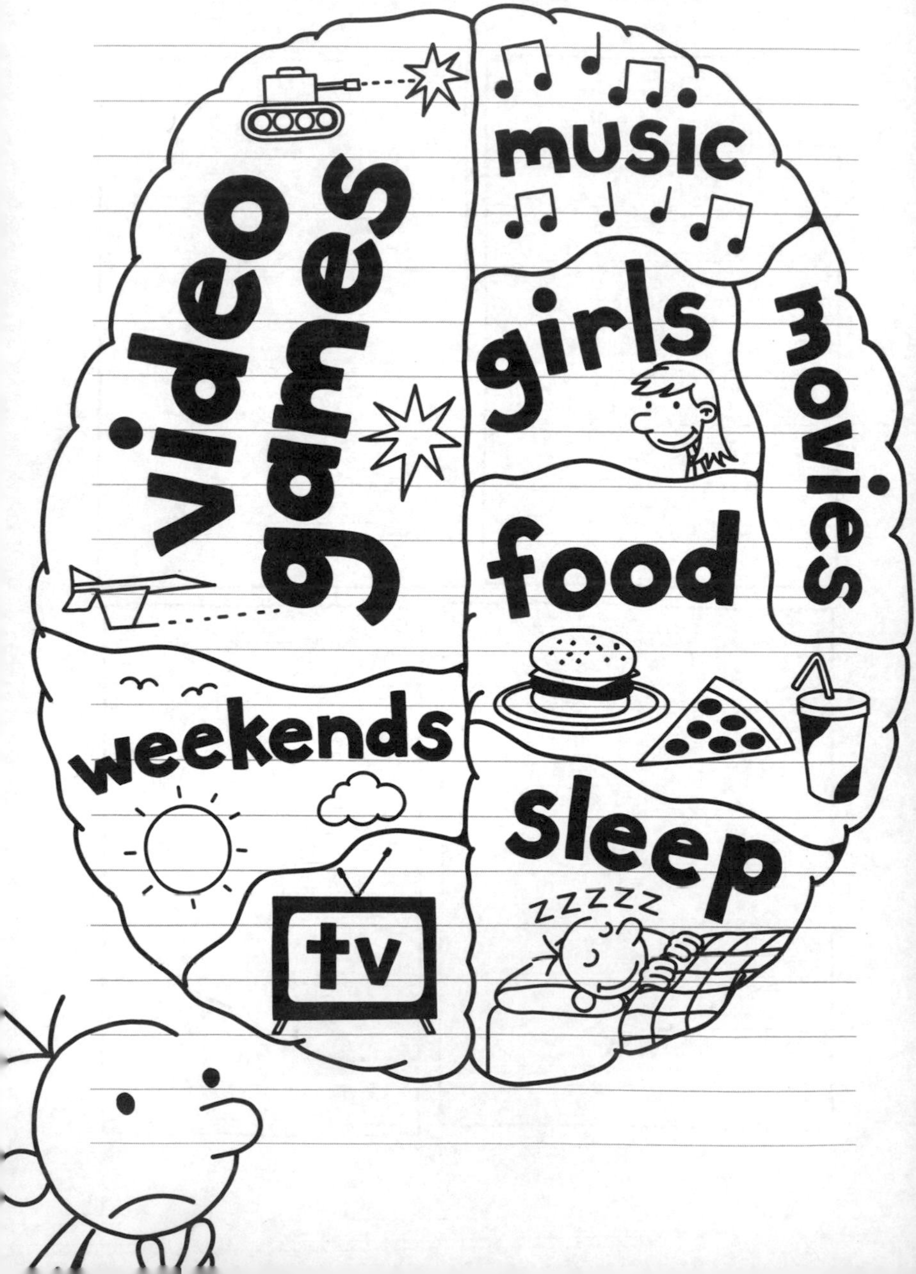
video games
music
girls
movies
food
weekends
sleep
ZZZZZ
tv

# BRAIN?

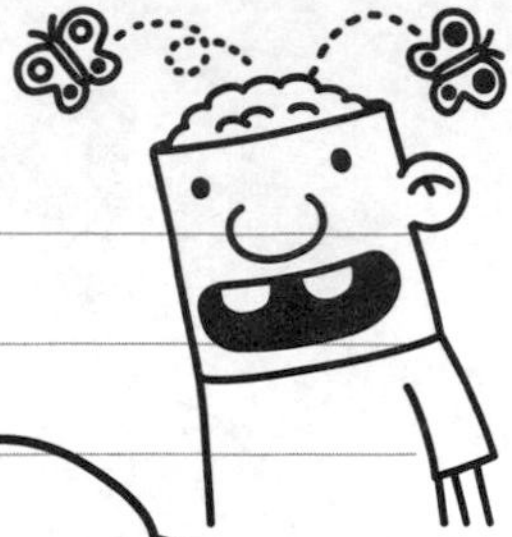

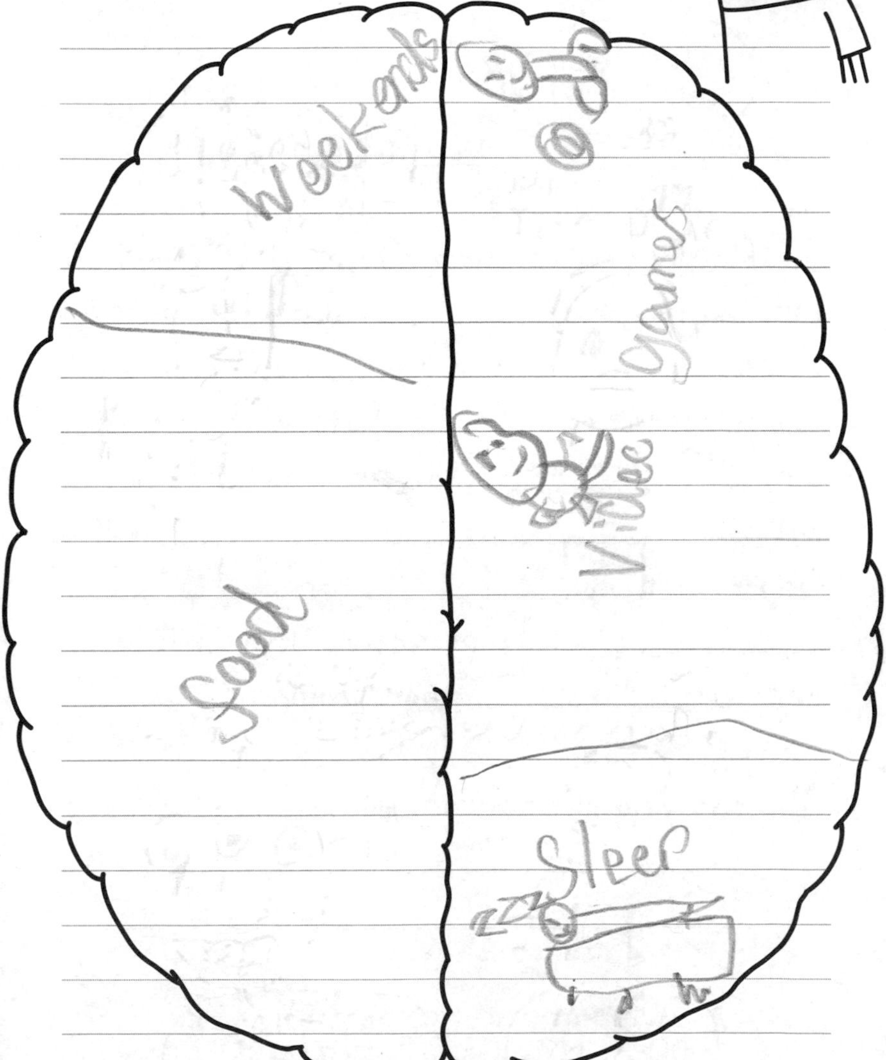

Weekends
Games
Food

# Predict the

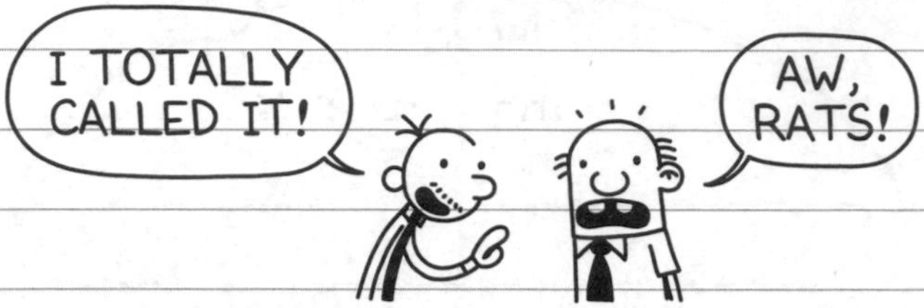
I TOTALLY CALLED IT!
AW, RATS!

I officially predict that twenty years from now cars will run on ____________ instead of petrol. A cheeseburger will cost $_____, and a ticket to the movies will cost $ _____. Pets will have their own ______________s. Underwear will be made out of ____________. _________________ will no longer exist. A ___________ named ____________ ____________ will be president. There will be more _______________ than people.

The annoying catchphrase will be:

____________________________________

____________________________________

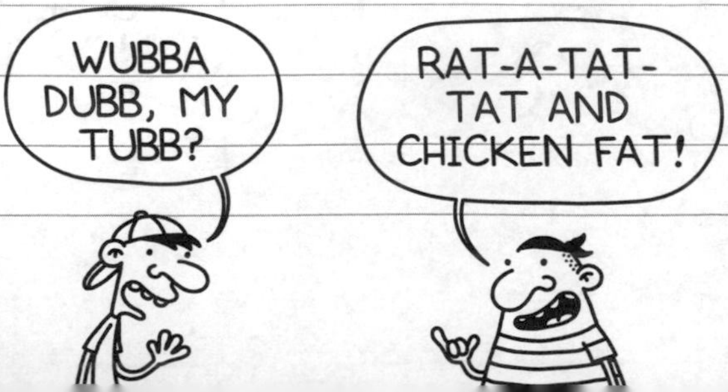
WUBBA DUBB, MY TUBB?
RAT-A-TAT-TAT AND CHICKEN FAT!

# FUTURE

Aliens will visit our planet in the year ____ and make the following announcement:

_______________

_______________

_______________

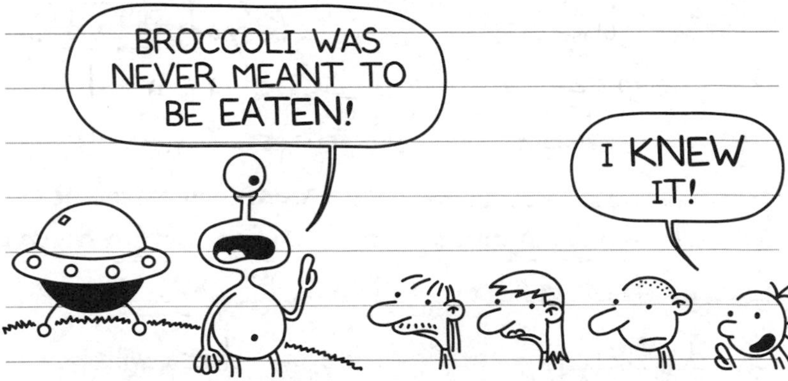
BROCCOLI WAS NEVER MEANT TO BE EATEN!
I KNEW IT!

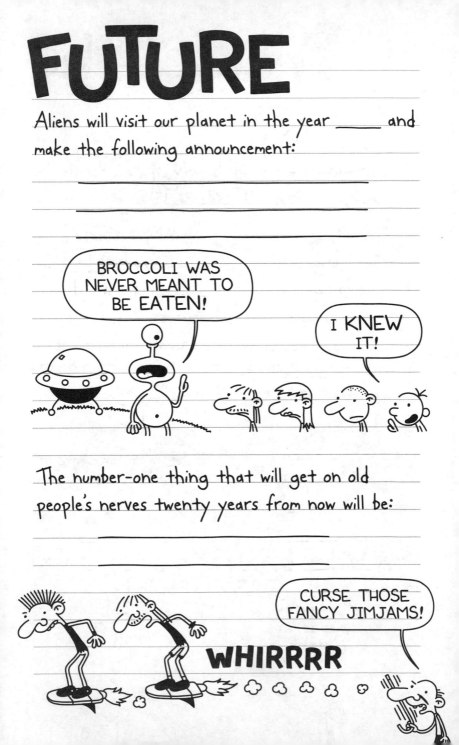

The number-one thing that will get on old people's nerves twenty years from now will be:

_______________

_______________

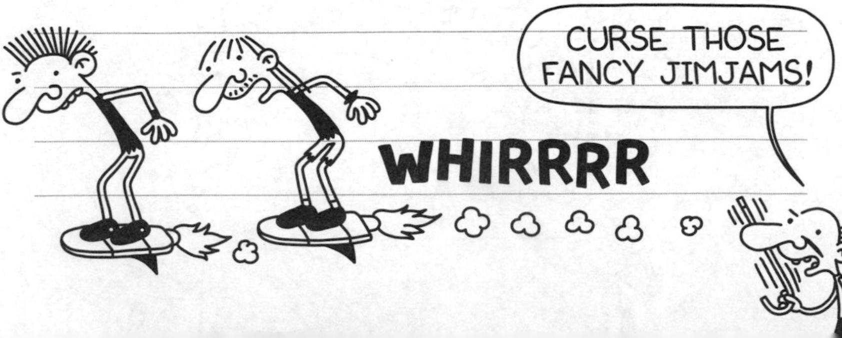
CURSE THOSE FANCY JIMJAMS!
WHIRRRR

# Predict the

IN FIFTY YEARS:

Robots and mankind will be locked in a battle for supremacy. TRUE ☐ FALSE ☐

HA!
DOINK
HEY! QUIT IT!

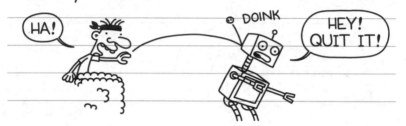

Parents will be banned from dancing within twenty feet of their children. TRUE ☐ FALSE ☐

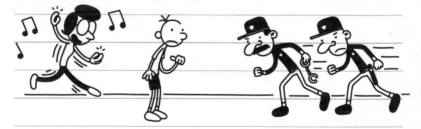

People will have instant-messaging chips implanted in their brains. TRUE ☐ FALSE ☐

u r a
dork
:(

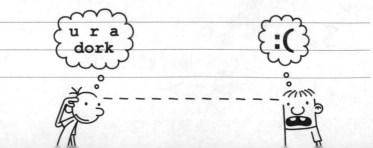

# FUTURE

YOUR FIVE BOLD PREDICTIONS FOR THE FUTURE:

**1.**

**2.**

**3.**

**4.**

**5.**

(WRITE EVERYTHING DOWN NOW
SO YOU CAN TELL YOUR FRIENDS
"I TOLD YOU SO" LATER ON.)

# Predict YOUR

Answer these questions, then check back when you're an adult to see how you did!

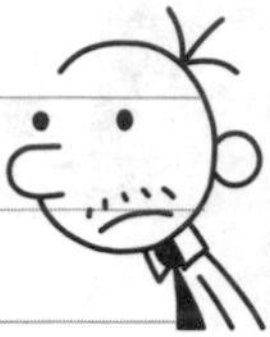

WHEN I'M THIRTY YEARS OLD

I will live ____ kilometres from my current home.

I will be: MARRIED ☐ SINGLE ☐

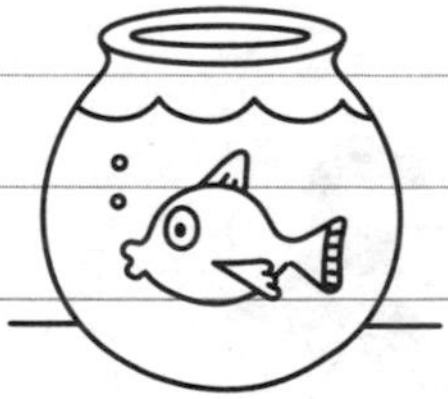

I will have _____ kids and a __________ named __________.

I will work as a ____________________ and make ________________ dollars a year.

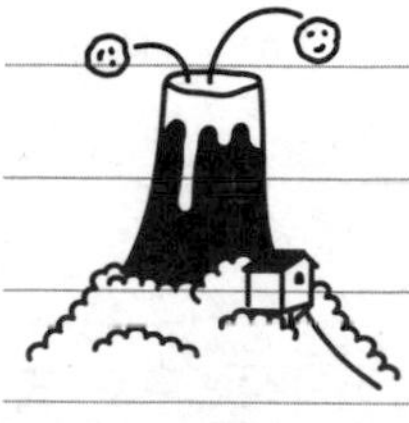

I will live in a ________________ on a ____________________.

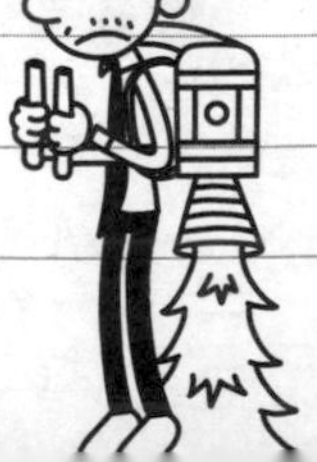

I will take a ________________ to work every day.

# future

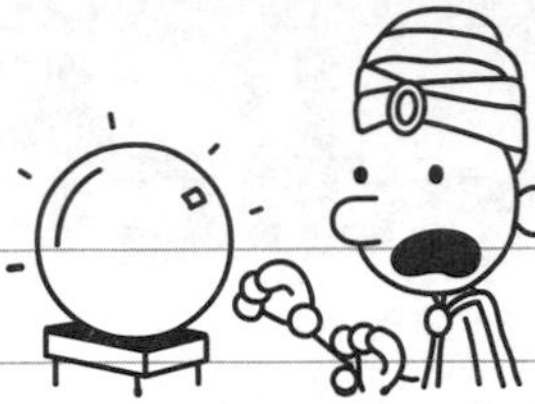

I will be ____ metres _____ centimetres tall.

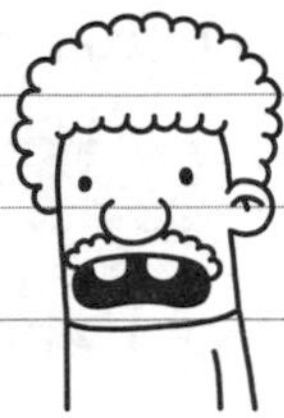

I will have the same basic haircut
I have now. TRUE ☐ FALSE ☐

I will have the same best friend I have right
now. TRUE ☐ FALSE ☐

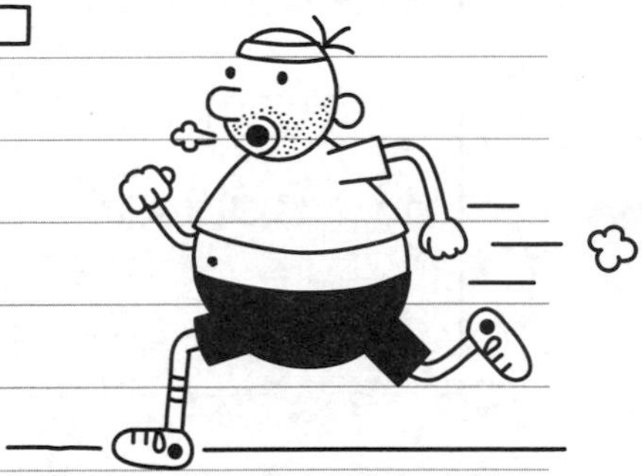

I will be in really
excellent shape.
TRUE ☐ FALSE ☐

I will listen to the same kind of music I listen to
now. TRUE ☐ FALSE ☐

I will have visited _____ different countries.

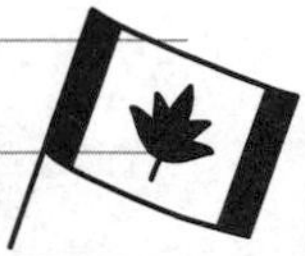

The thing that will change the most about me
between now and then will be: ____________________

______________________________________________

______________________________________________.

# Predict YOUR

What you're basically gonna do here is roll a dice over and over, crossing off items when you land on them, like this:

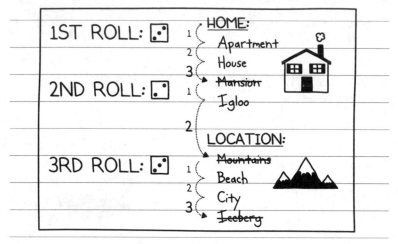

1ST ROLL: ⚁

HOME:
1 Apartment
2 House
3 ~~Mansion~~
1 Igloo

2ND ROLL: ⚀

2

LOCATION:
1 ~~Mountains~~
2 Beach
3 City

3RD ROLL: ⚂

~~Iceberg~~

Keep going through the list, and when you get to the end, jump back to the beginning. When there's only one item left in a category, circle it. Once you've got an item in each category circled, you'll know your future! Good luck!

MY LIFE STINKS.

# future

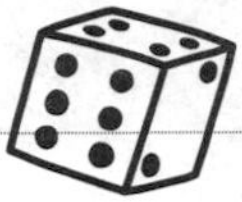

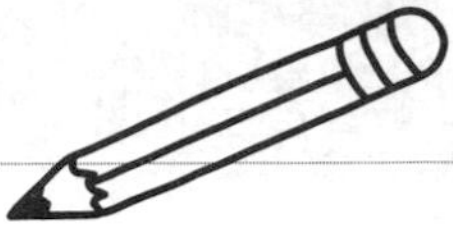

HOME:

Apartment
House
Mansion
Igloo

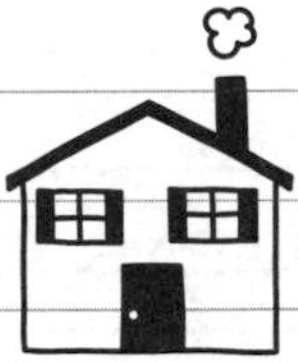

LOCATION:

Mountains
Beach
City
Iceberg

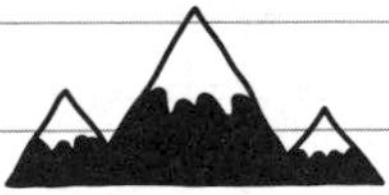

KIDS:

None
One
Two
Ten

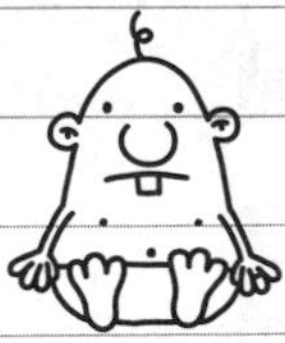

PET:

Dog
Cat
Bird
Turtle

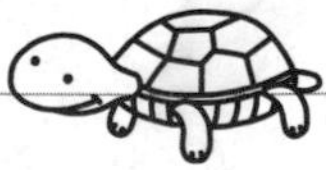

JOB:

Doctor
Actor
Clown
Mechanic
Lawyer
Pilot
Pro athlete
Dentist
Magician
Whatever you want

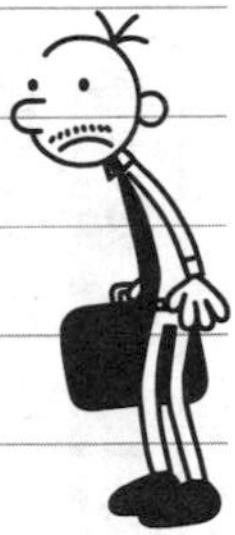

VEHICLE:

Car
Motorcycle
Helicopter
Skateboard

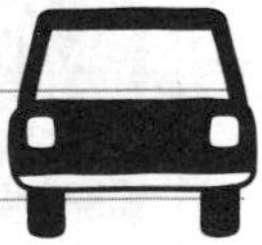

SALARY:

$100 a year
$100,000 a year
$1 million a year
$100 million a year

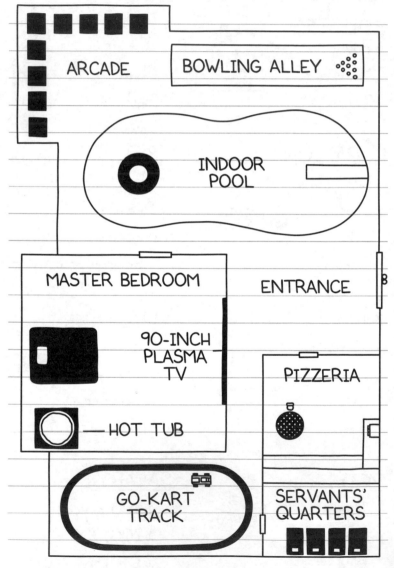

GREG HEFFLEY'S FUTURE HOUSE

ARCADE

BOWLING ALLEY

INDOOR POOL

MASTER BEDROOM

ENTRANCE

90-INCH PLASMA TV

PIZZERIA

HOT TUB

GO-KART TRACK

SERVANTS' QUARTERS

# DREAM HOUSE

YOUR FUTURE HOUSE

# FRIENDS

MOST LIKELY TO FALL
ASLEEP IN CLASS

MOST LIKELY TO FAINT
AT THE SIGHT OF BLOOD

MOST LIKELY TO
BECOME A BILLIONAIRE

MOST LIKELY TO BE ON
A REALITY TV SHOW

24

# HALL OF FAME

MOST LIKELY TO
BECOME PRESIDENT

MOST LIKELY TO
ACCIDENTALLY WEAR
PYJAMAS TO SCHOOL

MOST LIKELY TO
JOIN THE CIRCUS

MOST LIKELY TO SET
A WORLD RECORD

# A few questions

What's the most embarrassing thing that ever happened to someone who wasn't you?

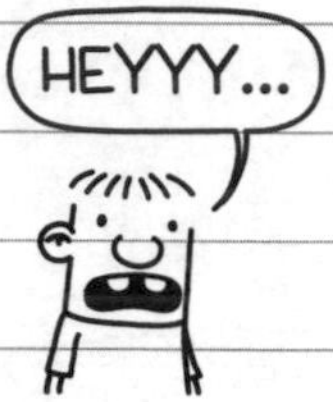
HEYYY...

What's the worst thing you ever ate? 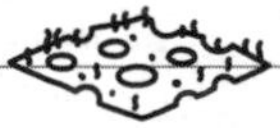

How many steps does it take you to jump into bed after you turn off the light?

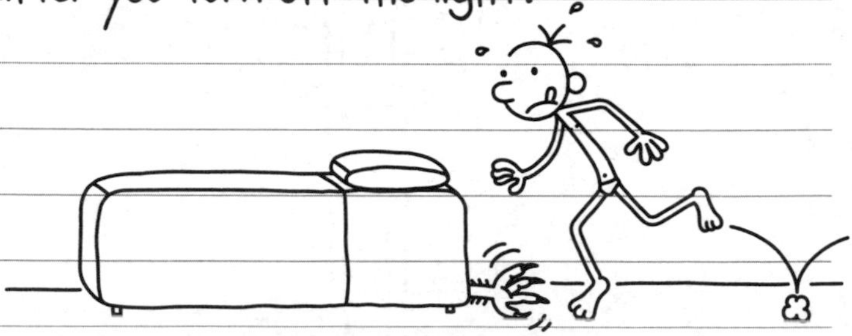

How much would you be willing to pay for an extra hour of sleep in the morning?

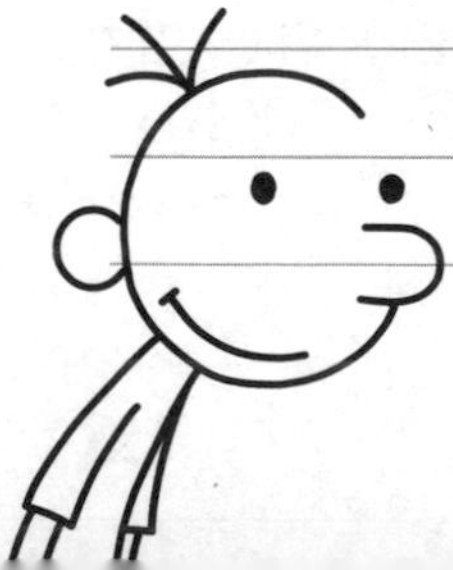

# from GREG

Have you ever pretended you were sick so you could stay home from school?

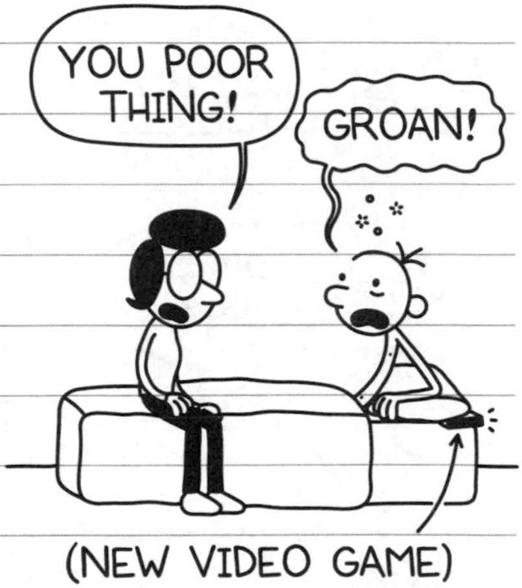
YOU POOR THING!
GROAN!
(NEW VIDEO GAME)

Does it get on your nerves when people skip?

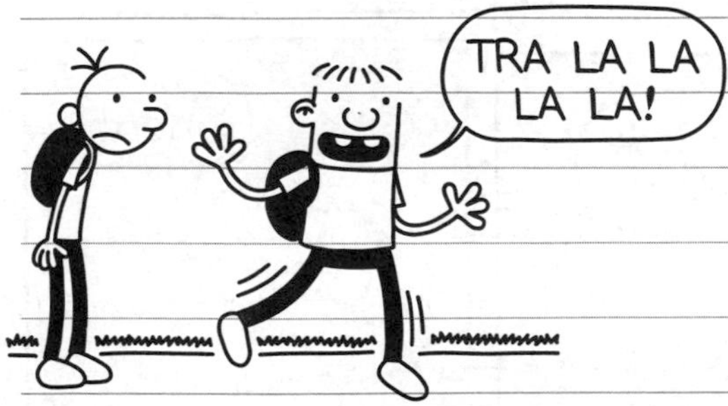
TRA LA LA LA LA!

Did you ever do something bad that you never got busted for?

# Unfinished

## Ugly Eugene

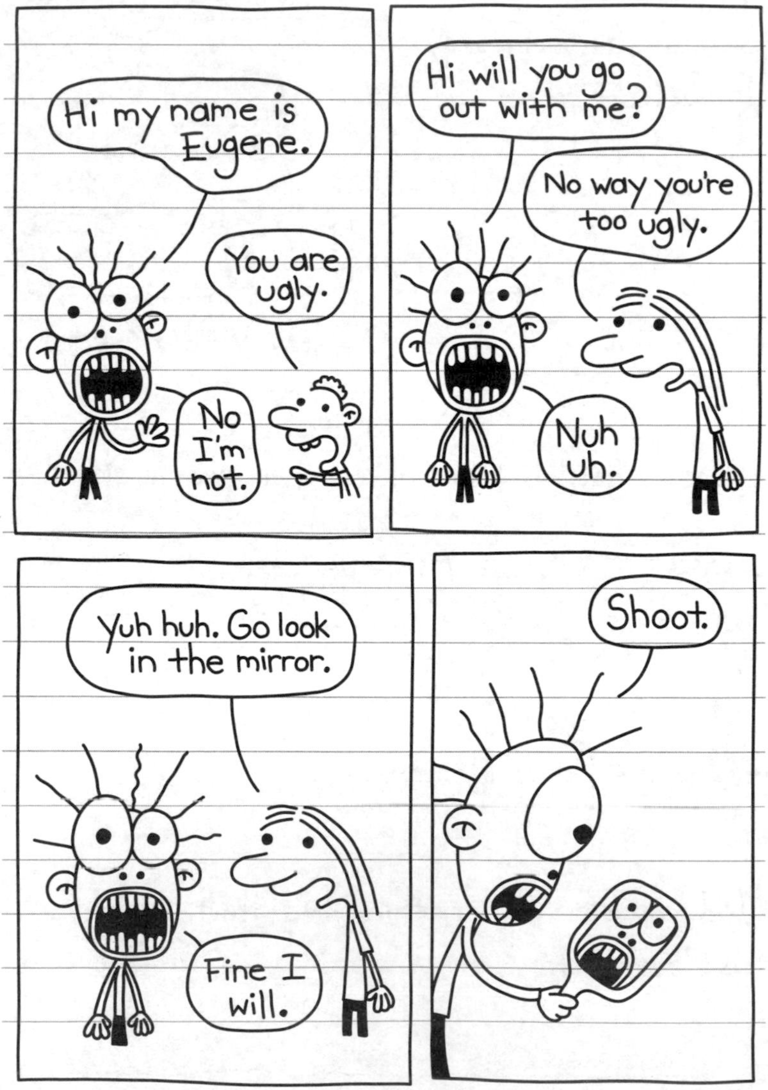
Hi my name is Eugene.
You are ugly.
No I'm not.
Hi will you go out with me?
No way you're too ugly.
Nuh uh.
Yuh huh. Go look in the mirror.
Fine I will.
Shoot.

# COMICS

## Ugly Eugene

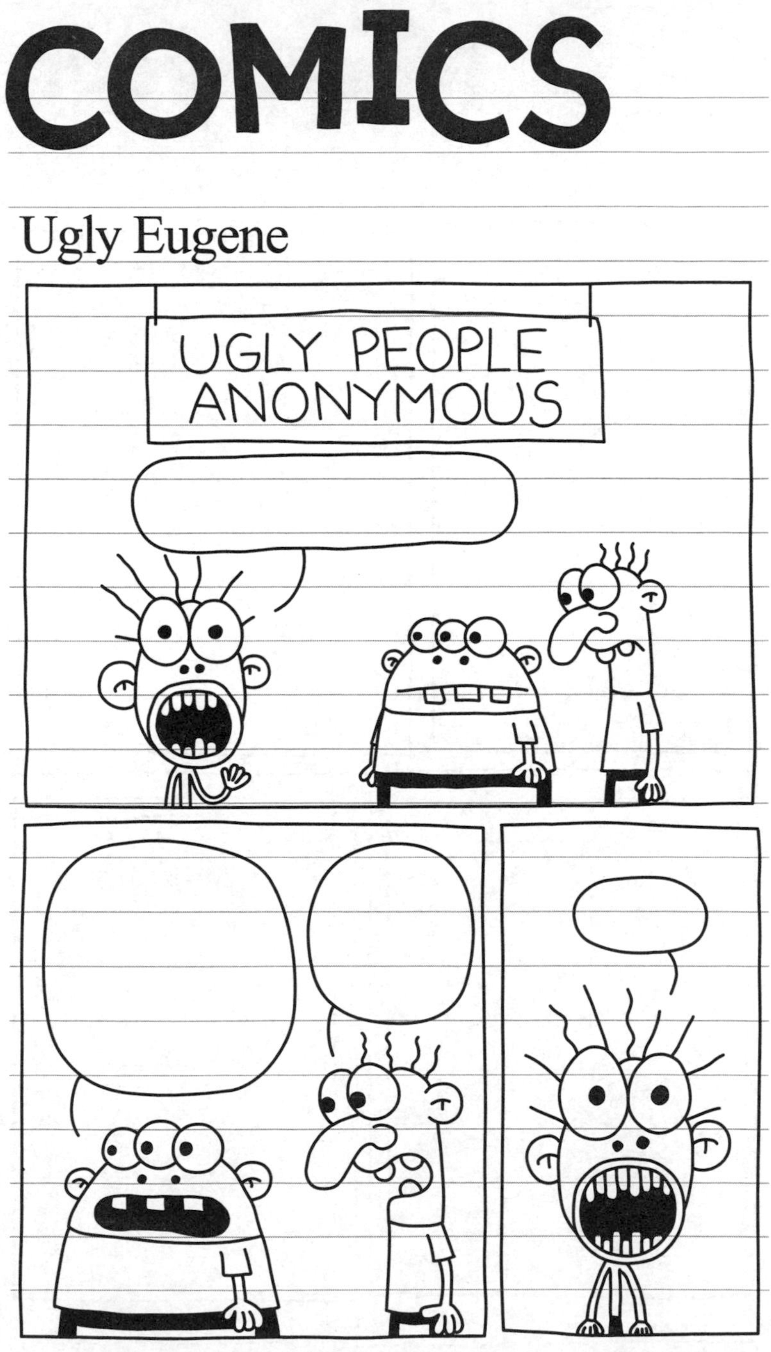
UGLY PEOPLE ANONYMOUS

# Make your

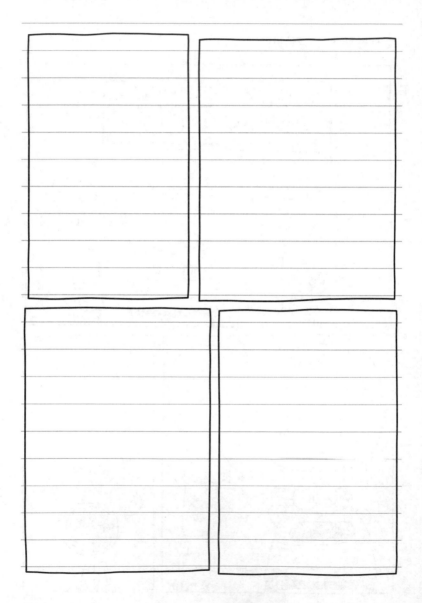

# OWN comics

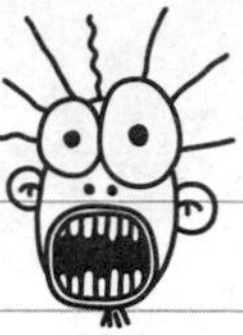

# Which would you

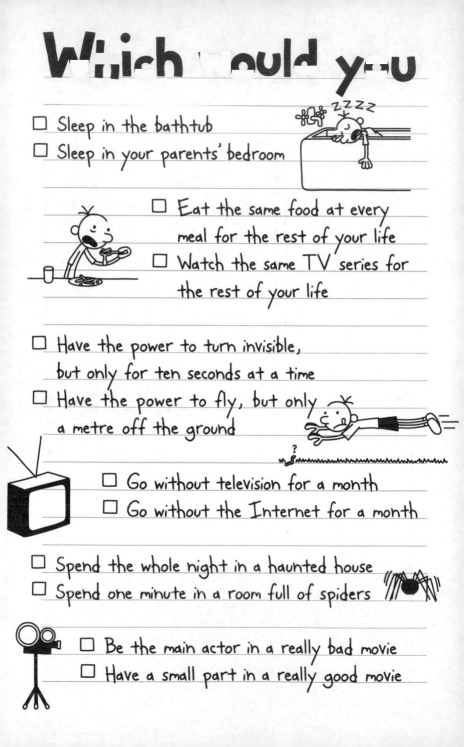

- [ ] Sleep in the bathtub
- [ ] Sleep in your parents' bedroom

- [ ] Eat the same food at every meal for the rest of your life
- [ ] Watch the same TV series for the rest of your life

- [ ] Have the power to turn invisible, but only for ten seconds at a time
- [ ] Have the power to fly, but only a metre off the ground

- [ ] Go without television for a month
- [ ] Go without the Internet for a month

- [ ] Spend the whole night in a haunted house
- [ ] Spend one minute in a room full of spiders

- [ ] Be the main actor in a really bad movie
- [ ] Have a small part in a really good movie

# RATHER DO?

- ☐ Wear the same Halloween costume every year
- ☐ Wear the same pair of socks for a week

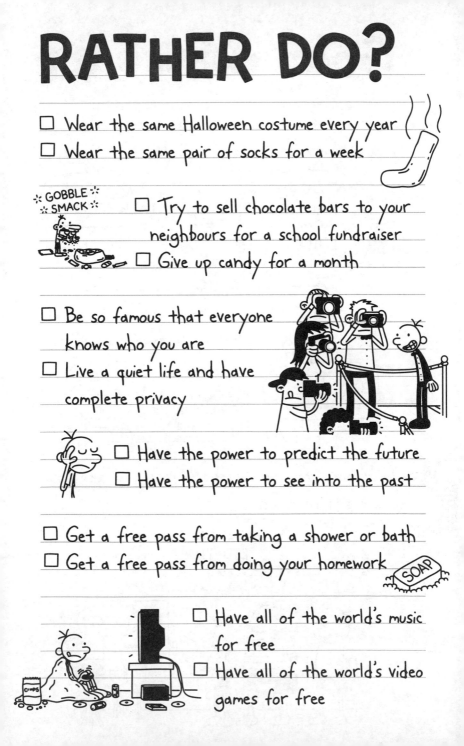

GOBBLE
SMACK

- ☐ Try to sell chocolate bars to your neighbours for a school fundraiser
- ☐ Give up candy for a month

- ☐ Be so famous that everyone knows who you are
- ☐ Live a quiet life and have complete privacy

- ☐ Have the power to predict the future
- ☐ Have the power to see into the past

- ☐ Get a free pass from taking a shower or bath
- ☐ Get a free pass from doing your homework

SOAP

- ☐ Have all of the world's music for free
- ☐ Have all of the world's video games for free

CHIPS

# Good advice for

**1.** Don't use the bathroom on the second floor, because there aren't any stall doors in there.

COULD YOU HAND ME SOME TOILET PAPER?
PLEASE DON'T TALK TO ME.

**2.** Be careful who you sit next to in the cafeteria.

THAT COOKIE IS MINE!
MMRF!

**3.** Don't pick your nose right before you get your school picture taken.

NOW WHERE DID THAT BOOGER GO?
NEXT!

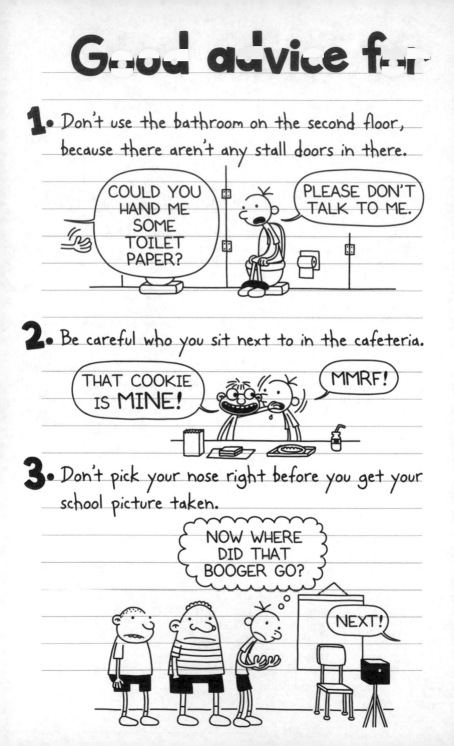

# next year's class

**1.**

**2.**

**3.**

**4.**

# Draw your FAMILY

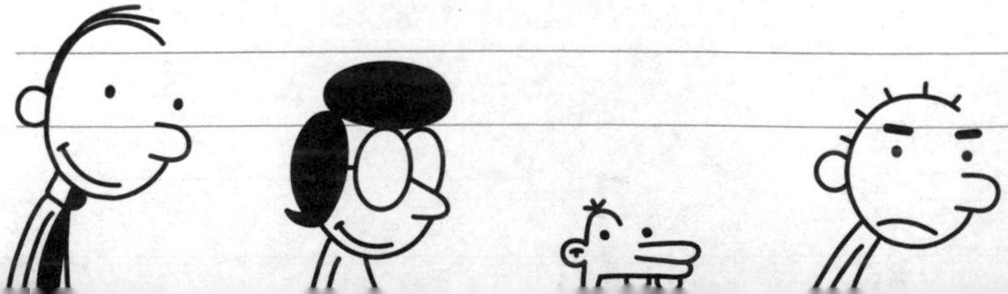

# the way Greg Heffley would

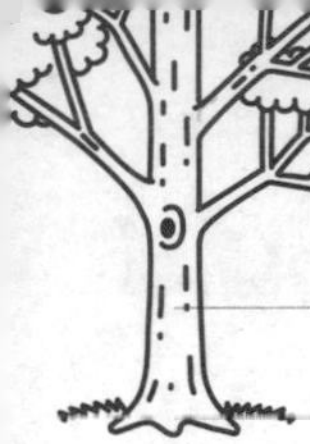

# Draw up your

How many generations can you trace your family history back?

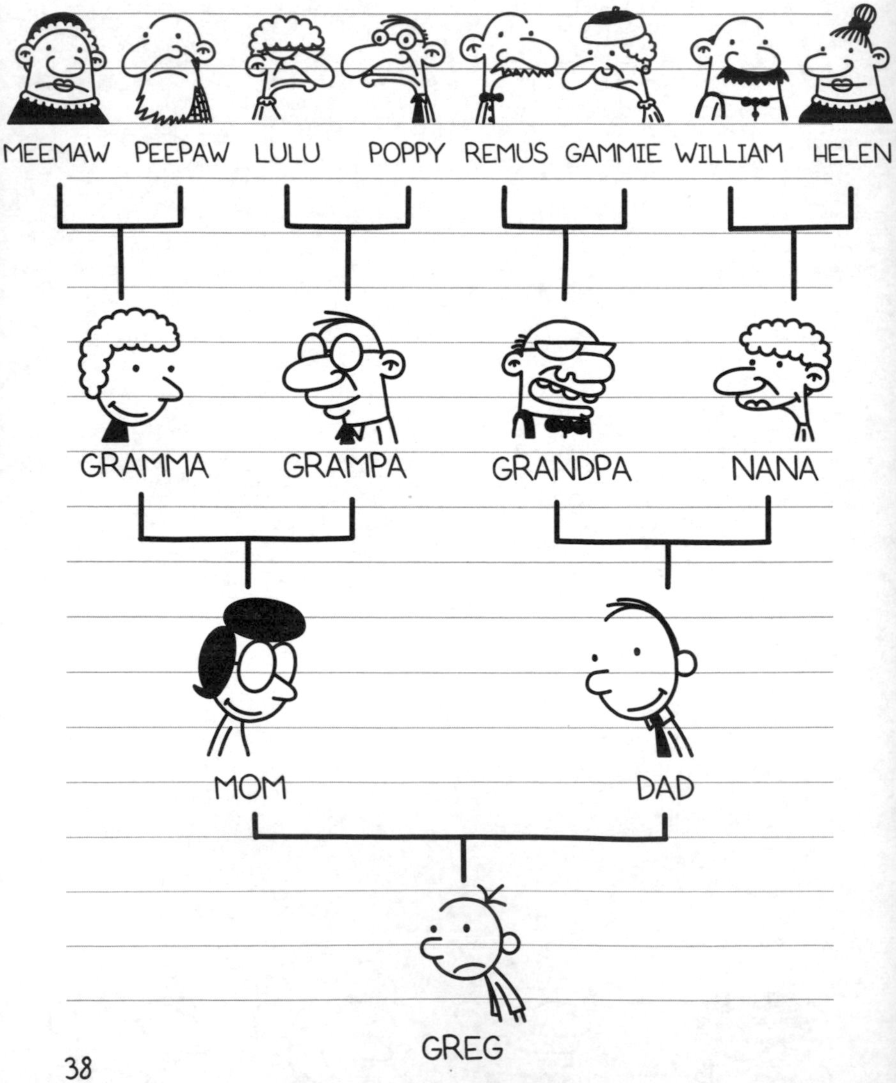
MEEMAW
PEEPAW
LULU
POPPY
REMUS
GAMMIE
WILLIAM
HELEN
GRAMMA
GRAMPA
GRANDPA
NANA
MOM
DAD
GREG

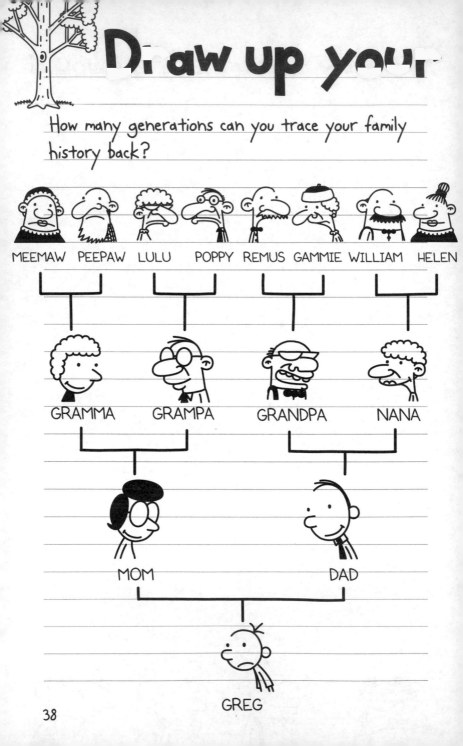

# FAMILY TREE

Create your OWN family tree in the space below!

# Your FAVOURITES

TV show:

Band:

Sports team:

Food:

Celebrity:

Smell:

Villain:

Shoe brand:

Store:

Drink:

Cereal:

Super hero:

Candy:

Restaurant:

Athlete:

Game system:

Comic strip:

Magazine:

Car:

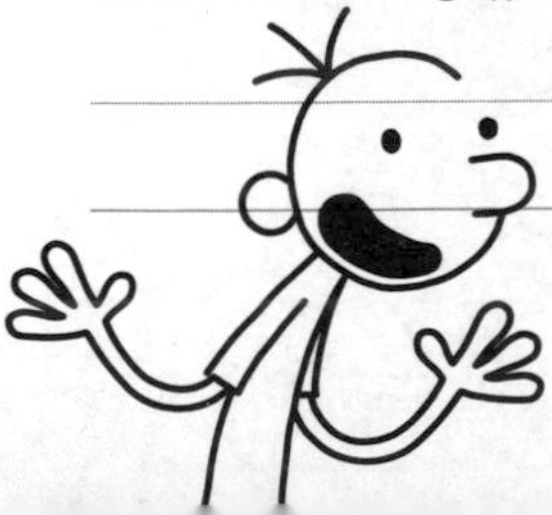

# Your LEAST favourites

TV show:

Band:

Sports team:

Food:

Celebrity:

Smell:

Villain:

Shoe brand:

Store:

Drink:

Cereal:

Super hero:

Candy:

Restaurant:

Athlete:

Game system:

Comic strip:

Magazine:

Car:

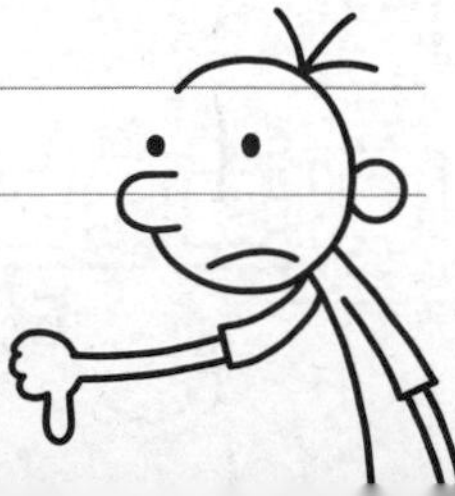

# Record your

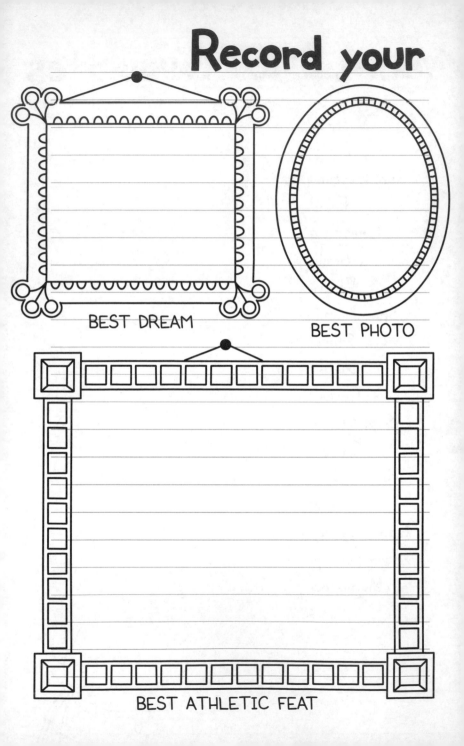

BEST DREAM

BEST PHOTO

BEST ATHLETIC FEAT

# FINEST MOMENTS

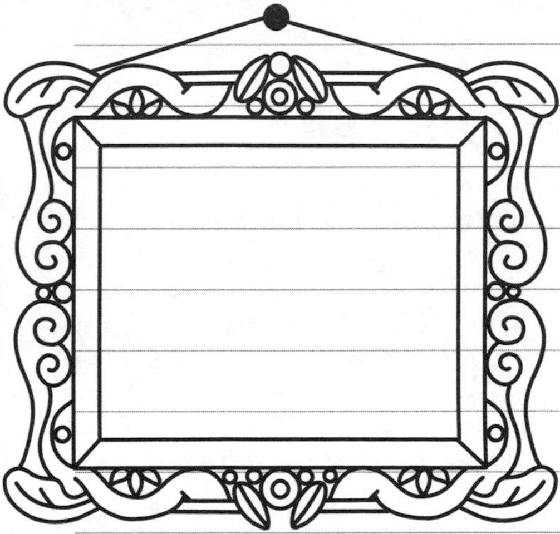

FUNNIEST QUOTE

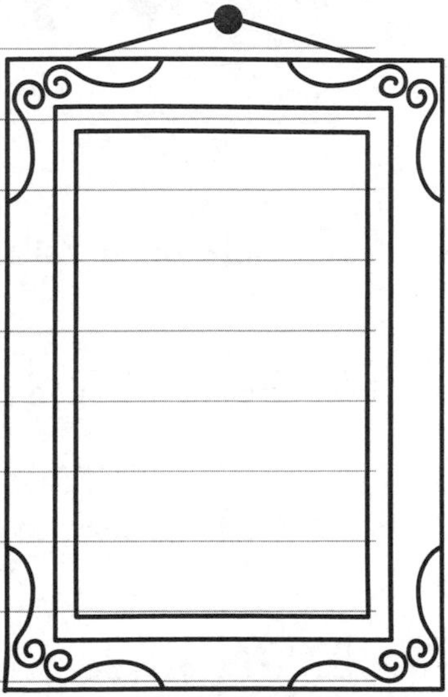

COOLEST
AWARD

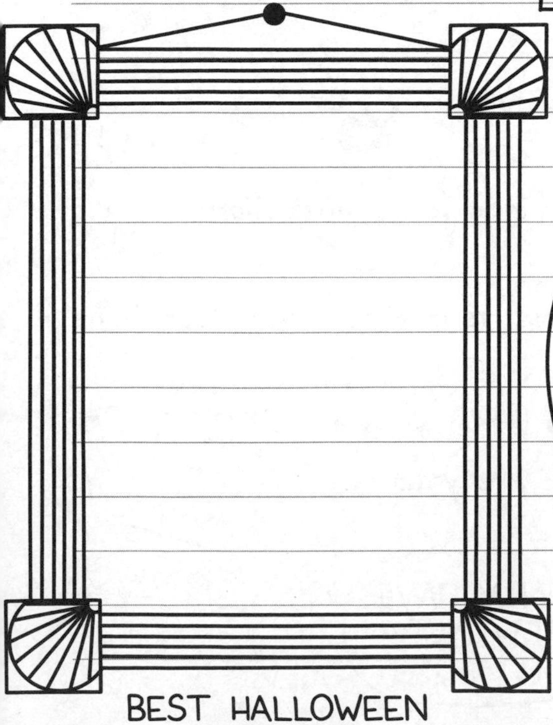

BEST HALLOWEEN
COSTUME

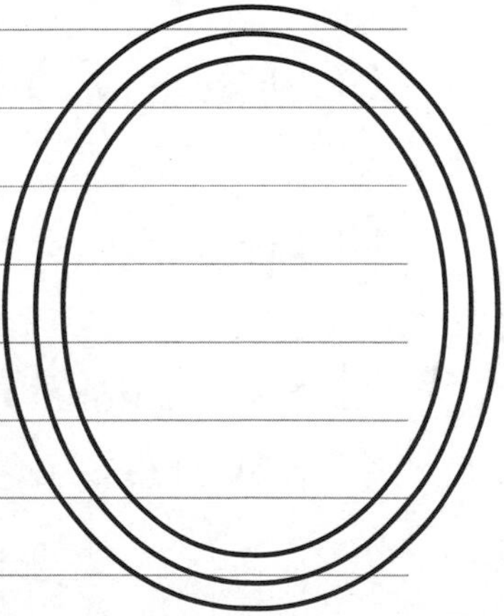

BEST MEAL

# Things you should do

☐ Stay up all night.

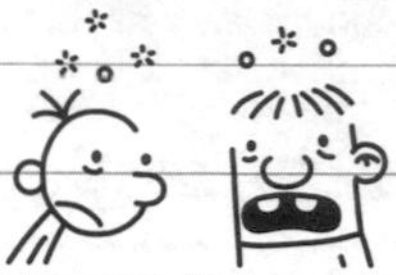

☐ Ride on a roller coaster with a loop in it.

☐ Get in a food fight.

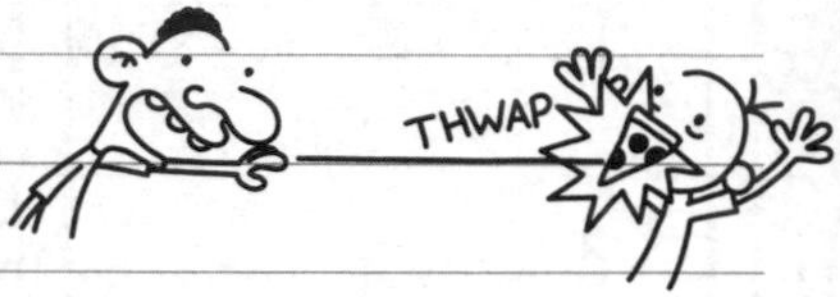
THWAP

☐ Get an autograph from a famous person.

☐ Get a hole-in-one in miniature golf.

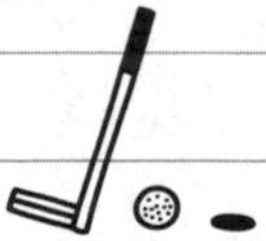

☐ Give yourself a haircut.

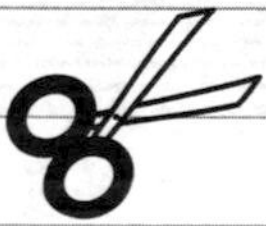

☐ Write down an idea for an invention.

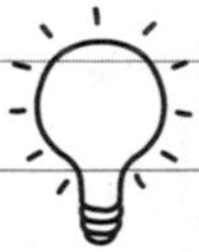

☐ Spend three nights in a row away from home.

☐ Mail someone a letter with a real stamp and everything.

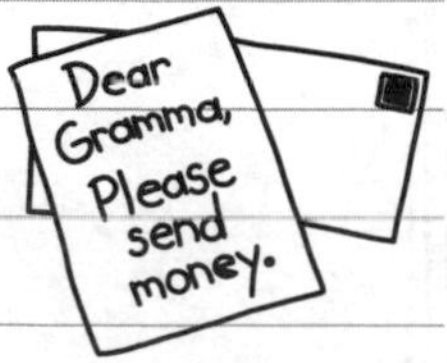
Dear Gramma,
Please send money.

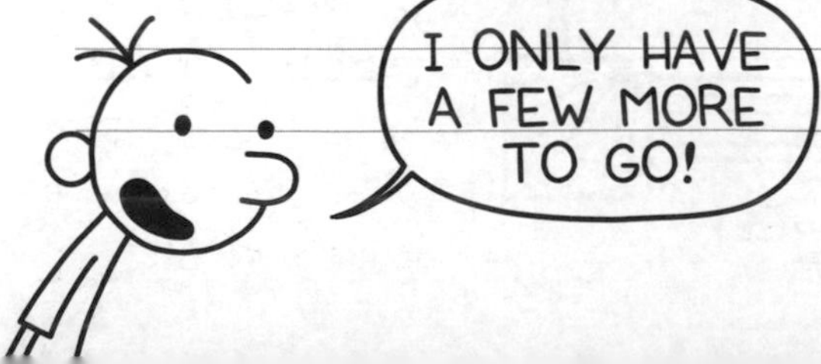
I ONLY HAVE A FEW MORE TO GO!

# before you get old

☐ Go on a campout.

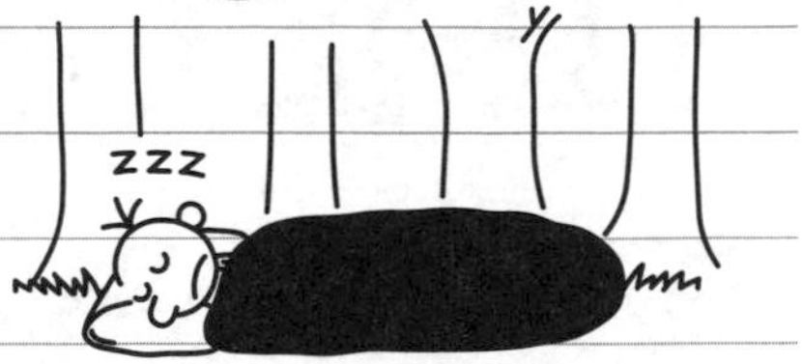
ZZZ

☐ Read a whole book with no pictures in it.

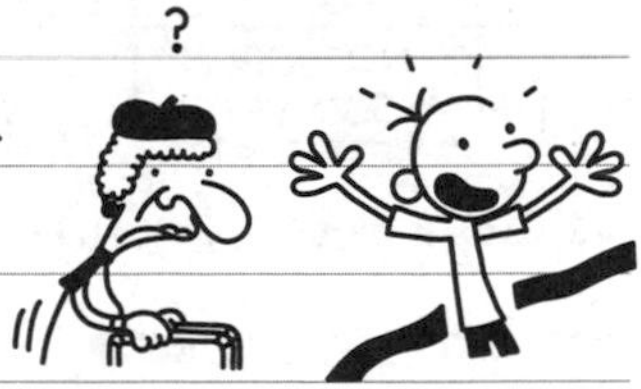
?

☐ Beat someone who's older than you in a footrace.

☐ Make it through a whole lollipop without biting it.

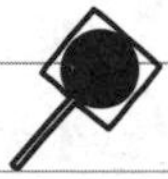

☐ Use a porta-potty.

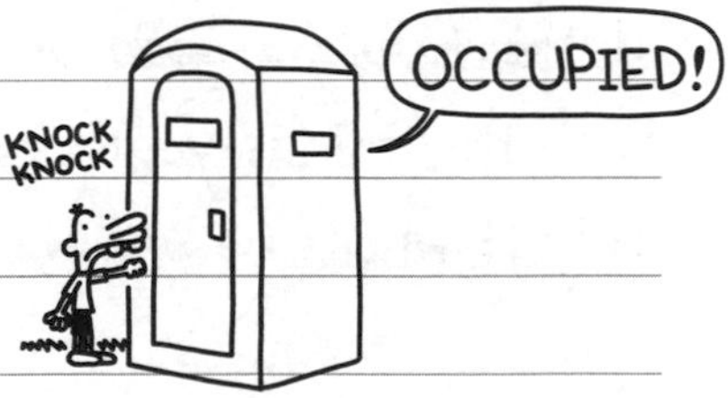
KNOCK KNOCK
OCCUPIED!

☐ Score at least one point in an organized sport.

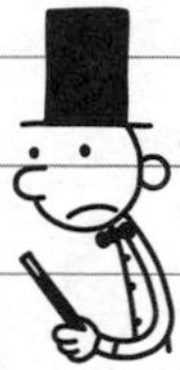

☐ Try out for a talent show.

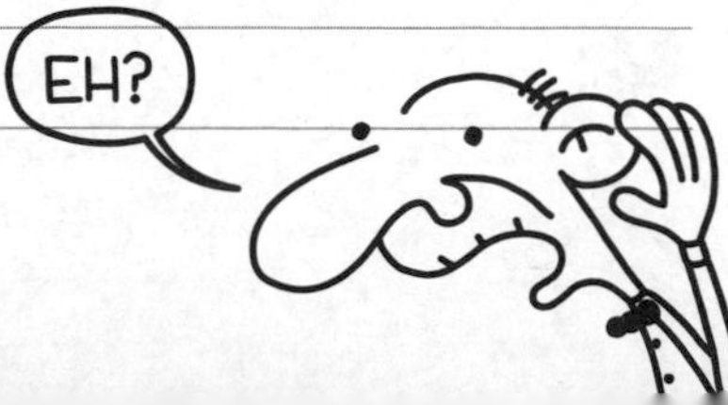
EH?

# Make your own TIME CAPSULE

TIME
CAPSULE
DO NOT OPEN
FOR 500 YEARS

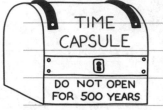

Hundreds of years from now, people are gonna want to know how you lived your life. What kinds of clothes did you wear? What kinds of stuff did you read? What did you do for entertainment?

Fill a box with things you think will give people in the future a good picture of what you're like. List the things you're gonna put in the box, then bury it where no one will dig it up for a long time!

**1.**

**2.**

**3.**

**4.**

**5.**

**6.**

**7.**

**8.**

# The BEST JOKE you've ever heard

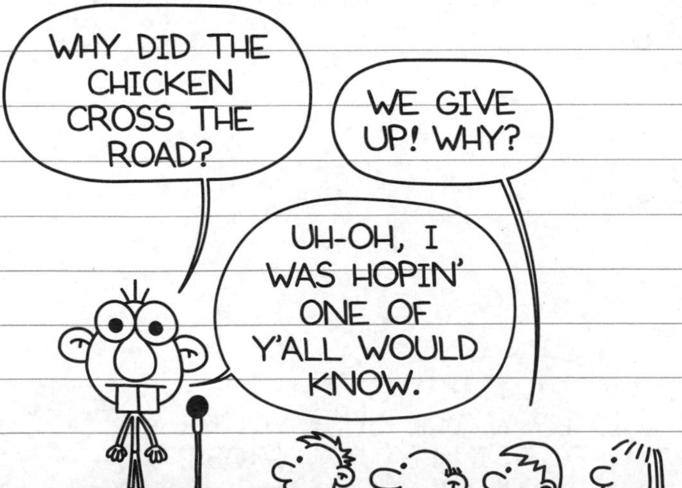
WHY DID THE CHICKEN CROSS THE ROAD?
WE GIVE UP! WHY?
UH-OH, I WAS HOPIN' ONE OF Y'ALL WOULD KNOW.

# Five things NOBODY KNOWS about you

BECAUSE THEY NEVER BOTHERED TO ASK

1.

2.

3.

4.

5.

I CAN PUT MY WHOLE FOOT IN MY MOUTH!
YOU'RE GROSS!

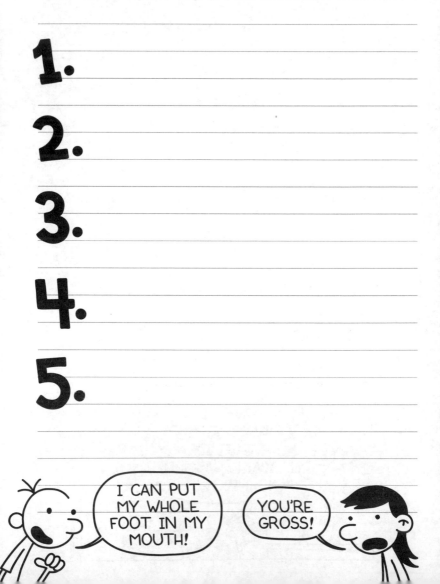

# The WORST NIGHTMARE you've ever had

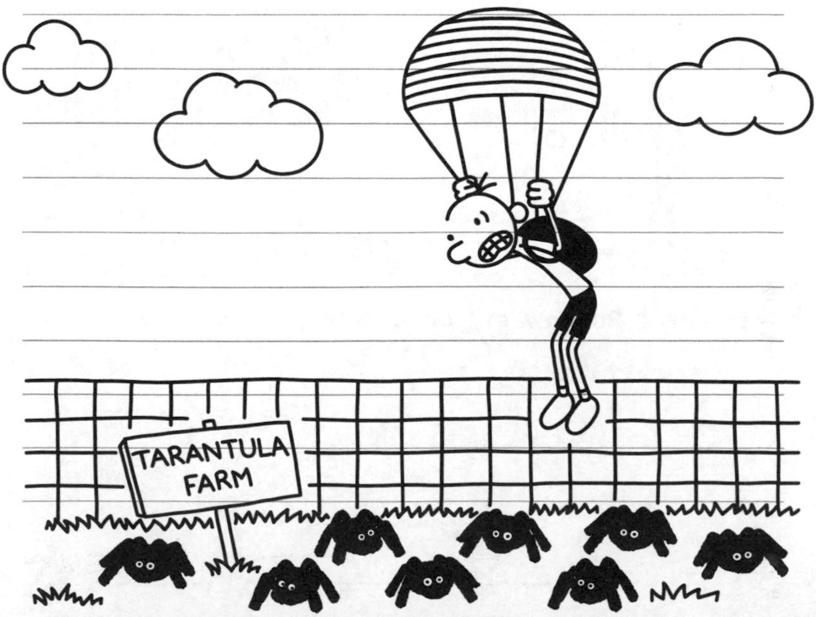
TARANTULA FARM

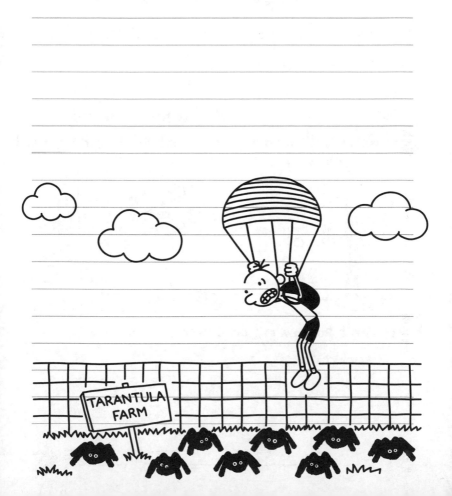

# Rules for your

1. Don't talk to me before 8:00 in the morning.

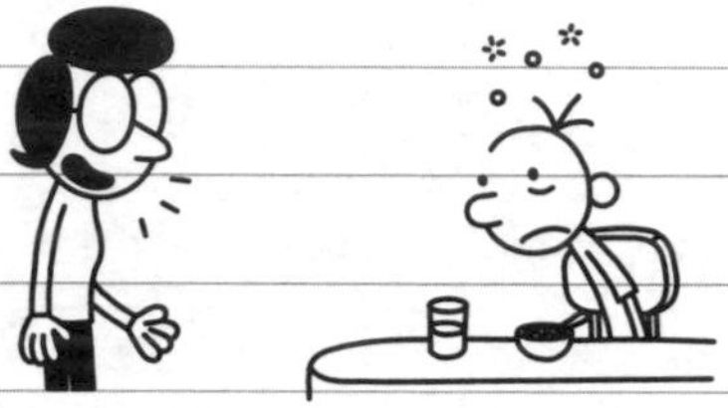

2. Don't make me sit next to my little brother on spaghetti night.

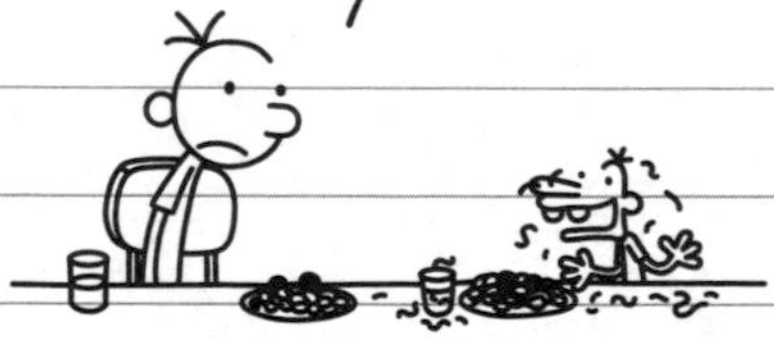

3. Don't walk into my room without knocking first.

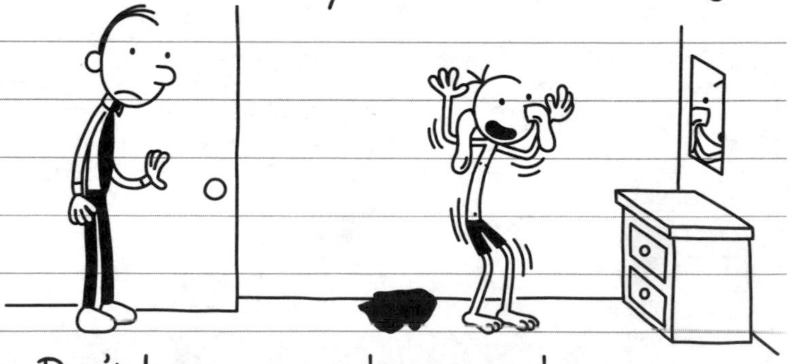

4. Don't borrow my underwear under any circumstances.

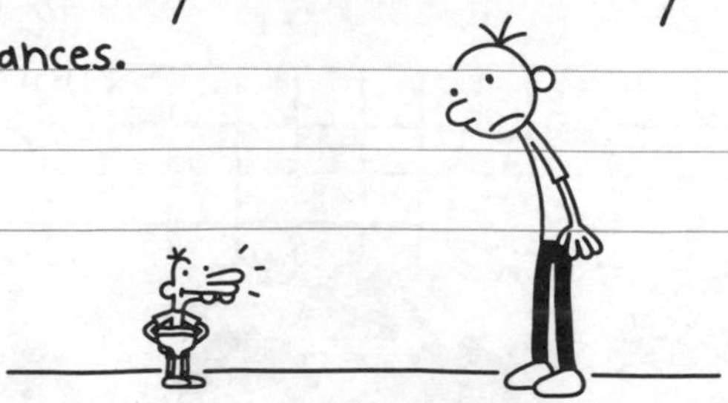

# FAMILY

**1.**

**2.**

**3.**

**4.**

# The SCOOP on your

The person you'd trust to keep
a secret: _____

The person who'd be a good
roommate in university: _____

The person you'd trust to go
clothes shopping for you: _____

The person you'd trust to give
you a haircut: _____

The person who's the worst liar: _____

The person who's most likely to
blame a fart on someone else: _____

The person who's most likely to
borrow something and forget to
give it back: _____

# CLASSMATES

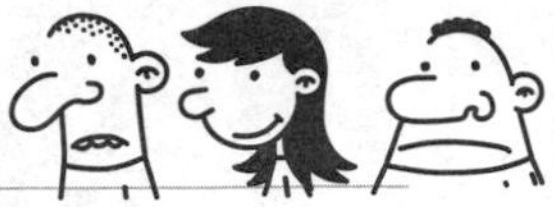

The person who'd have the best chance of surviving in the wild: ____________

The person you'd want to do your homework for you: ____________

The person who doesn't have a "whispering voice": ____________

The person you wouldn't want to get in a fistfight with: ____________

The person who you wish lived in your neighbourhood: ____________

The person who's most likely to do something crazy on a dare: ____________

The person you really wouldn't want to get hold of this book: ____________

# Your life, by

Longest you've ever gone without bathing:

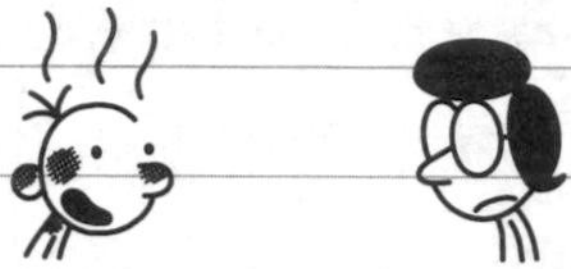

__________________

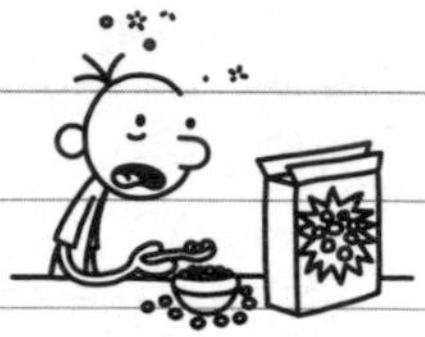

Most bowls of cereal you've ever eaten at one time:

__________________

Longest you've ever been grounded: __________________

Latest you've ever been for school:

__________________

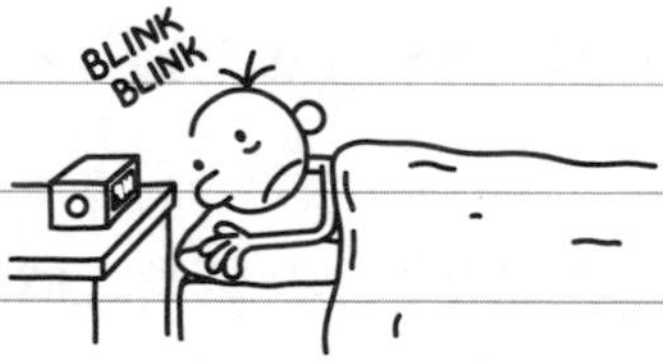
BLINK
BLINK

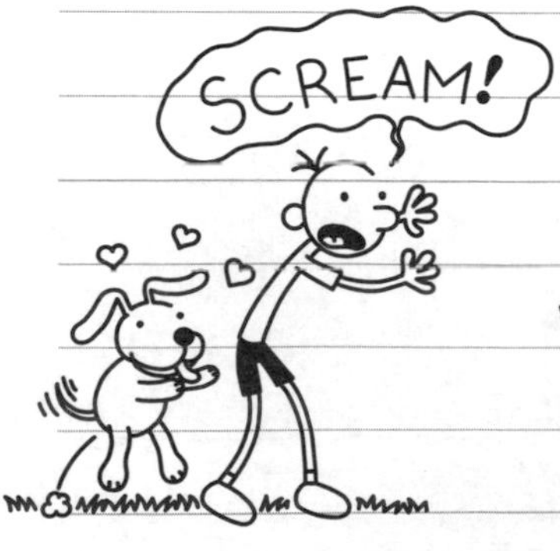
SCREAM!

Number of times you've been chased by a dog:

__________________

Number of times you've been locked out of the house:

__________________

# the numbers

Most hours you've spent doing homework in one night: ________

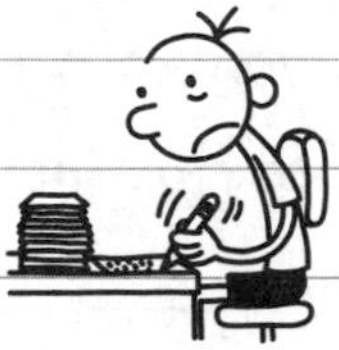

Most money you've ever saved up: ________

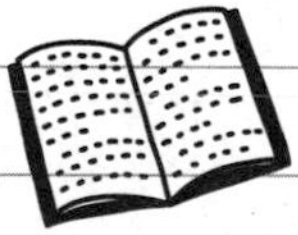

Length of the shortest book you've ever used for a book report: ________

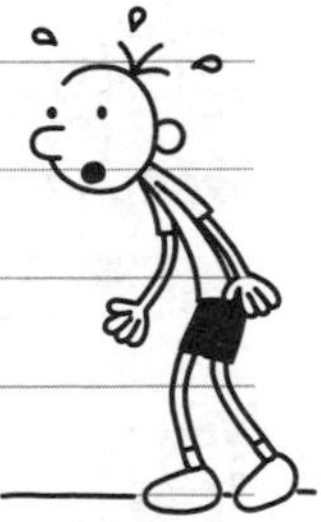

Furthest distance you've ever walked: ________

Longest you've ever gone without watching TV: ________

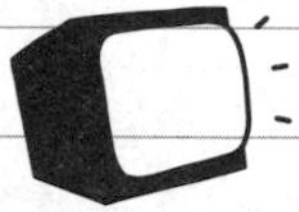

Number of times you've been caught picking your nose: ________

Number of times you've got away with picking your nose: ________

# Your life, by

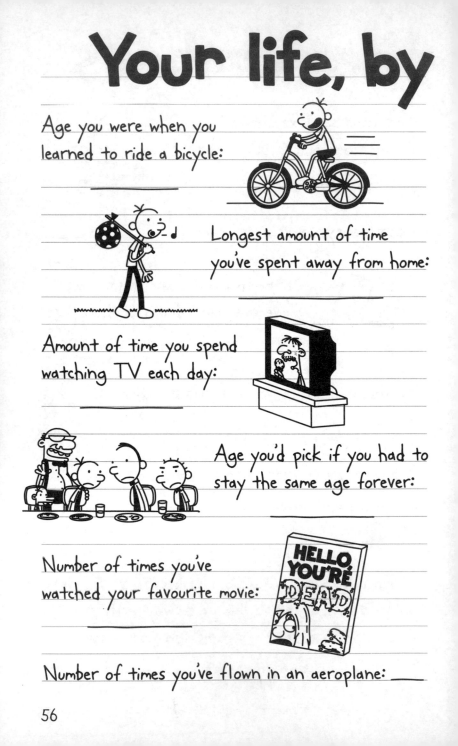

Age you were when you learned to ride a bicycle:

Longest amount of time you've spent away from home:

Amount of time you spend watching TV each day:

Age you'd pick if you had to stay the same age forever:

Number of times you've watched your favourite movie:

Number of times you've flown in an aeroplane:

# the numbers

Most number of times you've eaten fast food in a single day:

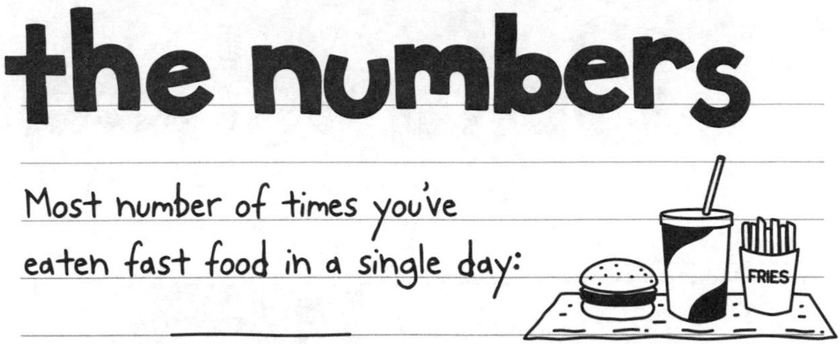
FRIES

________

Number of states you've been to: ________

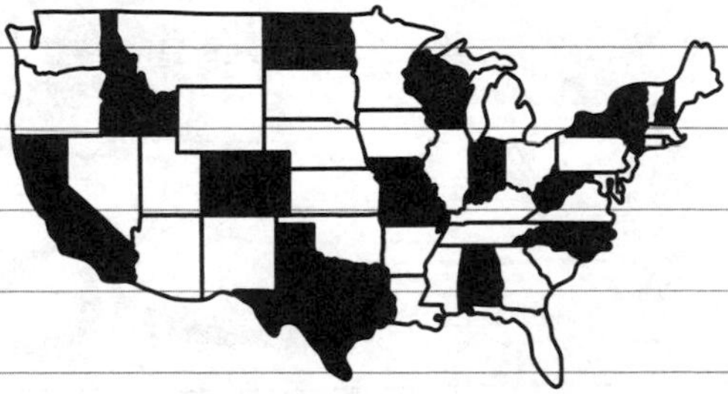

Most pets you've had at one time: ________

Most cavities you've ever had in one dental appointment:

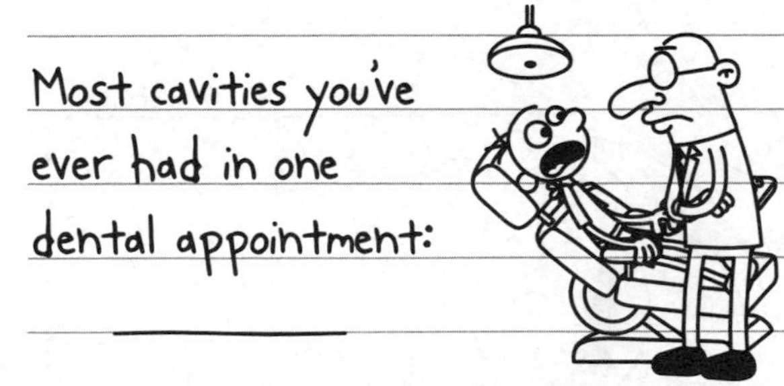

________

Longest you've ever waited in a queue: ________

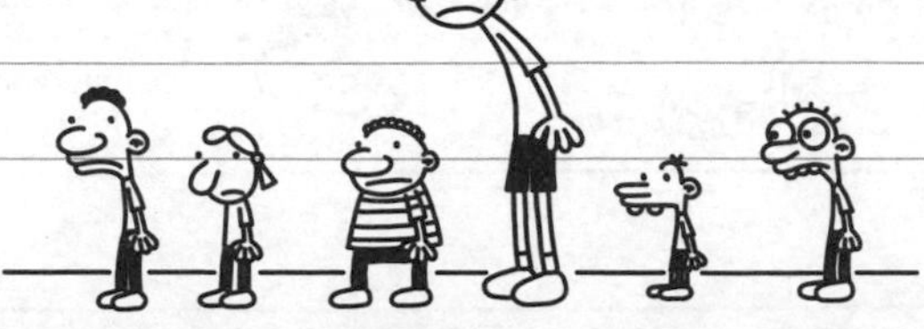

# Unfinished

## Li'l Cutie

66 *Mommy, did my pencil go to heaven?* 99

## Li'l Cutie

66 _____ 99

# COMICS

## Li'l Cutie

66 _____ 99

## Li'l Cutie

66 _____ 99

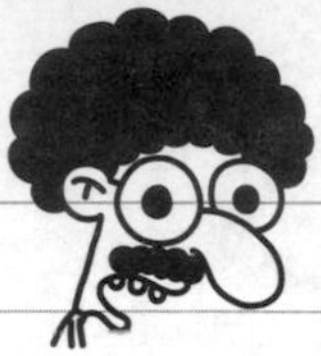

# Make your

“ ”

# OWN comics

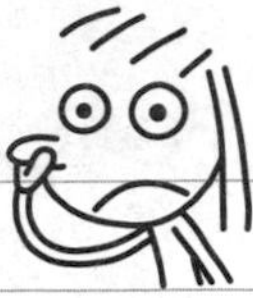

“ ”

# Come up with your own CATCHPHRASE

You know how some character in a movie or a TV show says something funny, and the next thing you know, EVERYONE is saying it? Well, why not come up with your OWN catchphrase, print up a bunch of T-shirts and totally cash in?

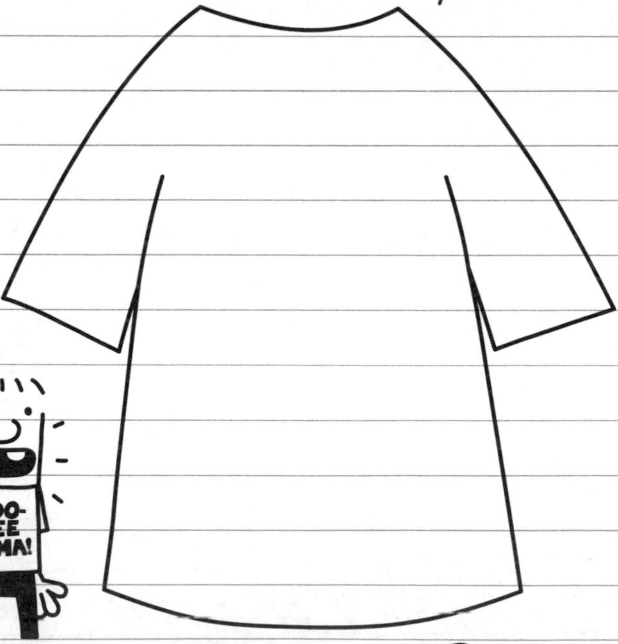

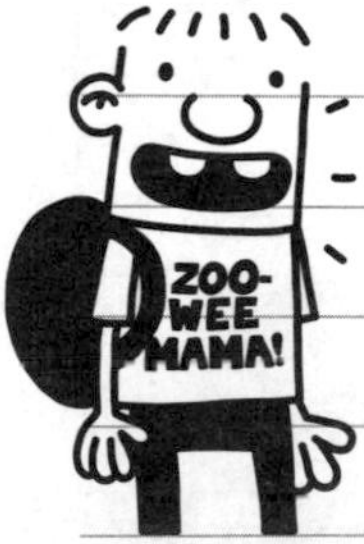
ZOO-
WEE
MAMA!

BONUS: Come up with another catchphrase and put it on a hat!

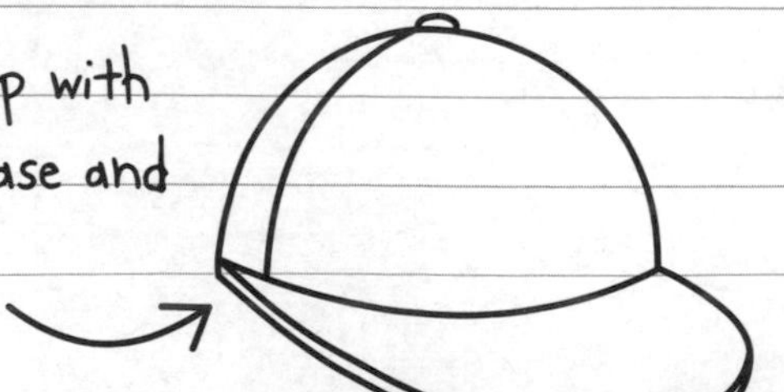

# In case you get AMNESIA...

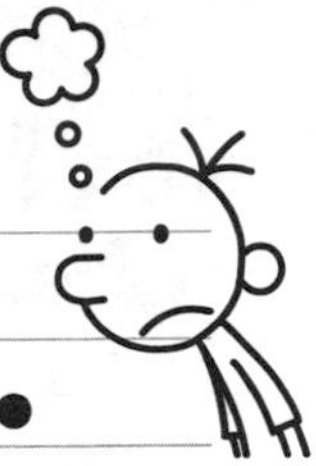

People in the movies are always getting clonked on the head, then waking up and not remembering who they are or where they came from. In case that ever happens to you, you should write down the most important facts about yourself now so you can get a head start on getting your memory back!

**1.**

**2.**

**3.**

**4.**

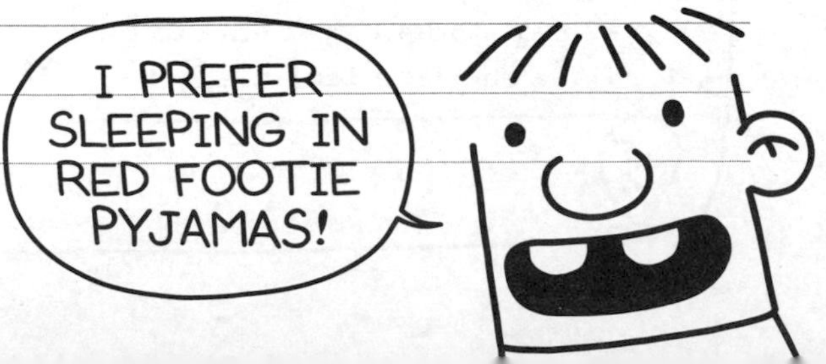
I PREFER SLEEPING IN RED FOOTIE PYJAMAS!

# The FIRST FOUR LAWS you'll pass when you get elected president

1.

2.

3.

4.

"I hereby decree that no middle school student shalt have to take a shower after Phys Ed."

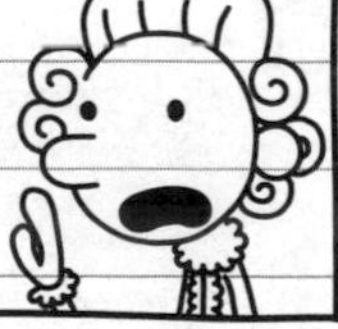

# The BADDEST THING
## you ever did as a little kid

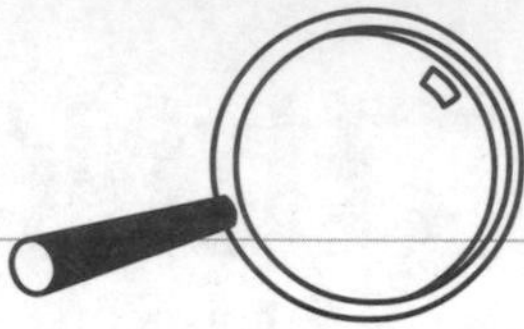

# Probing

Have you ever eaten food that was in the bin?

YES ☐ NO ☐

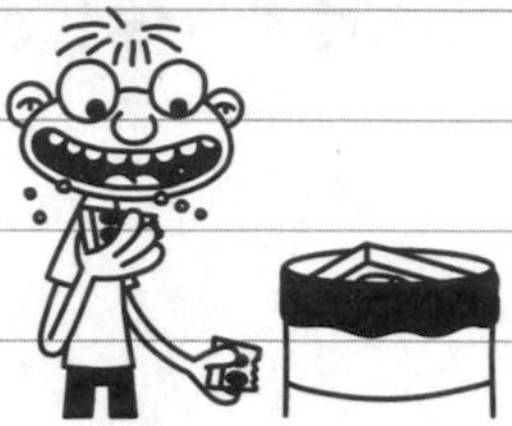

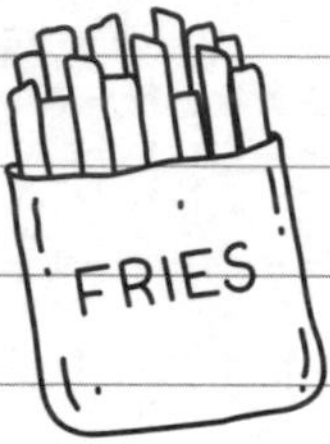
FRIES

Which restaurant do you think makes the best french fries?

___

What's something you tried once but will never try again?

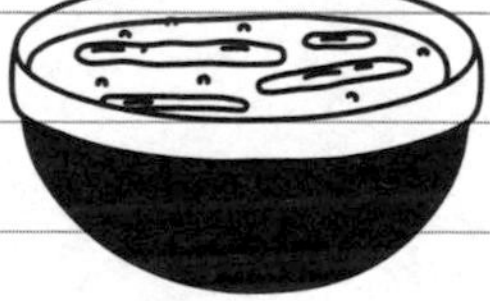

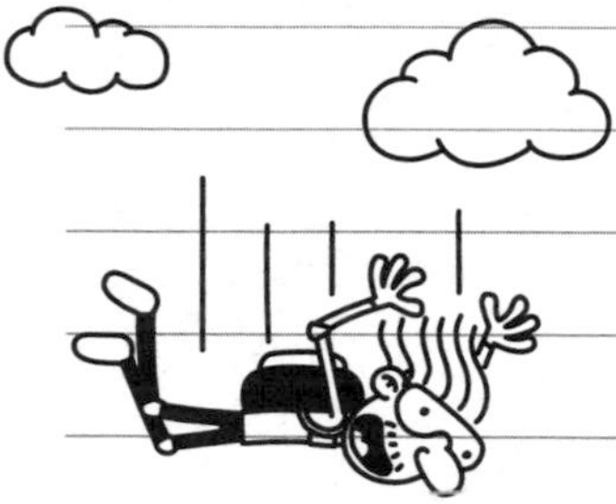

What's something you wish you were brave enough to do?

___

If you could eliminate one holiday, which one would you choose?

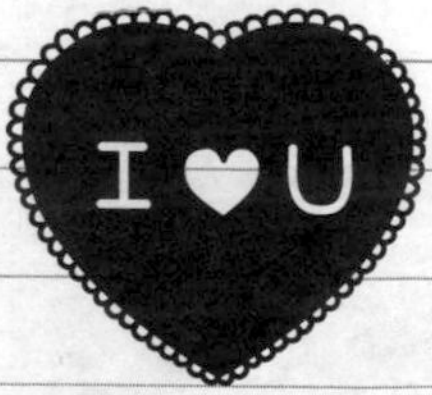
I ♥ U

___

# QUESTIONS

How old do you think a person should have to be before they get their first mobile phone?

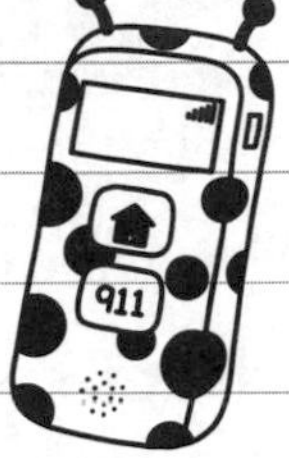
911

What's the most boring sport to watch on TV?

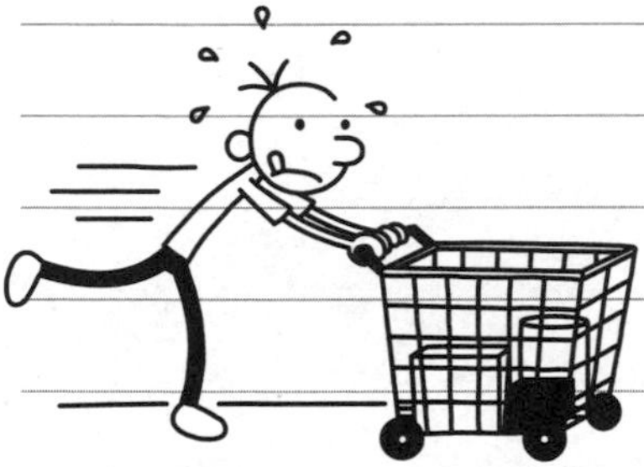

If you could go on a shopping spree at any store, which store would you choose?

If someone wrote a book about your life, what would the title be?

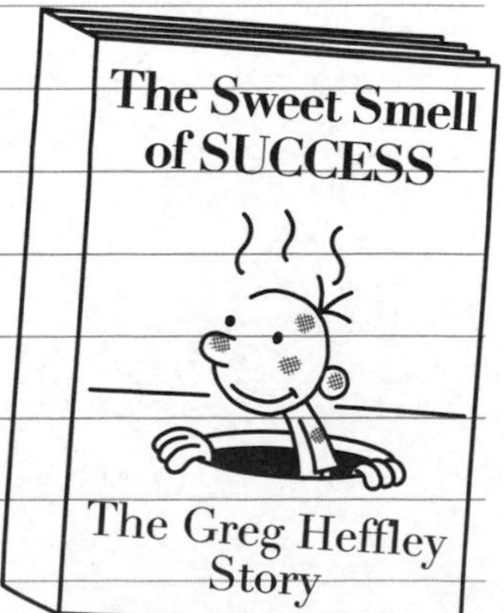
The Sweet Smell of SUCCESS
The Greg Heffley Story

# Practise your
# SIGNATURE

You'll be famous one day, so let's face it...that signature of yours is gonna need some work. Use this page to practise your fancy new autograph.

# List your INJURIES

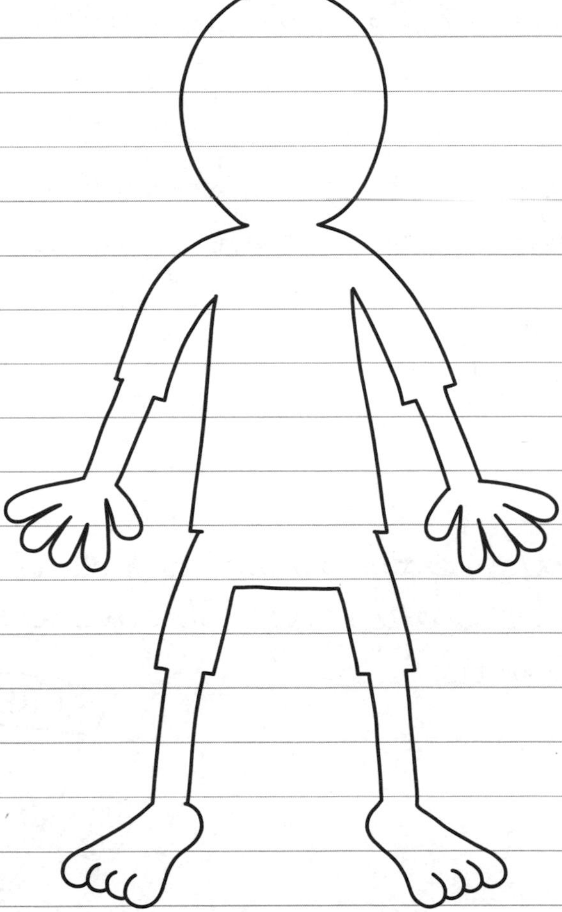

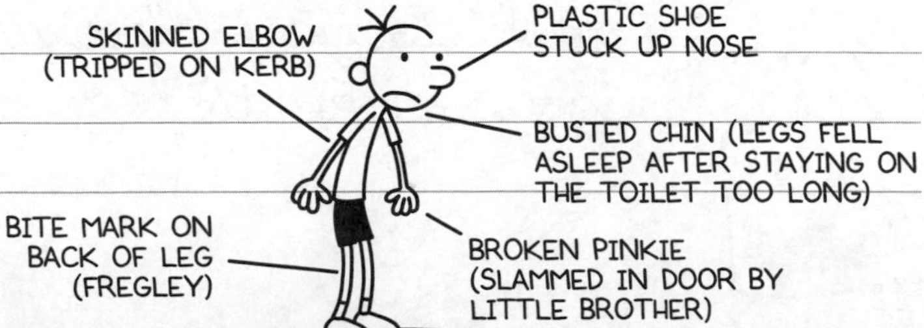
SKINNED ELBOW (TRIPPED ON KERB)
PLASTIC SHOE STUCK UP NOSE
BUSTED CHIN (LEGS FELL ASLEEP AFTER STAYING ON THE TOILET TOO LONG)
BITE MARK ON BACK OF LEG (FREGLEY)
BROKEN PINKIE (SLAMMED IN DOOR BY LITTLE BROTHER)

# A few questions

Do you believe in unicorns?

If you ever got to meet a unicorn, what would you ask it?

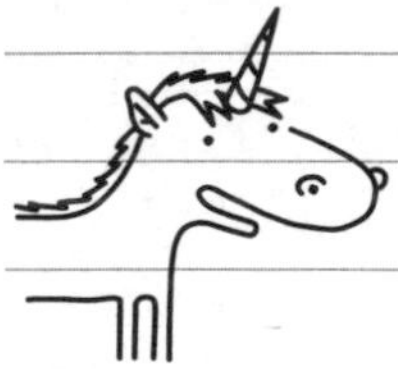

Have you ever drawn a picture that was so scary that it gave you nightmares?

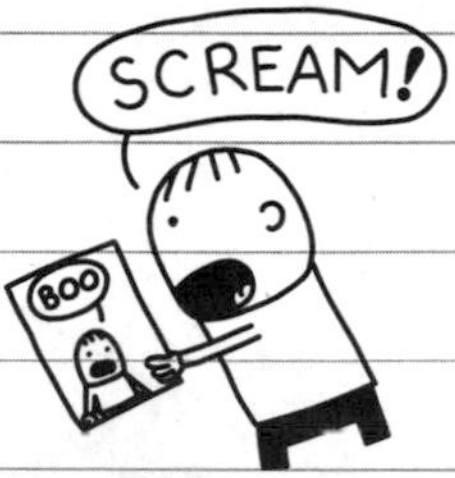
SCREAM!
BOO

How many nights a week do you sleep in your parents' bed?

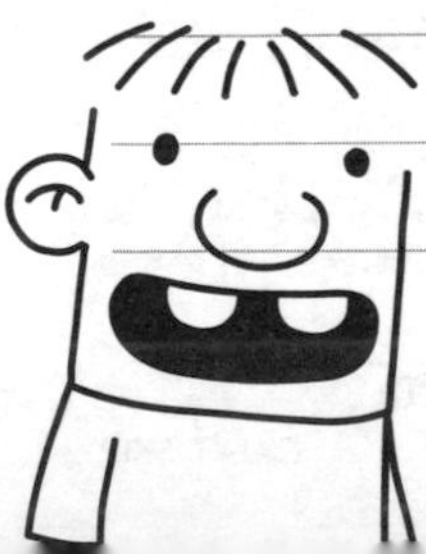

# from ROWLEY 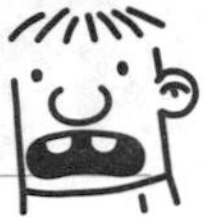

Have you ever tied your shoes without help from a grown-up?

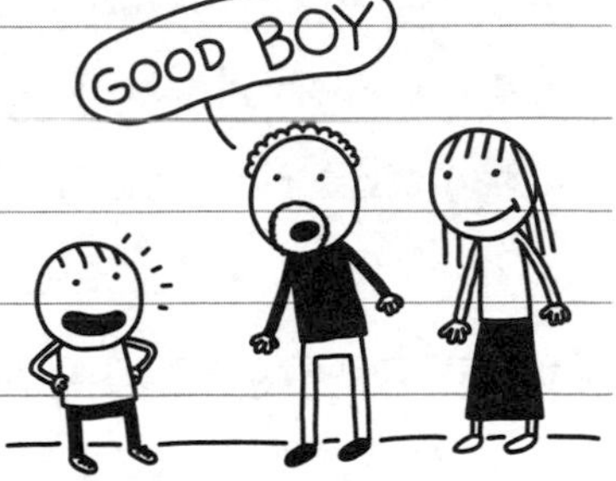
GOOD BOY

Have you ever got sick from eating cherry lip gloss?

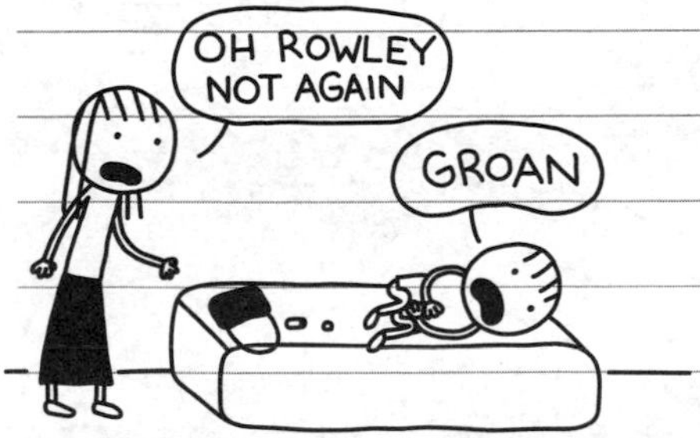
OH ROWLEY NOT AGAIN
GROAN

Are your friends jealous that you're a really good skipper?

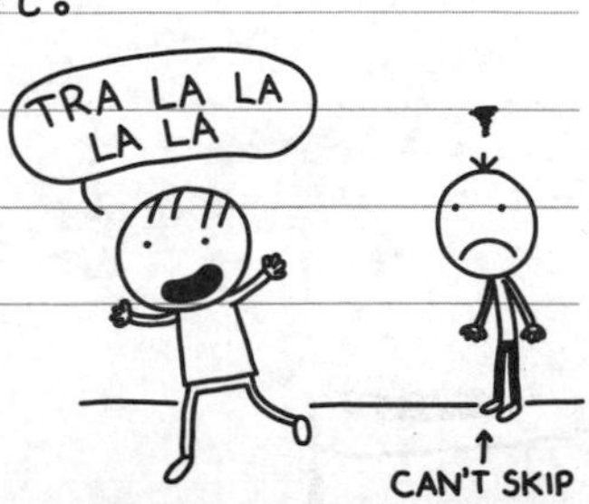
TRA LA LA LA LA
CAN'T SKIP

# Design your own

When you're famous, people are gonna want to name stuff after you. In fact, a few years from now, restaurants could be selling a sandwich with your name on it. So you might as well pick out the ingredients now.

WHITE BREAD

SWISS CHEESE

CHICKEN TENDER

KETCHUP

PEPPERONI

LETTUCE

BARBECUE SAUCE

# "The Rowley"

# SANDWICH

STACK YOUR SANDWICH HERE
⬇

# The BIGGEST MISTAKES

**1.** Believing my older brother when he said it was "Pyjama Day" at my school.

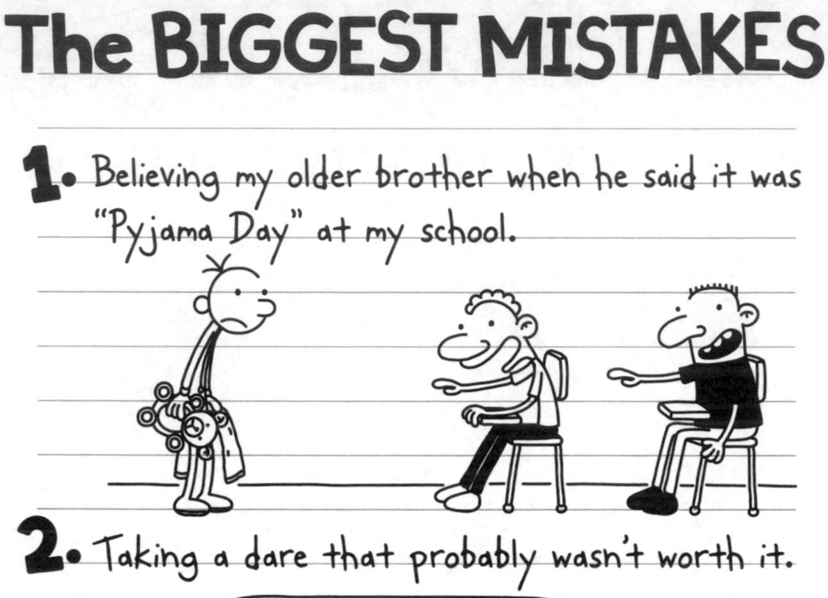

**2.** Taking a dare that probably wasn't worth it.

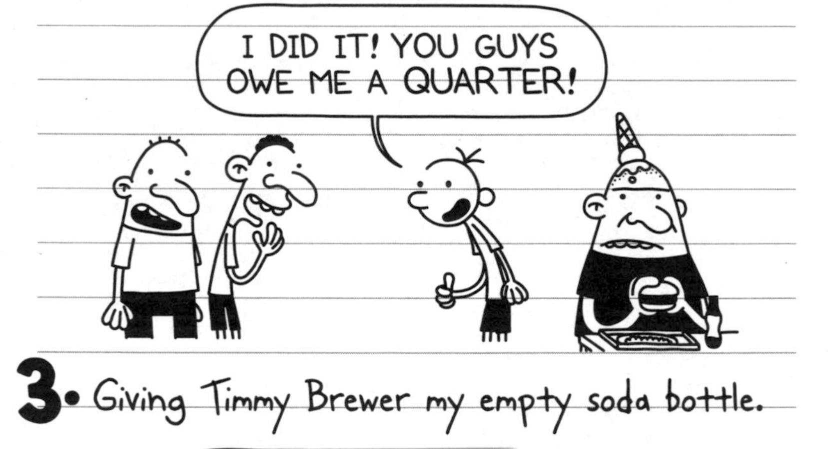
I DID IT! YOU GUYS OWE ME A QUARTER!

**3.** Giving Timmy Brewer my empty soda bottle.

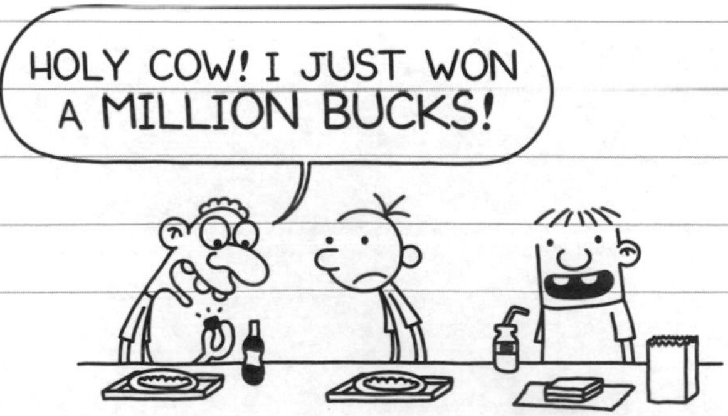
HOLY COW! I JUST WON A MILLION BUCKS!

# you've made so far

**1.**

**2.**

**3.**

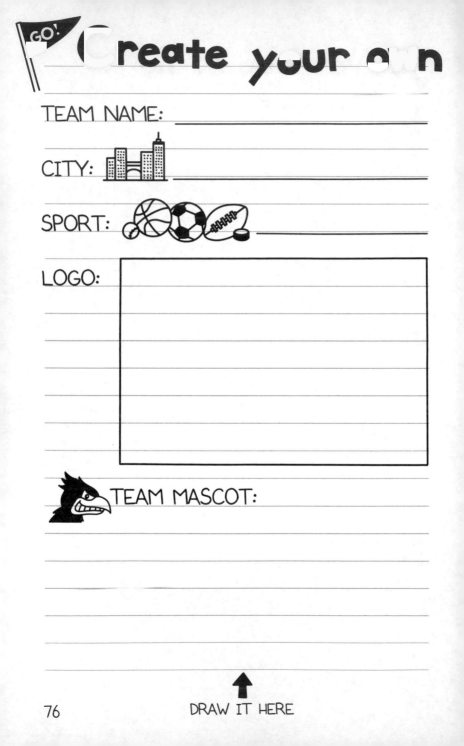

GO! **Create your own**

TEAM NAME: _____

CITY: _____

SPORT: _____

LOGO:

TEAM MASCOT: _____

↑
DRAW IT HERE

# SPORTS TEAM

## STARTING ROSTER

| | NAME | POSITION |
|---|---|---|
| 1. | | |
| 2. | | |
| 3. | | |
| 4. | | |
| 5. | | |

UNIFORM:

# Unfinished

## Creighton the Cretin

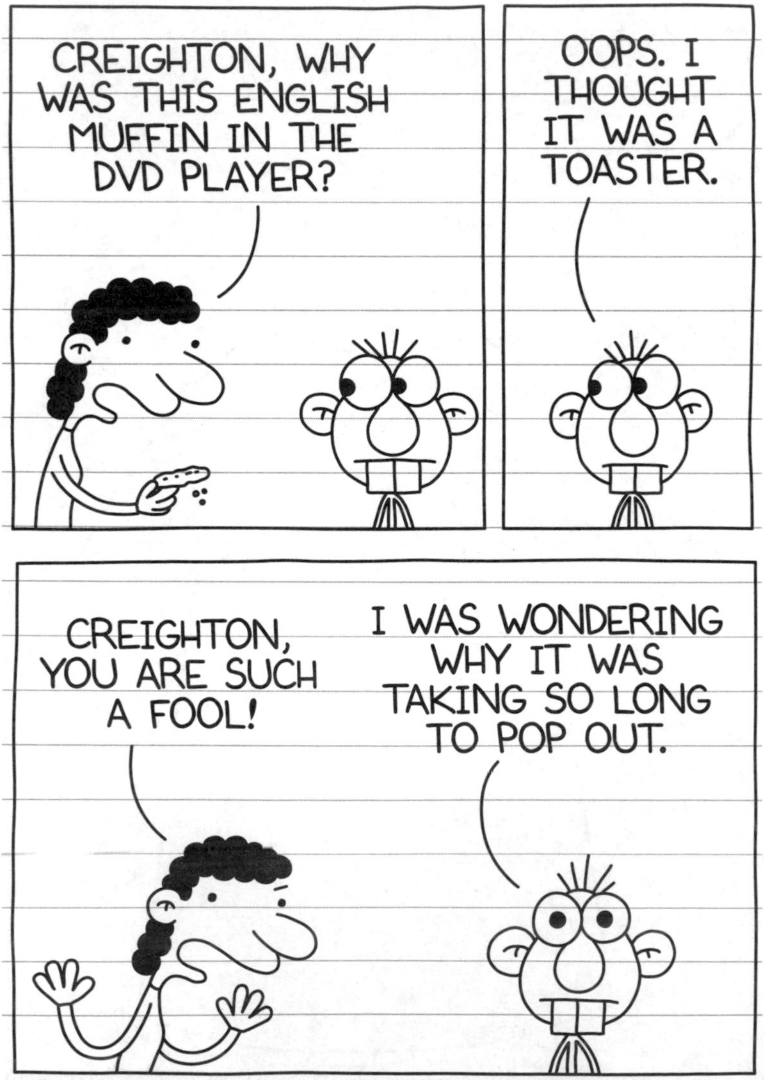
CREIGHTON, WHY WAS THIS ENGLISH MUFFIN IN THE DVD PLAYER?
OOPS. I THOUGHT IT WAS A TOASTER.
CREIGHTON, YOU ARE SUCH A FOOL!
I WAS WONDERING WHY IT WAS TAKING SO LONG TO POP OUT.

# COMICS

## Creighton the Cretin

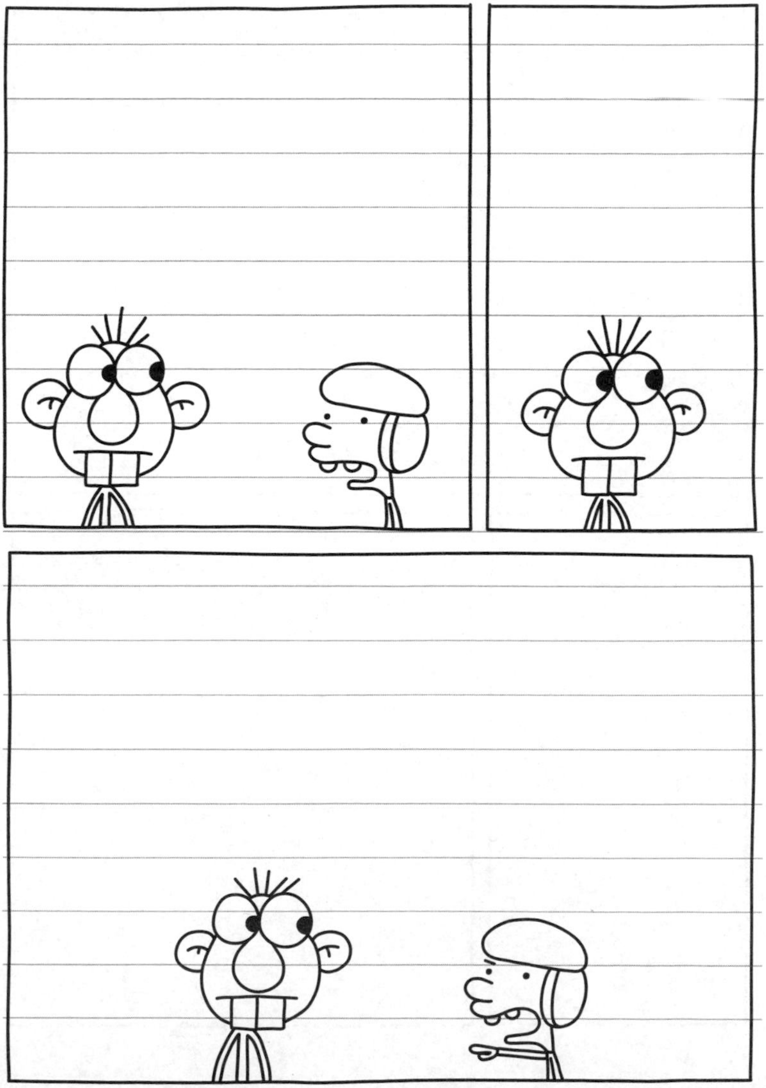

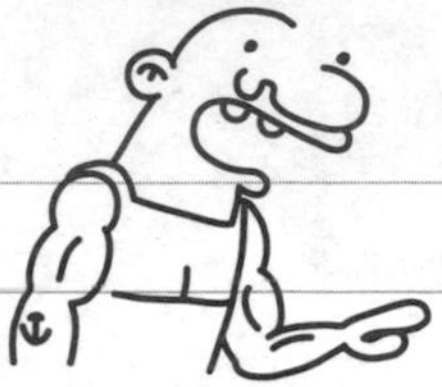

# Make your

# OWN comics

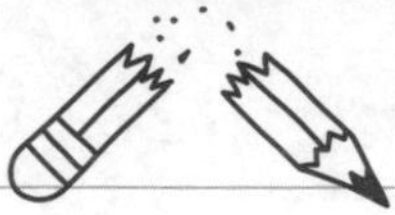 RODRICK'S

INTELLIGENCE TESTER:

Do this maze and then check to see if you're dumb or smart.

START

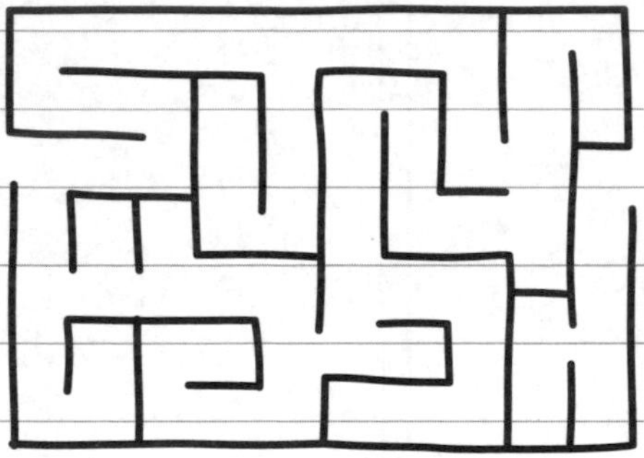

FINISH

(If you can finish this, you're smart, and if you can't, you're dumb.)

Put this sentence up to a mirror and then read it as loud as you can:

.NOЯOM A MA I

Fill in the blank below:

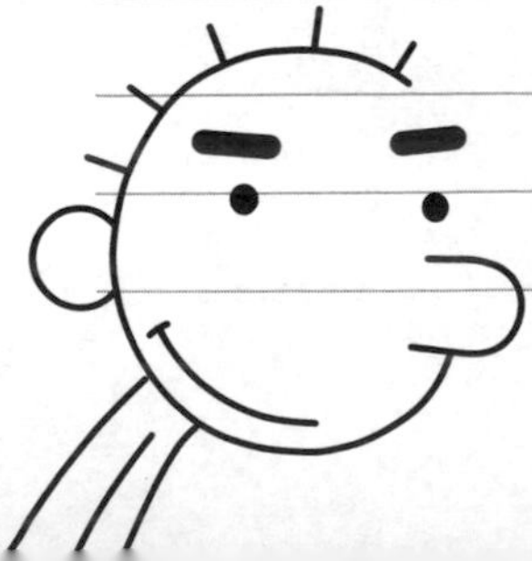

Q: Who is awesome?

A: RODR_CK

(Hint: "I")

# ACTIVITY PAGES

Answer this question yes or no <u>only</u>:

Q: Are you embarrassed that you
pooped in your diaper today?

_____

Do you want to start a band? Well, I
guess you're out of luck because the
best name is already taken and
that's Löded Diper. But if you still
want to start a band then you can
use this mix-and-match thing:*

| FIRST HALF | SECOND HALF |
|------------|-------------|
| Wikkid | Lizzerd |
| Nästy | Pigz |
| Vilent | Vömmit |
| Rabbid | Dagger |
| Killer | Syckle |
| Ransid | Smellz |

* P.S. If you use one of these names,
you owe me a hundred bucks.

# Form your own

BAND NAME:

GENRE:

(ROCK, POP, RAP, COUNTRY, ETC.)

LOGO →

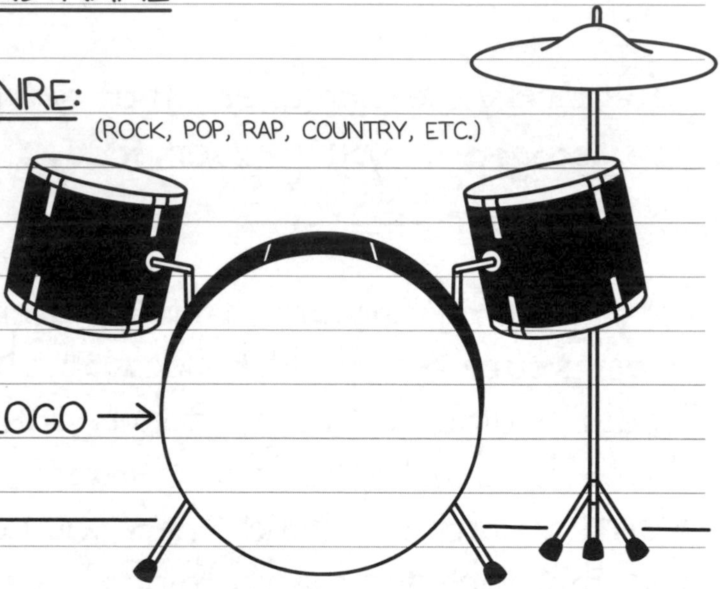

LEAD SINGER:

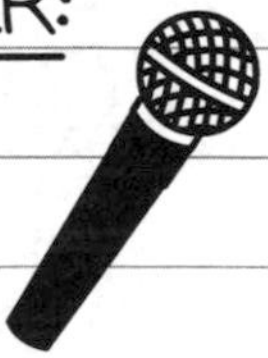

DRUMMER:

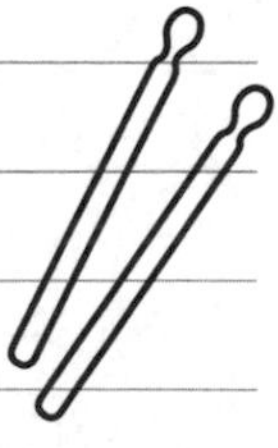

LEAD GUITARIST:

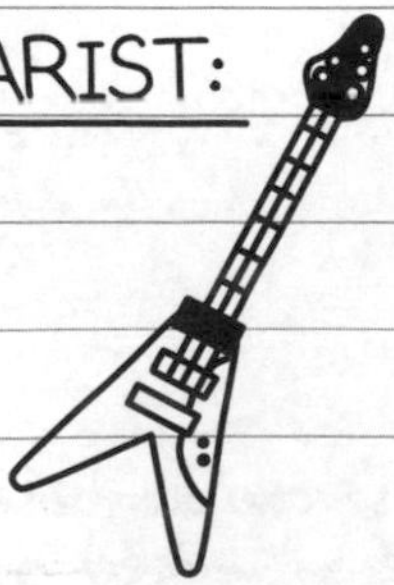

BASS GUITARIST:

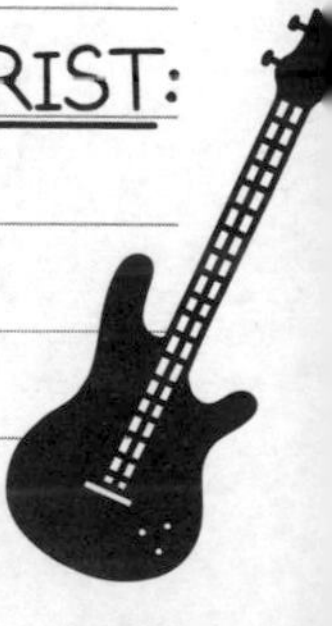

# BAND

Design a poster to advertise your first show!

# Write your own

DIPER OVERLÖDE by Rodrick Heffley

We're coming through your speakers
Runnin' through your town
We're pourin' through your headphones
And your eyes are turnin' brown.

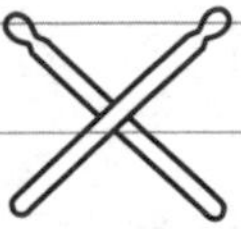

We're pumpin' up the volume
And we can't be stopped!
Your brains are leakin' out your ears
Your head's about to pop.

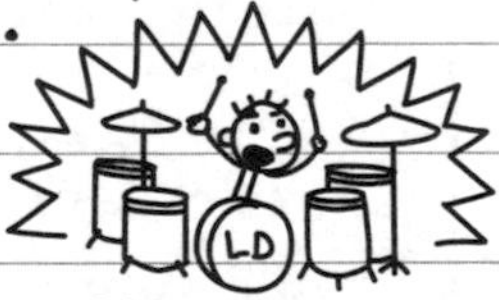
LD

This is a Diper!
A Diper Overlöde.
And you better run for cover
'Cause we're 'bout to explode.

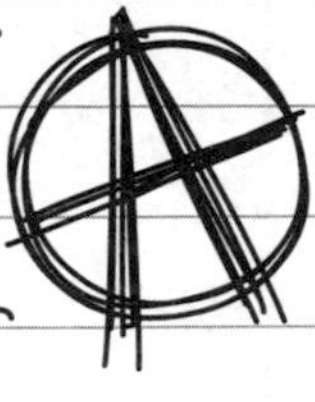

Said it's a Diper!
A Diper Overlöde.
And your mother's gonna shudder
When this Diper hits the road.

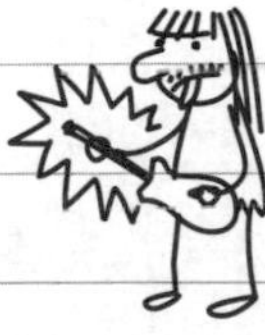

The pressure's buildin' up now
And we're about to bust out!
Rockin' stadiums, gymnasiums,
If you're feelin' us, shout!

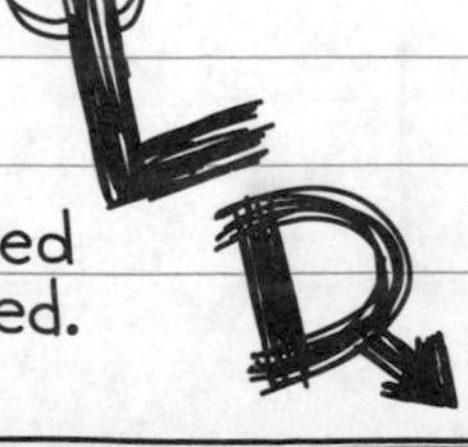

Yes, it's a Diper!
A Diper Overlöde.
And you ain't been this covered
Since the last time it snowed.

# SONG

# Design your own

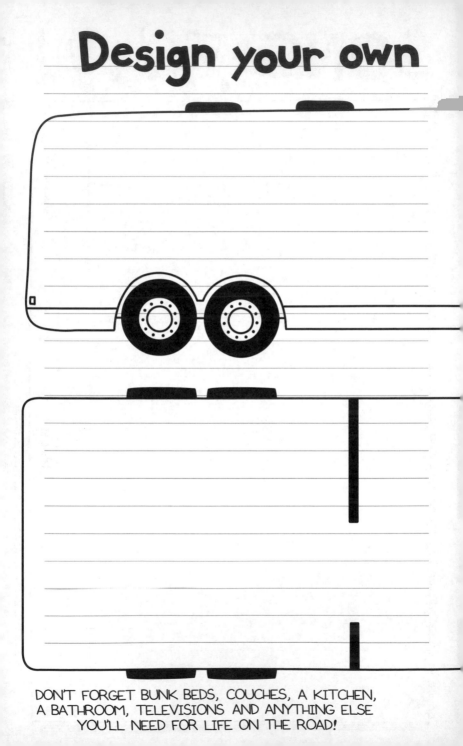

DON'T FORGET BUNK BEDS, COUCHES, A KITCHEN,
A BATHROOM, TELEVISIONS AND ANYTHING ELSE
YOU'LL NEED FOR LIFE ON THE ROAD!

# TOUR BUS

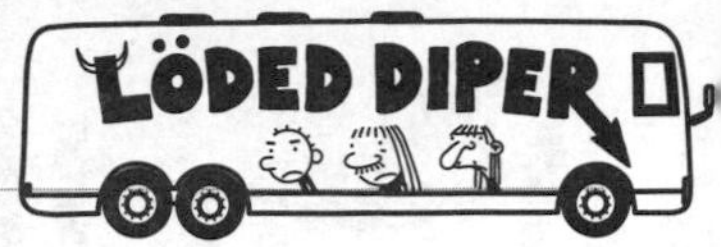
LÖDED DIPER

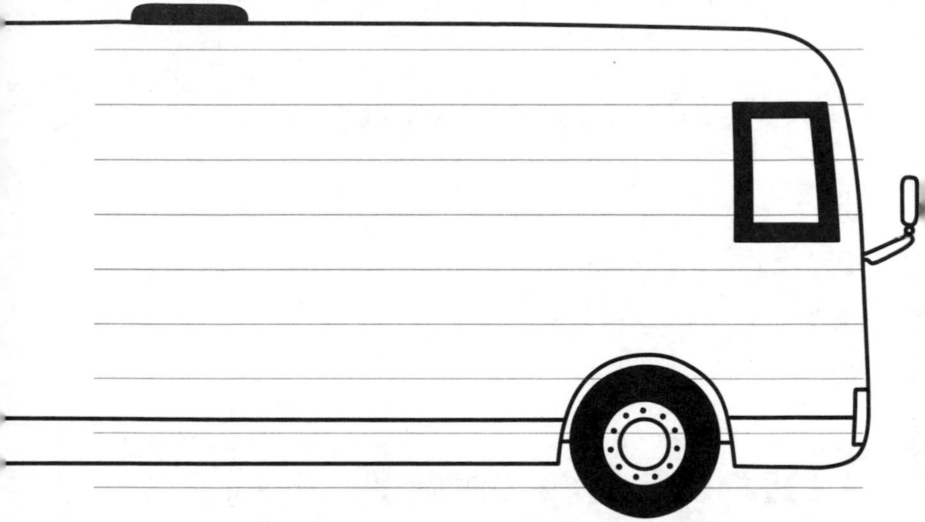

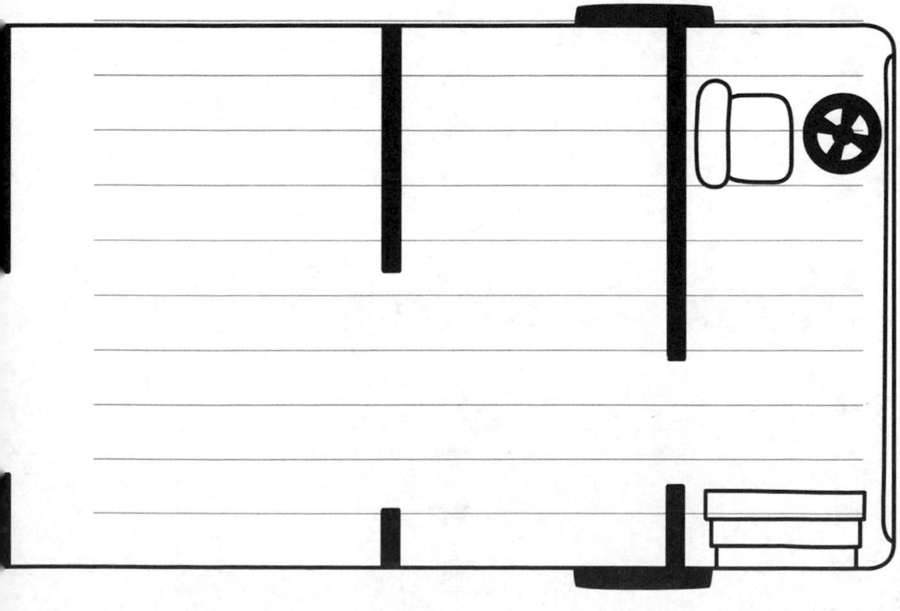

# Plan the ultimate

## People to invite

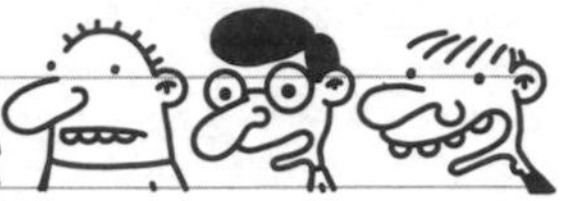

★
★
★
★

## Things to pack

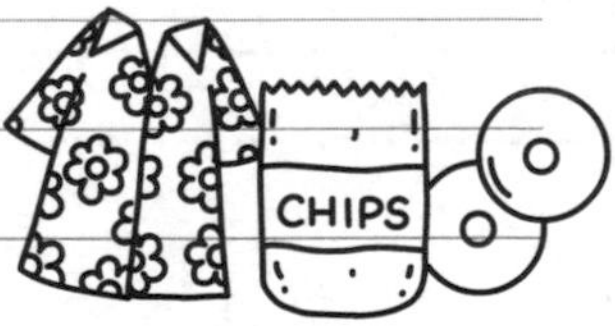
CHIPS

★
★
★
★
★
★
★
★

## Music to bring

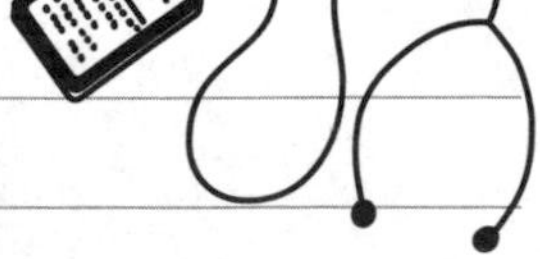

★
★
★
★
★
★
★
★

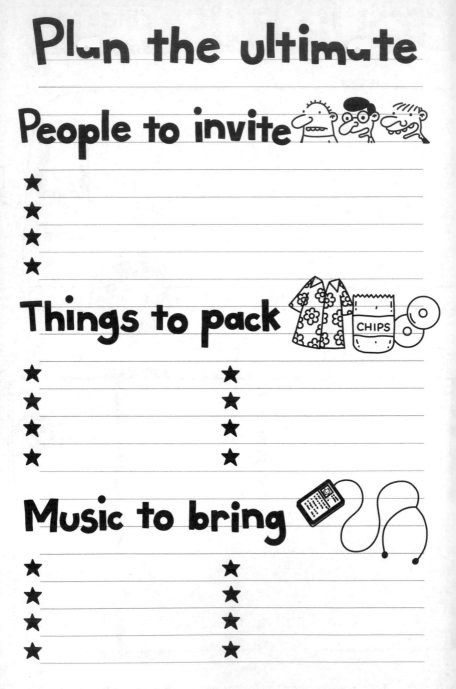

# ROAD TRIP

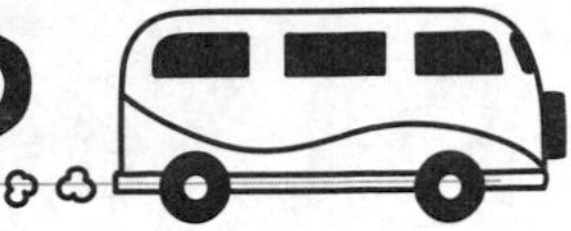

## Places to see

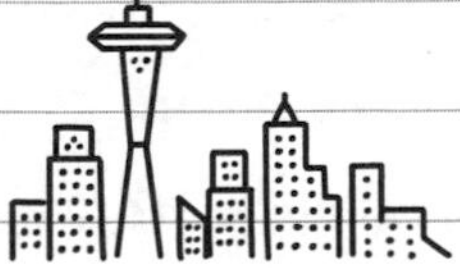

★ ★

★ ★

★ ★

★ ★

## Map your route

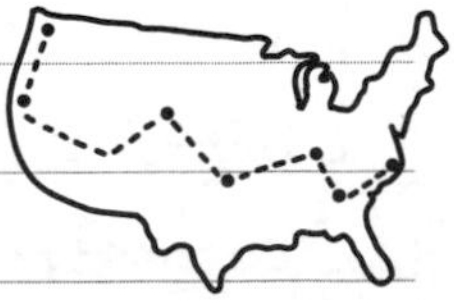

# Your DRESSING

If you end up being a famous musician or a movie star, you're gonna need to put together a list of things you'll need in your dressing room.

Requirements for Greg Heffley - page 1 of 9

3 litres of grape soda

2 extra-large pepperoni pizzas

2 dozen freshly baked chocolate-chip cookies

1 bowl of jelly beans (no pink or white ones)

1 popcorn machine

1 52-inch plasma TV

3 video-game consoles with 10 games apiece

1 soft-serve ice-cream machine

10 waffle cones

1 terry-cloth robe

1 pair of slippers

*** bathroom must have heated toilet seat

*** toilet paper must be name brand

# ROOM requirements

You might as well get your list together now so that you're ready when you hit the big time.

# How well do you

Answer these questions, and then ask your friend the same things. Keep track of how many answers you got right.

FRIEND'S NAME: _____

Has your friend ever been
carsick?                                        _____

If your friend could meet any
celebrity, who would it be?      _____

Where was your friend born?    _____

Has your friend ever laughed
so hard that milk came out
of their nose?                              _____

Has your friend ever been
sent to the principal's office?   _____

9—10: YOU KNOW YOUR FRIEND SO WELL IT'S SCARY
6—8: NOT BAD...YOU KNOW YOUR FRIEND PRETTY WELL!

# know your FRIEND?

What's your friend's favourite junk food? __________

Has your friend ever broken a bone? __________

When was the last time your friend wet the bed? __________

If your friend had to permanently transform into an animal, what animal would it be? __________

Is your friend secretly afraid of clowns? __________

Now count up your correct answers and look at the scale below to see how you did.

2–5: DID YOU GUYS JUST MEET OR SOMETHING?
0–1: TIME TO GET A NEW FRIEND

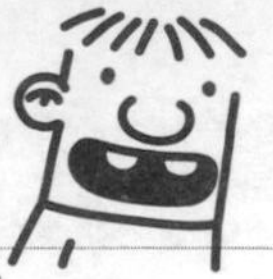

# Take a friendship

Want to see if you and your friend are a good match? First, go through each pair of items below and circle the one you like best.

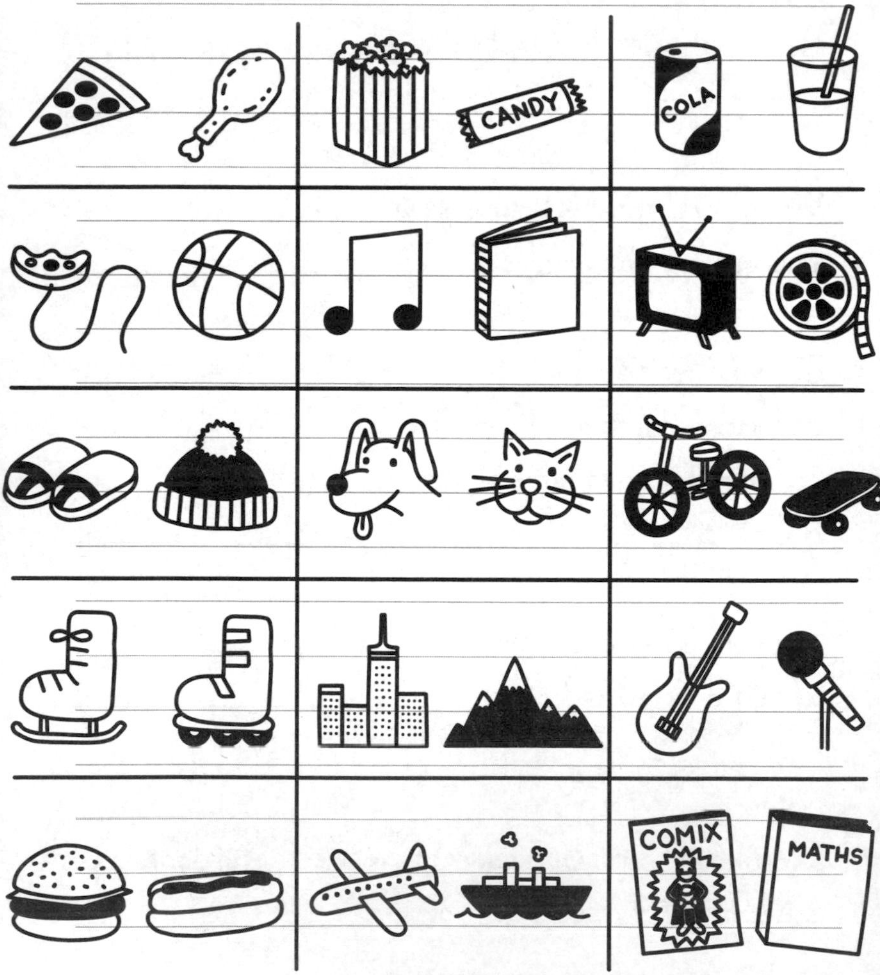
CANDY
COLA
COMIX
MATHS

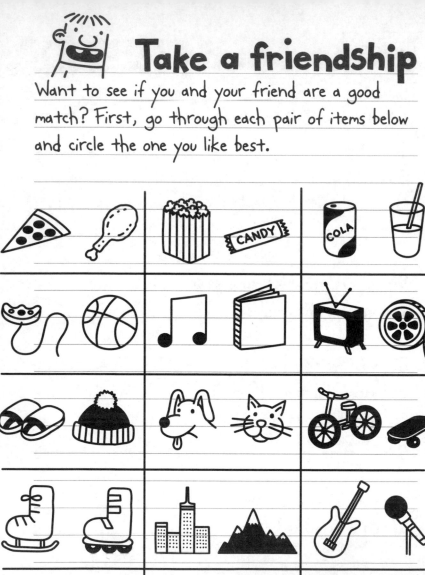

# COMPATIBILITY TEST

Then have your friend go through the same list and make their selections. See how well your answers match up!

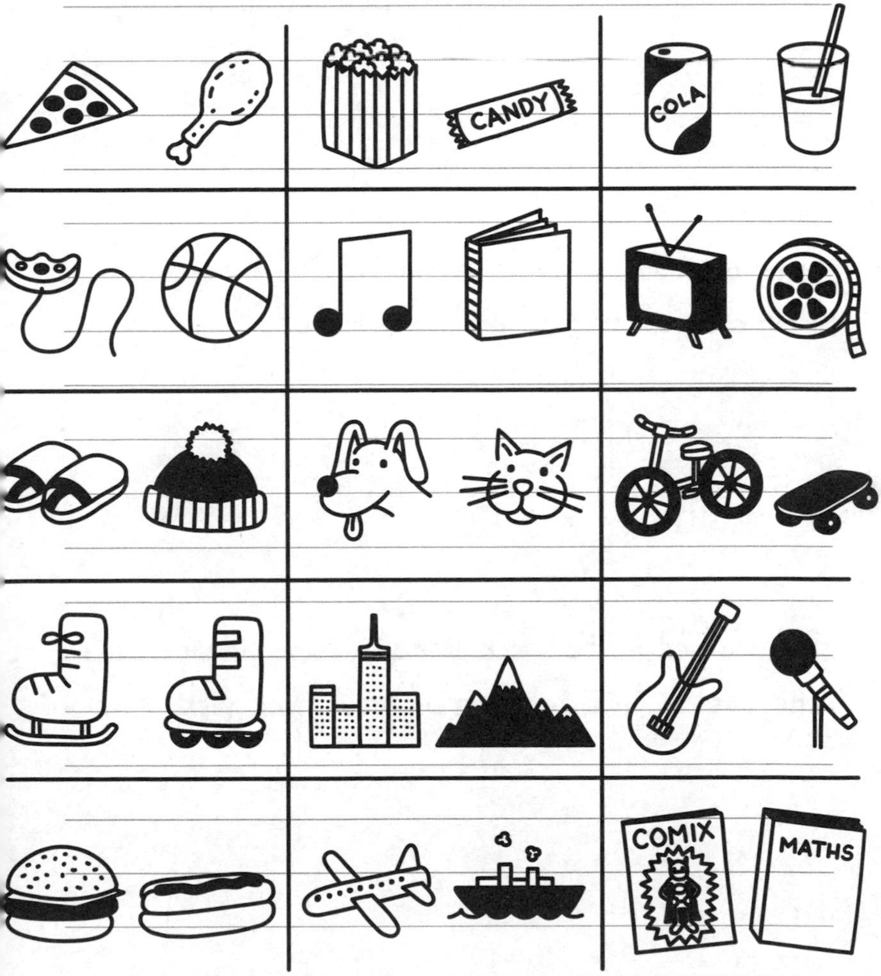
CANDY
COLA
COMIX
MATHS

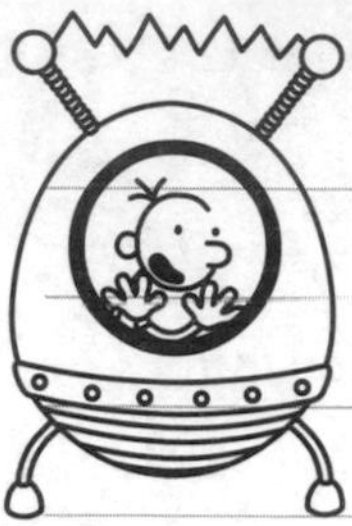

# If you had a

If you could go back in time and change the future, but you only had five minutes, where would you go?

If you could go back in time and witness any event in history, what would it be?

If you had to be stuck living in some time period in the past, what time period would you pick?

# TIME MACHINE...

If you could go back and videotape one event from your own life, what would it be?

If you could go back and tell your past self one thing, what would it be?

If you could go forward in time and tell your future self something, what would it be?

YOU LOOK RIDICULOUS IN THOSE SOCKS!
FAH!

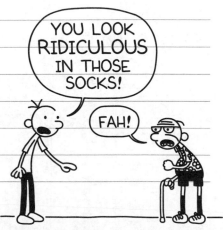

SPROING

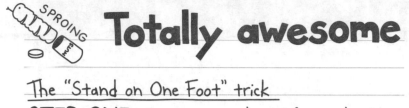

# Totally awesome

The "Stand on One Foot" trick

STEP ONE: On your way home from school, bet your friend they can't stand on one foot for three minutes without talking.

THAT'S SO CINCHY!

STEP TWO: While your friend stands on one foot, knock real hard on some crabby neighbour's front door.

KNOCK KNOCK KNOCK
?

STEP THREE: Run.

WHADDA YOU WANT?
ZIP

# PRACTICAL JOKES

## A JOKE YOU'VE PLAYED ON A FRIEND:

## A JOKE YOU'VE PLAYED ON A FAMILY MEMBER:

## A JOKE YOU'VE PLAYED ON A TEACHER:

# Draw your BEDROOM

Joshie

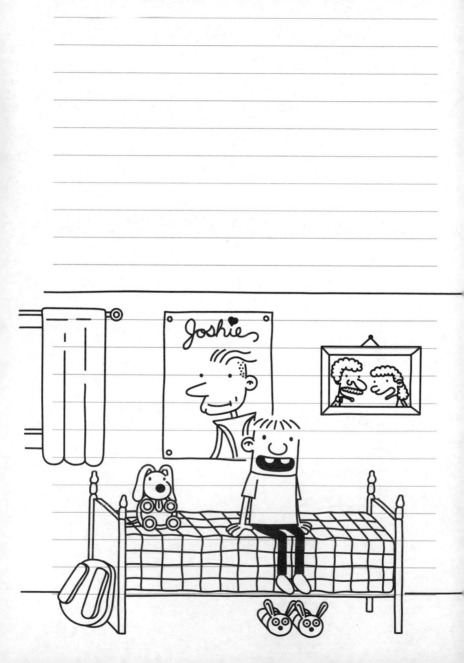

# the way it looks right now

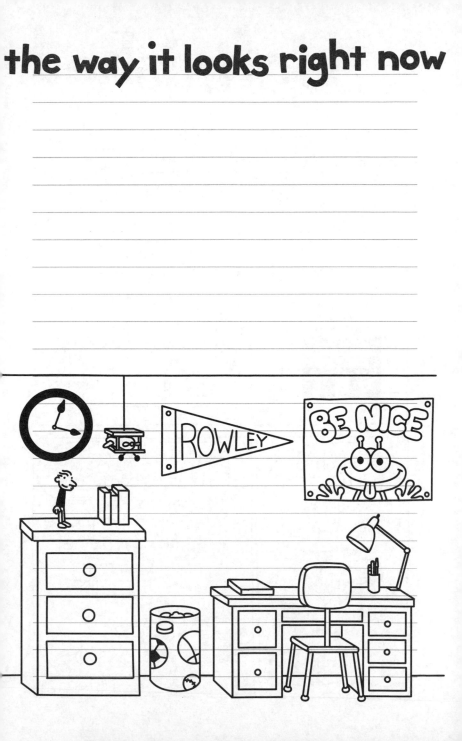

# Unfinished

## The Amazing Fart Police

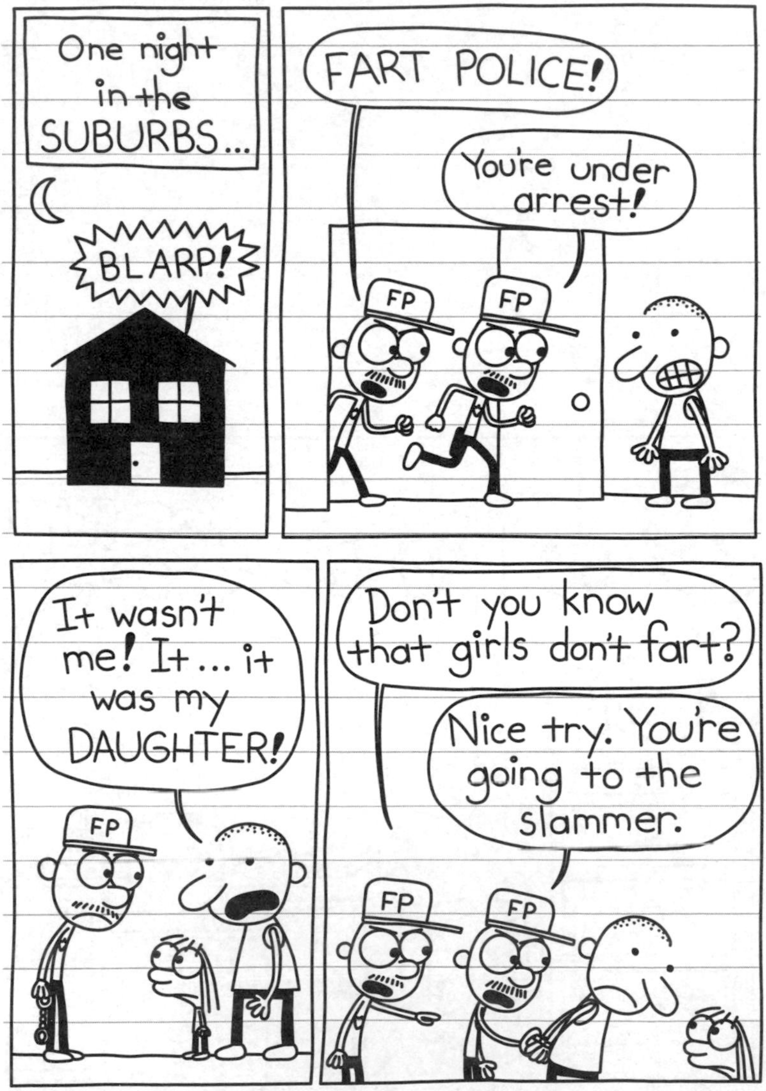

One night in the SUBURBS...
BLARP!
FART POLICE!
You're under arrest!
FP
FP
It wasn't me! It... it was my DAUGHTER!
FP
Don't you know that girls don't fart?
Nice try. You're going to the slammer.
FP
FP

# COMICS

## The Amazing Fart Police

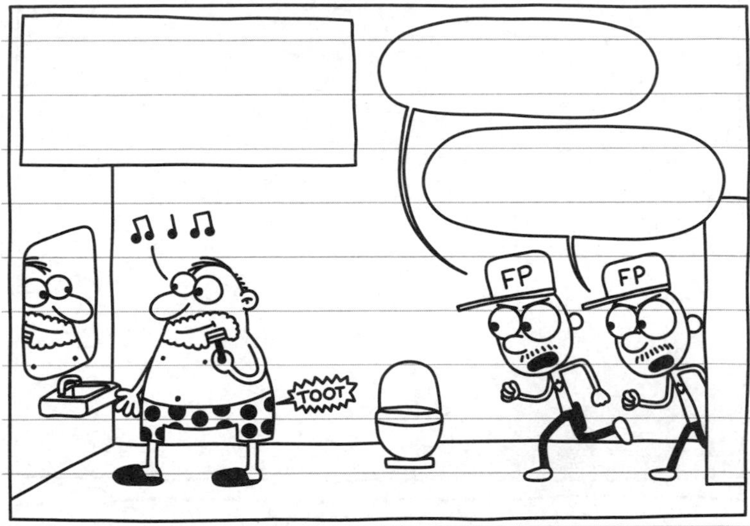

TOOT
FP
FP


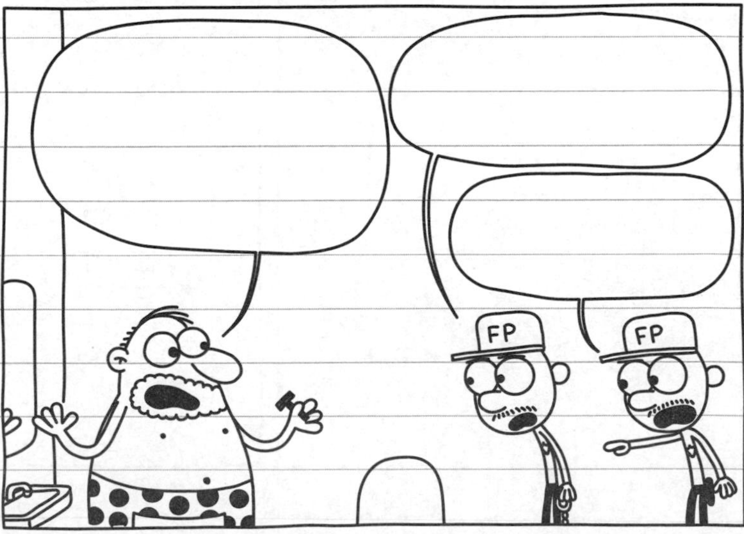

FP
FP

# Make your

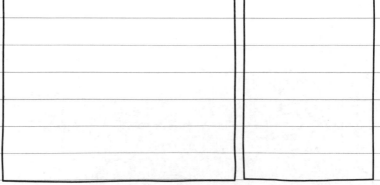

# OWN comics

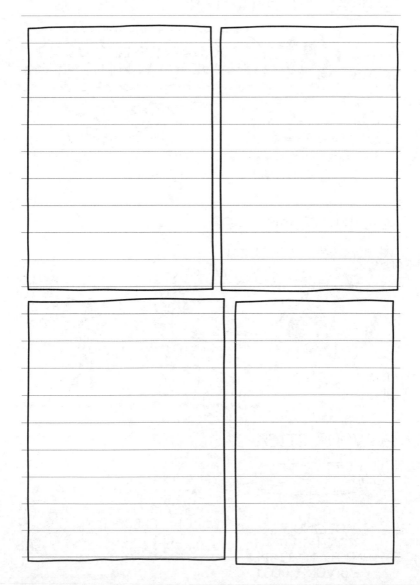

# Your best ideas for

## BAD-BREATH DEFLECTOR

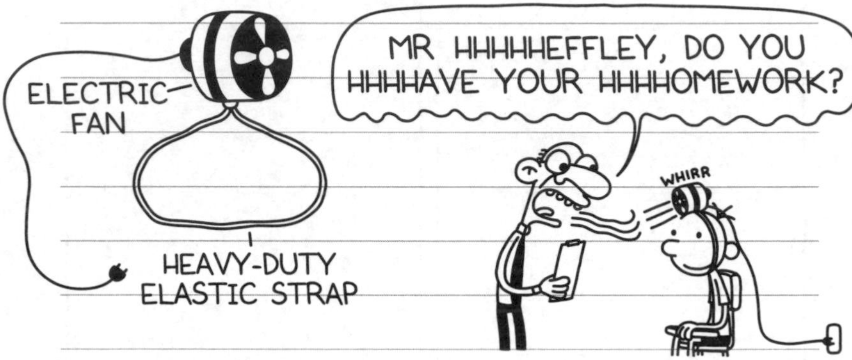
ELECTRIC FAN
HEAVY-DUTY ELASTIC STRAP
MR HHHHHEFFLEY, DO YOU HHHHAVE YOUR HHHHOMEWORK?
WHIRR

## ANIMAL TRANSLATOR

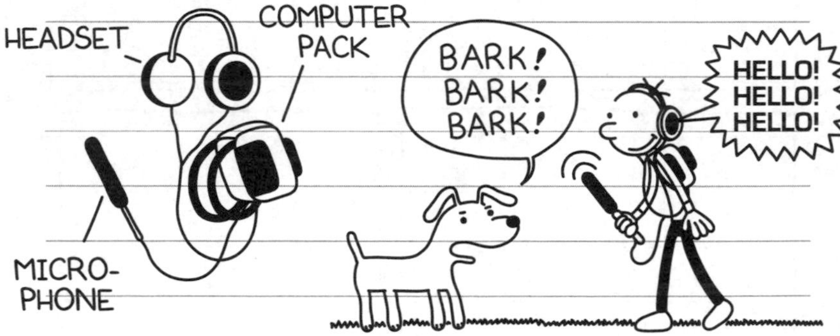
HEADSET
COMPUTER PACK
MICRO-PHONE
BARK! BARK! BARK!
HELLO! HELLO! HELLO!

## FLAVOUR STICK

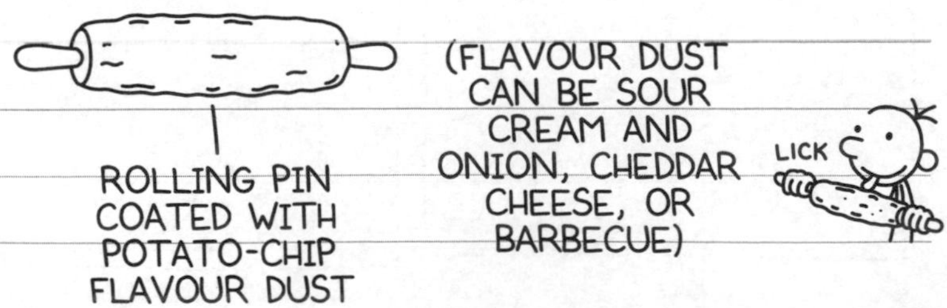
ROLLING PIN COATED WITH POTATO-CHIP FLAVOUR DUST
(FLAVOUR DUST CAN BE SOUR CREAM AND ONION, CHEDDAR CHEESE, OR BARBECUE)
LICK

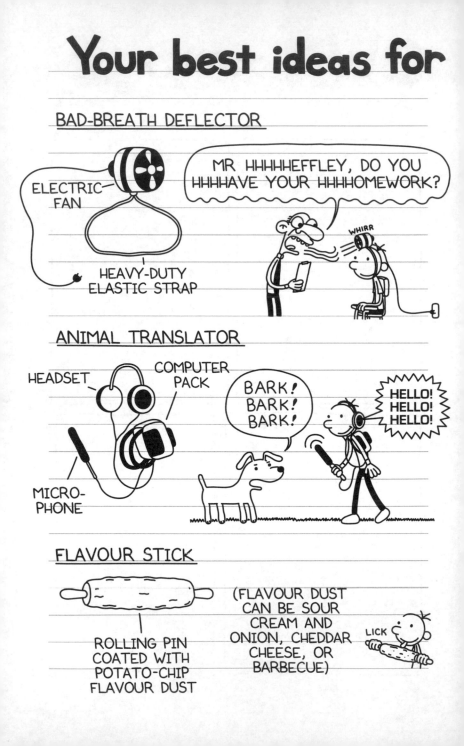

# INVENTIONS

WRITE DOWN YOUR OWN AWESOME IDEAS
SO YOU CAN PROVE YOU CAME UP WITH
THEM BEFORE ANYONE ELSE.

# Design your own SHOES

Famous athletes have their own custom-designed shoes, so why shouldn't you? Design a basketball shoe and a sneaker that fit your personality.

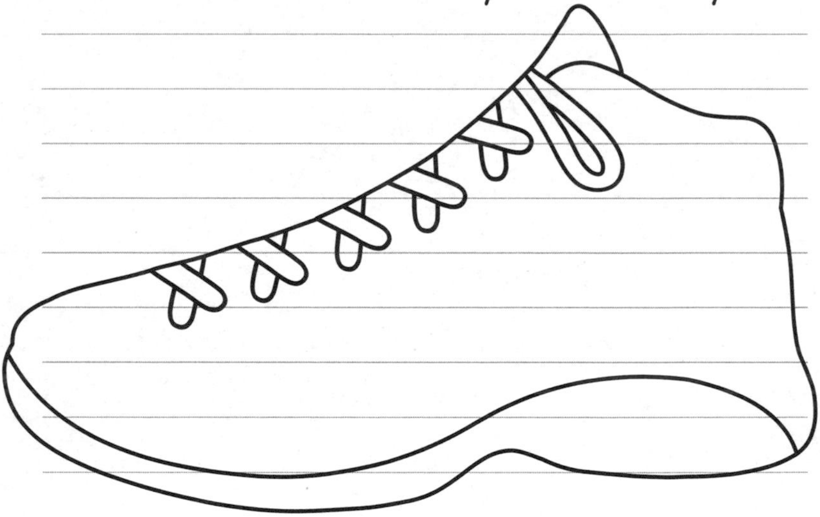

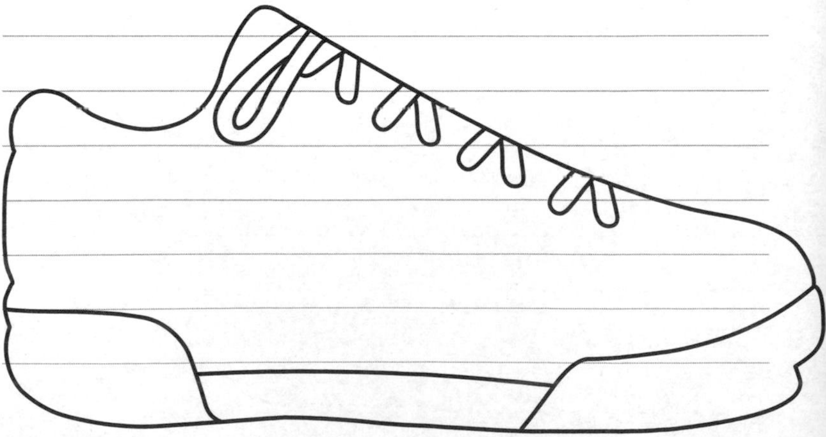

# All-Purpose EXCUSE MAKER

Did you forget to do your homework? Were you late for school? Whatever the situation, you can use this handy Excuse Maker to get yourself out of a bind. Just pick one item from each column and you're all set!

| | | |
|---|---|---|
| MY MOTHER | TORE UP | MY HOMEWORK |
| MY DOG | ATE | MY BUS |
| MY PINKY TOE | STEPPED ON | MY BEDROOM |
| A RANDOM GUY | INJURED | MY CLOTHES |
| THE TOILET | SMACKED | MY LUNCH |
| A COCKROACH | SMOOSHED | YOUR MONEY |

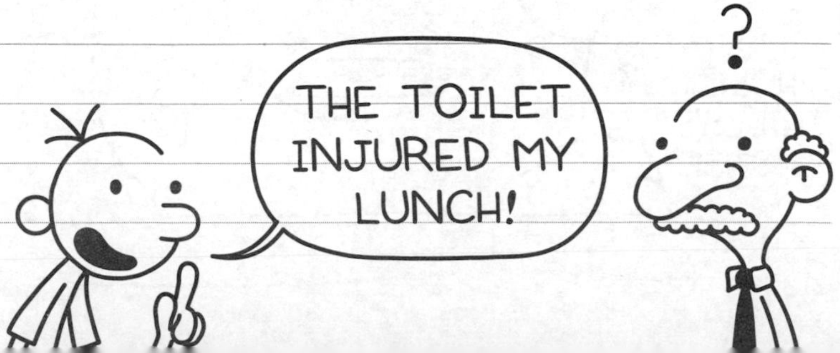
THE TOILET INJURED MY LUNCH!
?

# Make a map of your...

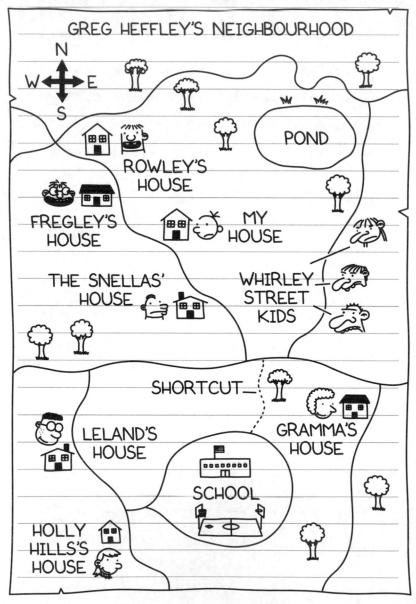

GREG HEFFLEY'S NEIGHBOURHOOD

N
W    E
S

ROWLEY'S HOUSE

POND

FREGLEY'S HOUSE

MY HOUSE

THE SNELLAS' HOUSE

WHIRLEY STREET KIDS

SHORTCUT

LELAND'S HOUSE

GRAMMA'S HOUSE

SCHOOL

HOLLY HILLS'S HOUSE

# NEIGHBOURHOOD

## YOUR NEIGHBOURHOOD

HAPPY
BIRTHDAY

# Make your own

FRONT

Dear Aunt Jean,

**THANK YOU**

for the wonderful socks you knitted for me.

INSIDE

But next time, could we just stick with cash?

DORK!
SHOVE

FRONT

*I'm sorry*

that it didn't work out with you and Lyndsey.

INSIDE

P.S. Could you find out if she thinks I'm "cute"?

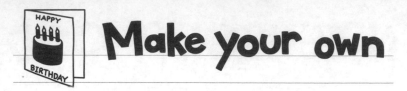

# GREETING CARDS

FRONT | INSIDE

FRONT | INSIDE

# The BEST VACATION
## you ever went on

# Pearls of WISDOM

Write down great quotes from famous people or from people you know!

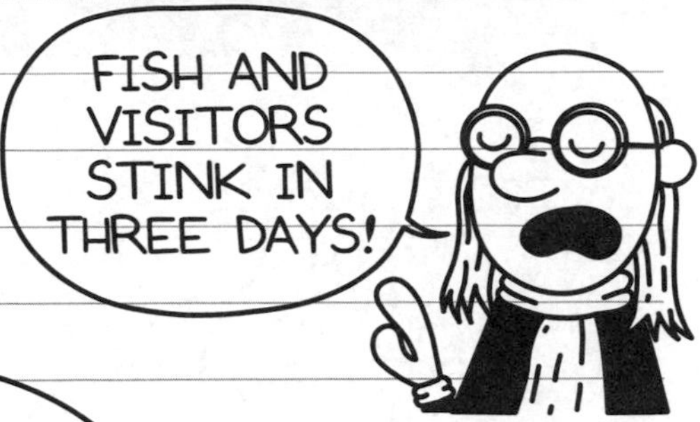
FISH AND VISITORS STINK IN THREE DAYS!

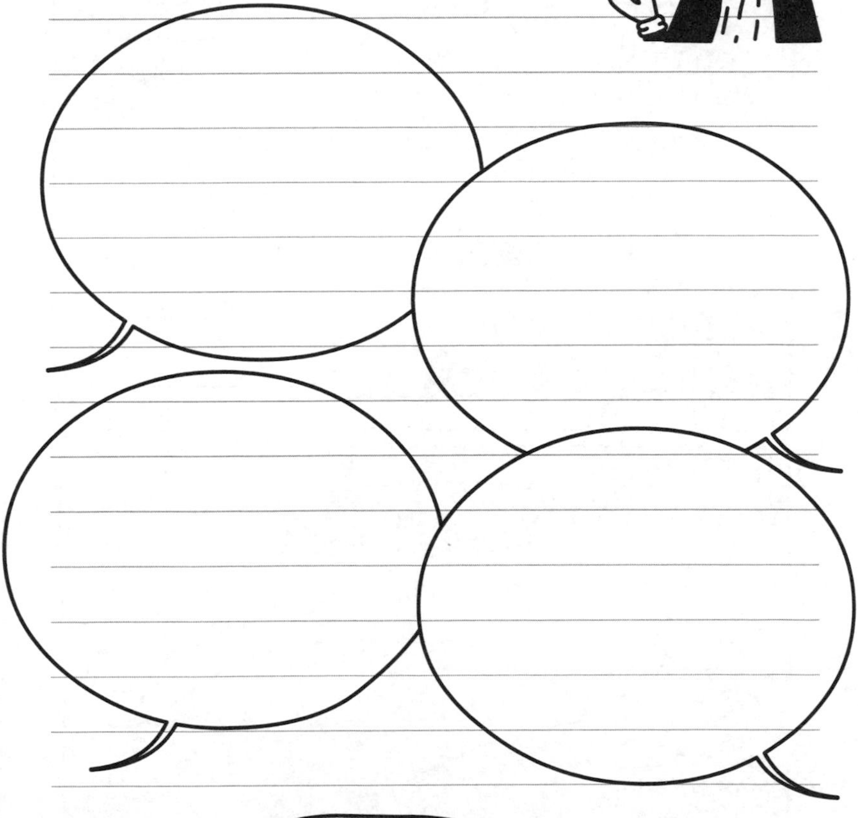

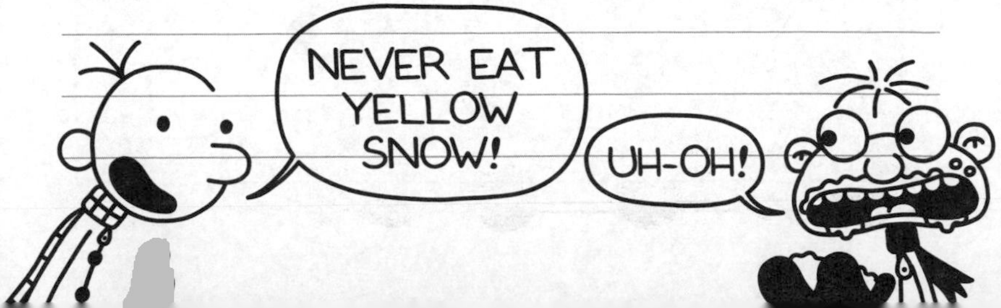
NEVER EAT YELLOW SNOW!
UH-OH!

# Unfinished

## Xtreme Sk8ers

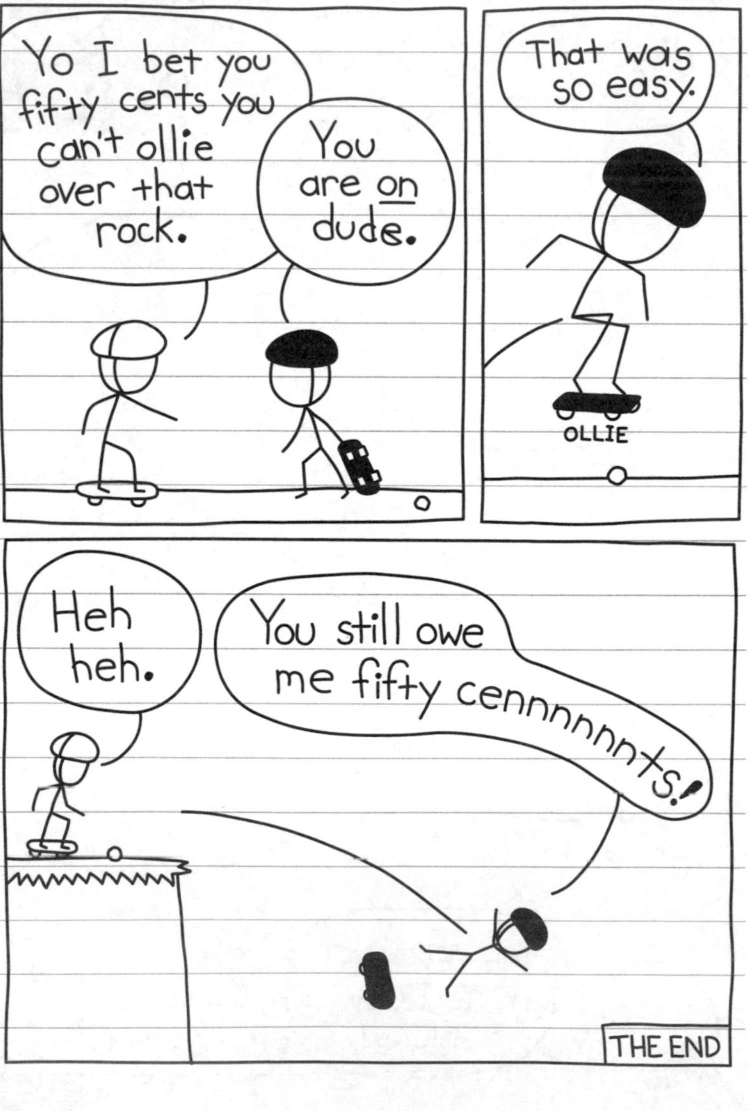

Yo I bet you fifty cents you can't ollie over that rock.
You are on dude.
That was so easy.
OLLIE
Heh heh.
You still owe me fifty cennnnnnnts!
THE END

# COMICS

## Xtreme Sk8ers

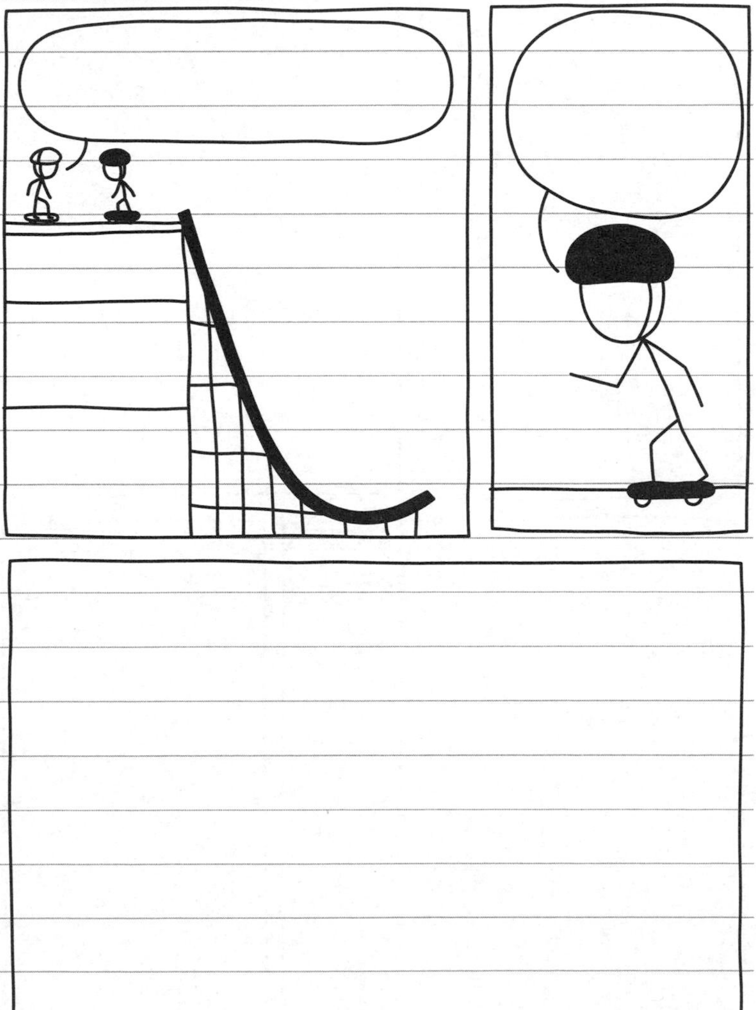
THE END

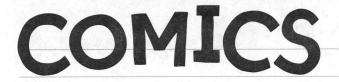

# Make your

# OWN comics

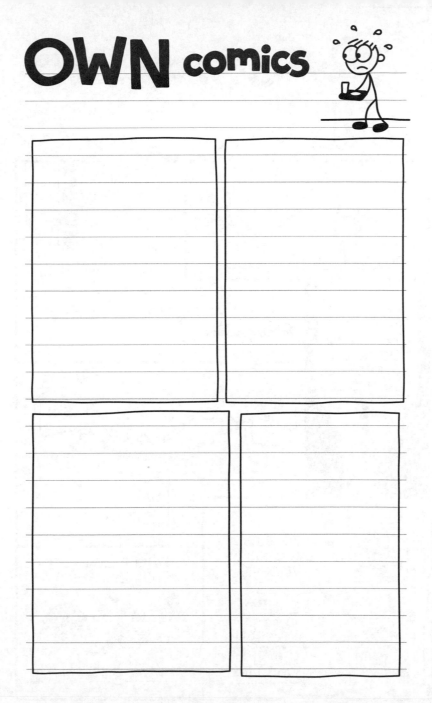

# Design your own

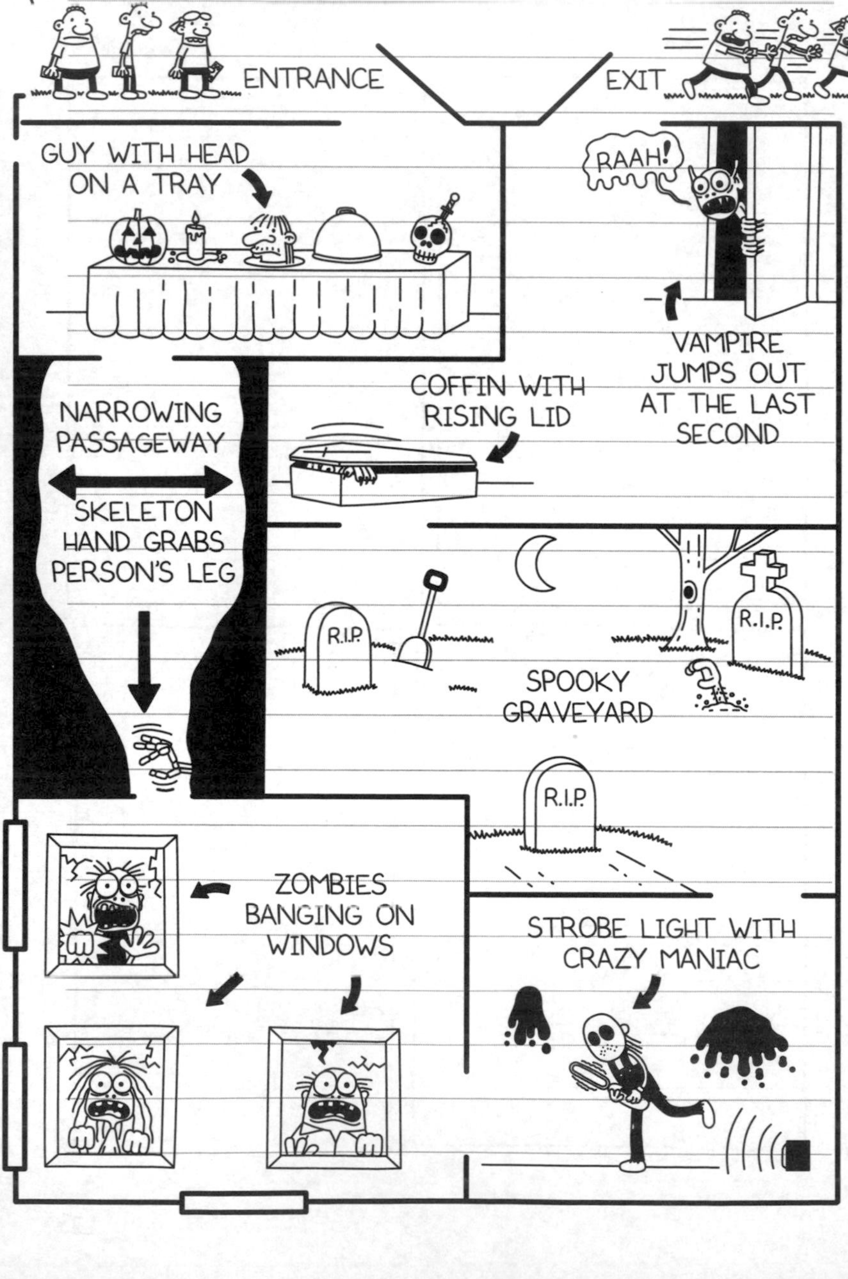
ENTRANCE
EXIT
GUY WITH HEAD ON A TRAY
RAAH!
VAMPIRE JUMPS OUT AT THE LAST SECOND
COFFIN WITH RISING LID
NARROWING PASSAGEWAY
SKELETON HAND GRABS PERSON'S LEG
R.I.P.
R.I.P.
SPOOKY GRAVEYARD
R.I.P.
ZOMBIES BANGING ON WINDOWS
STROBE LIGHT WITH CRAZY MANIAC

# HAUNTED HOUSE

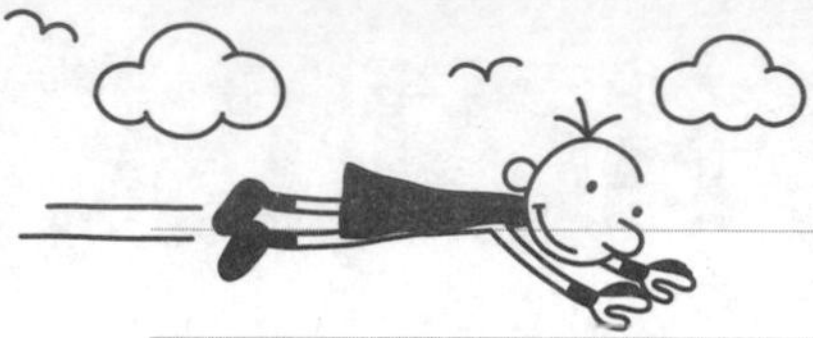

# If you had

If you had the power to read other people's thoughts, would you really want to use it?

YES ☐ NO ☐

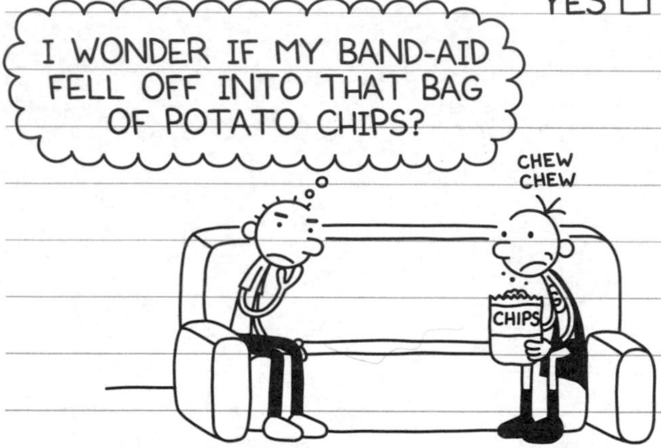

I WONDER IF MY BAND-AID FELL OFF INTO THAT BAG OF POTATO CHIPS?
CHEW CHEW
CHIPS


If you were a super hero, would you want to have a sidekick? YES ☐ NO ☐

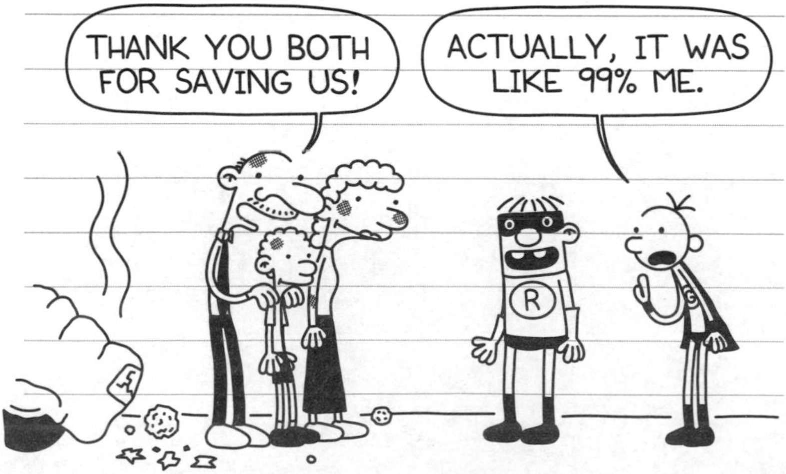

THANK YOU BOTH FOR SAVING US!
ACTUALLY, IT WAS LIKE 99% ME.

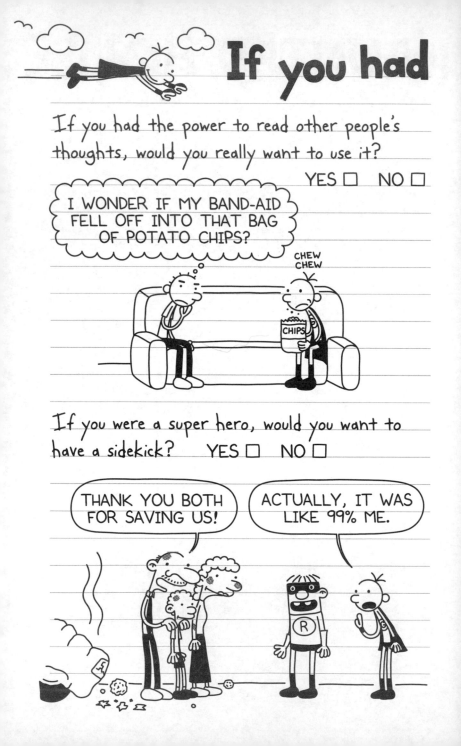

# SUPERPOWERS...

If you were a super hero, would you keep your identity secret? YES ☐ NO ☐

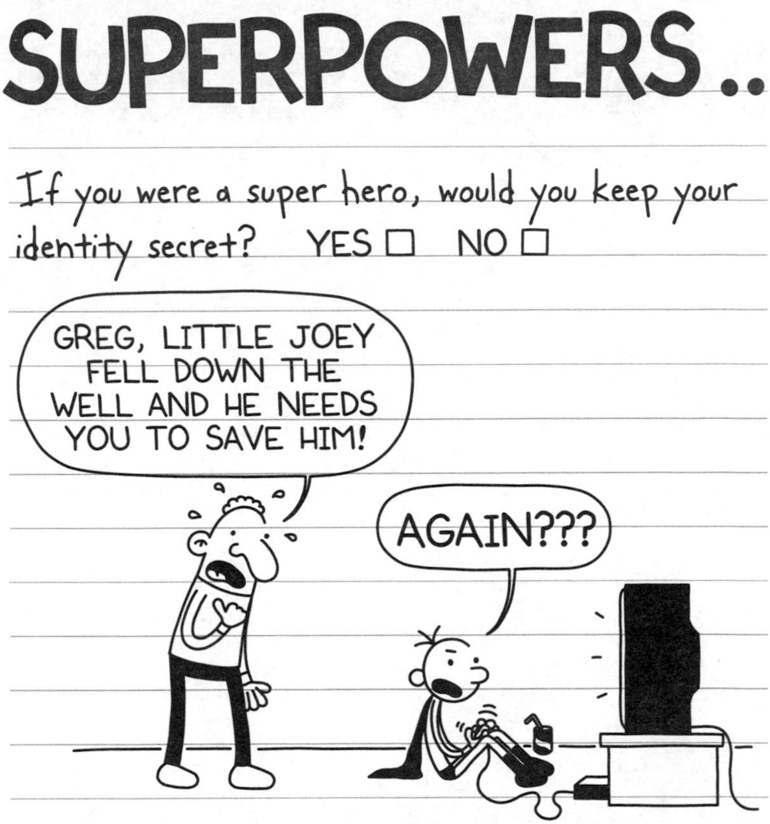
GREG, LITTLE JOEY FELL DOWN THE WELL AND HE NEEDS YOU TO SAVE HIM!
AGAIN???

Would you want to have X-ray vision if you couldn't turn it off? YES ☐ NO ☐

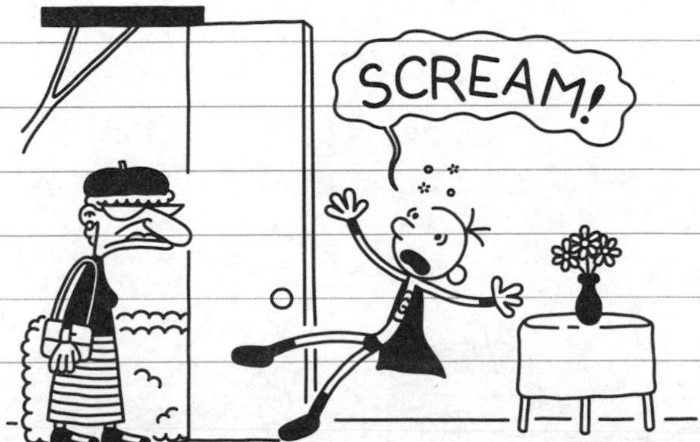
SCREAM!

# Draw your FRIENDS

the way Greg Heffley would

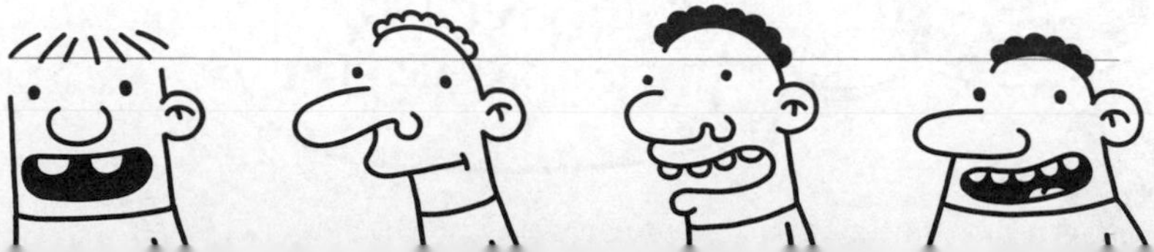

# A few questions

Do you ever put food in your belly button so you can have a snack later on?

Do animals ever use their thoughts to talk to you?

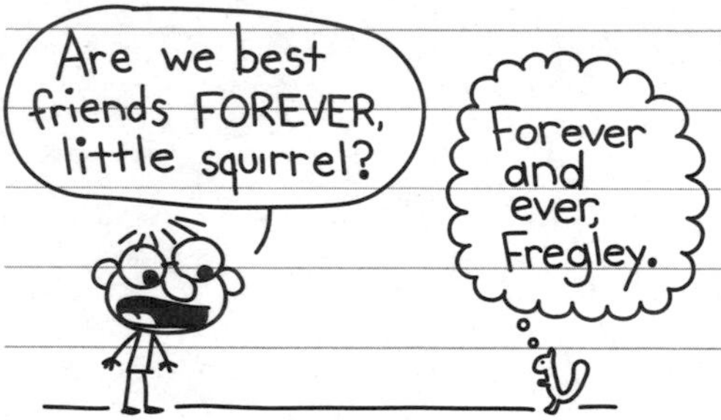
Are we best friends FOREVER, little squirrel?
Forever and ever, Fregley.

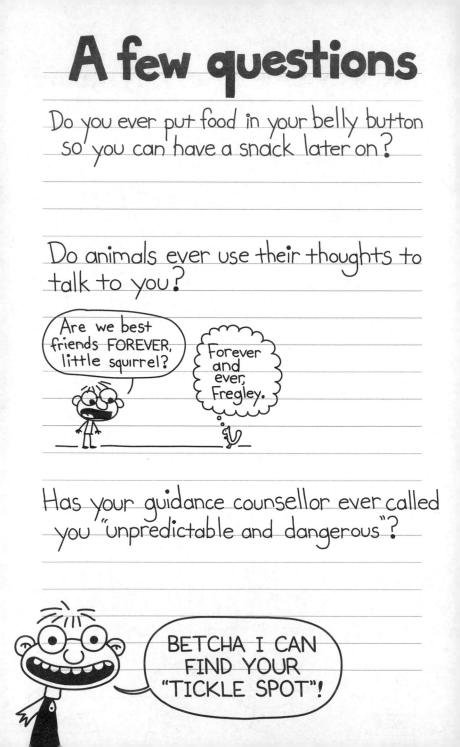

Has your guidance counsellor ever called you "unpredictable and dangerous"?

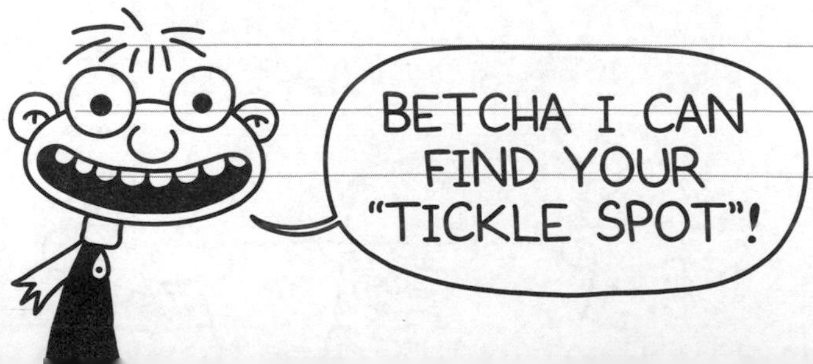
BETCHA I CAN FIND YOUR "TICKLE SPOT"!

# from FREGLEY

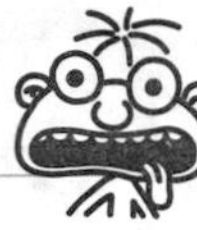

If you had a tail, what would you do with it?

Have you ever eaten a scab?

Do you wanna play "Diaper Whip"?

Have you ever been sent home from school early for "hygiene issues"?

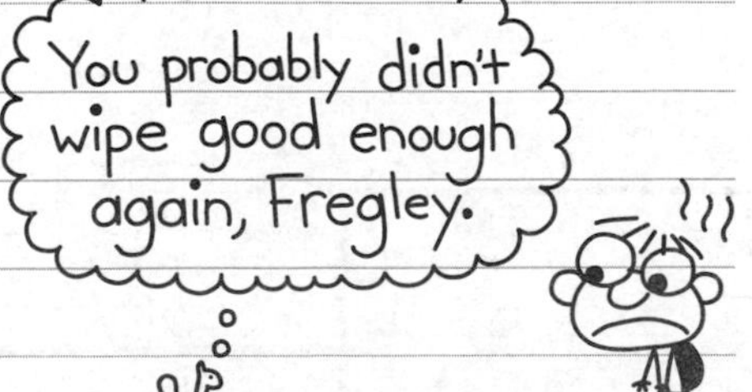
You probably didn't wipe good enough again, Fregley.

# Create your own

Dream up the ultimate competition, then pick the winner! Here's how it works. First, come up with a category for your tournament (Movie Villains, Sports Stars, Cartoon Characters, Bands, Breakfast Foods, TV Shows, etc.)

Then write an entry on each one of the numbered lines. Judge the winner of each individual match and move the winner to the next round.

ROUND 1

ROUND 2

ROUND 3

1.

2.

3.

4.

V

# TOURNAMENT

For example, in a battle of breakfast foods, you might pick cereal over eggs, so cereal would make it to the next round.

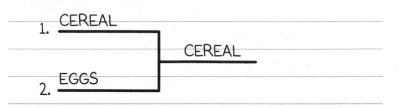

1. CEREAL

2. EGGS

CEREAL

Keep going until only two entries remain. When your final two teams face off, circle the one you think is the best. That's your winner!

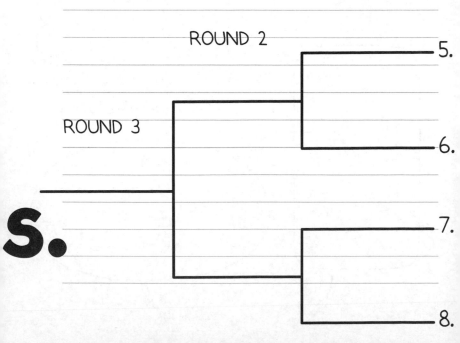

ROUND 1

ROUND 2

ROUND 3

5.

6.

7.

8.

S.

# Autographs

GET YOUR FRIENDS TO WRITE STUFF IN THIS BOOK.

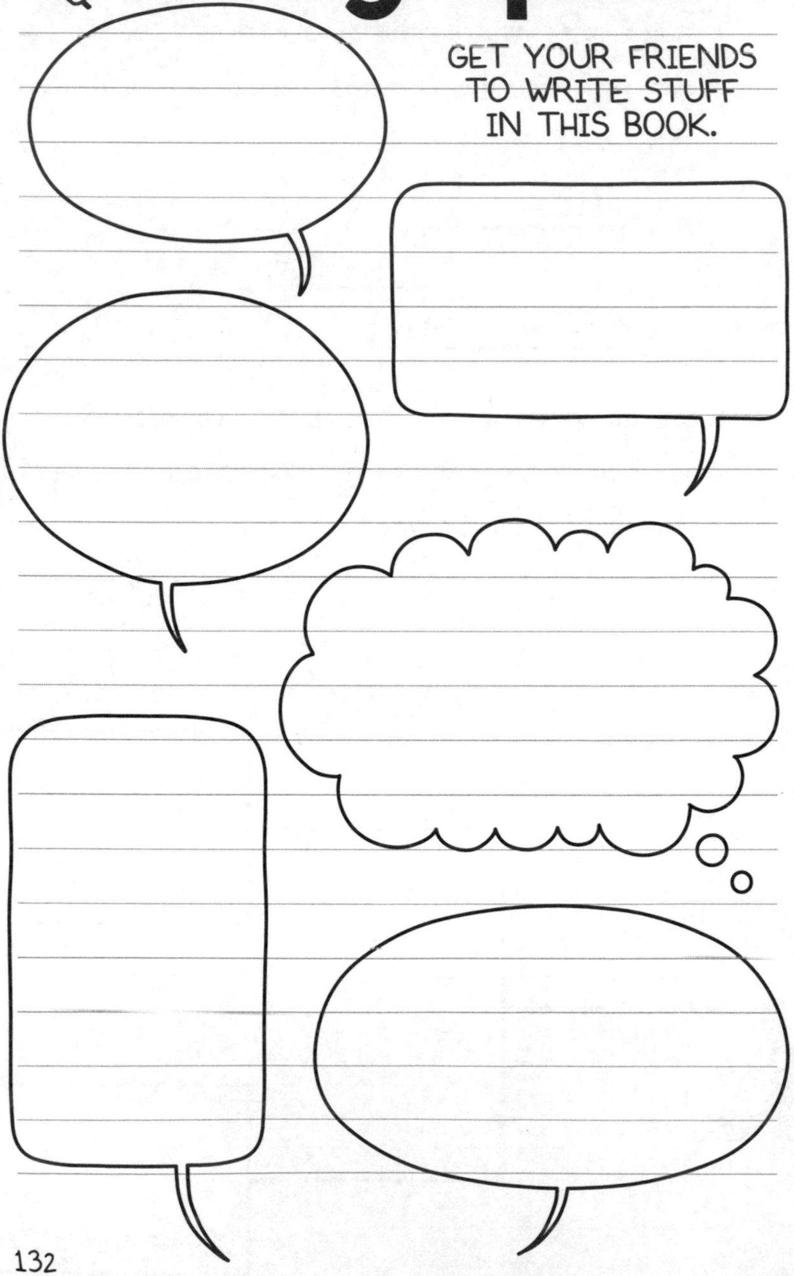

# Autographs

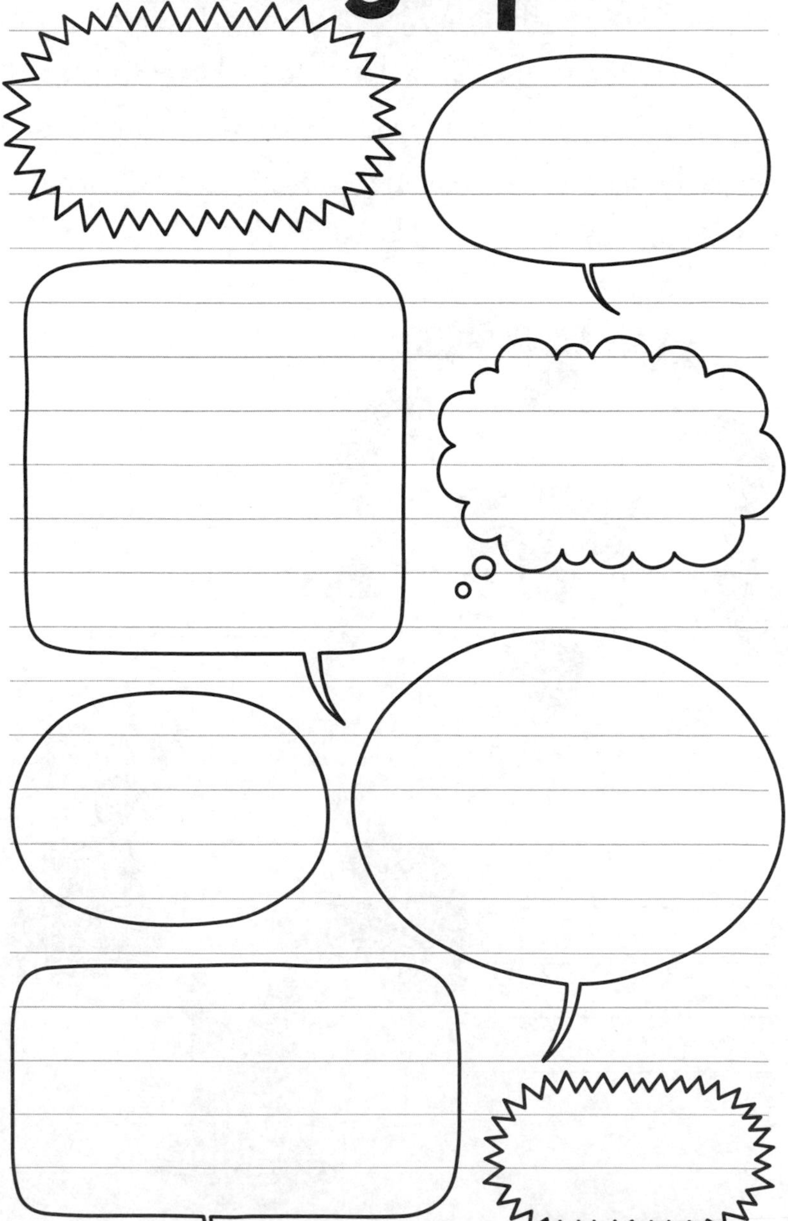

# What do you see in these

Take a look at these inkblots and write down what you think they look like. You'll have to use your imagination! What you see in these inkblots probably says something about your personality... but it's up to you to decide WHAT!

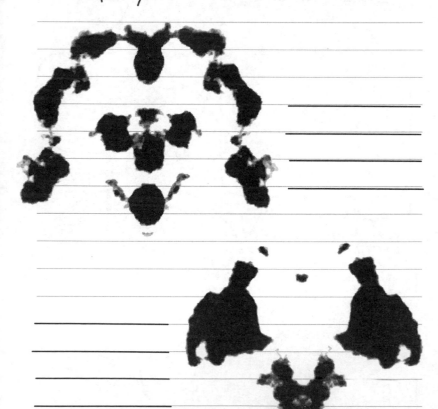

# INKBLOTS?

TWO TURTLES PLAYING TENNIS!

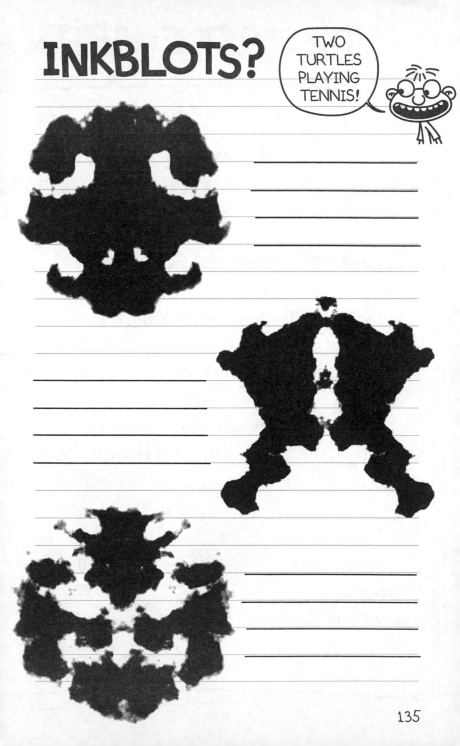

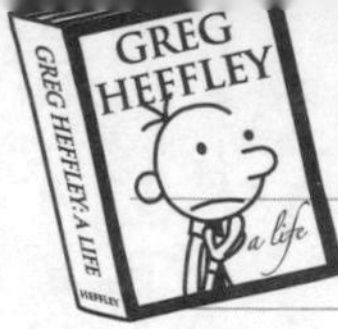
GREG HEFFLEY
GREG HEFFLEY: A LIFE
a life
HEFFLEY

# The FIRST CHAPTER

## *Chapter One*

## CHILDHOOD

I was born in ______________________ on ____________, ______. I was ___ centimetres long and ______ kilos, and I looked like a ______________________.

I spent my first few months doing a lot of ____________ and ______________, until I was ____ months old and I finally started to ________________.

From a very early age, I had a talent for ________________, but I never really got the hang of ____________________. I liked to eat ________________, but I never could stand ________________.

When I turned ____, I started to get really interested in __________________, but I got bored with that when I turned ___ and moved on to __________________________ instead.

As a little kid, I was brave enough to
_____, but I was
scared to death of _____.
In fact, to this day, I won't go near a _____
_____.

My best friend growing up was a kid named
_____, who now works as a
_____ in _____.
My most treasured possession as a kid was a
_____. My best birthday
party was when I turned _____ and I got a new
_____ from _____.
My favourite TV show was _____
_____, and when I wasn't
watching television, I'd _____
_____ for hours at a time.

When I was a little kid, everyone always told
me that one day I'd grow up to become a
_____. Who knew that I'd
actually become a _____?

# ZOO-WEE MAMA by Rowley

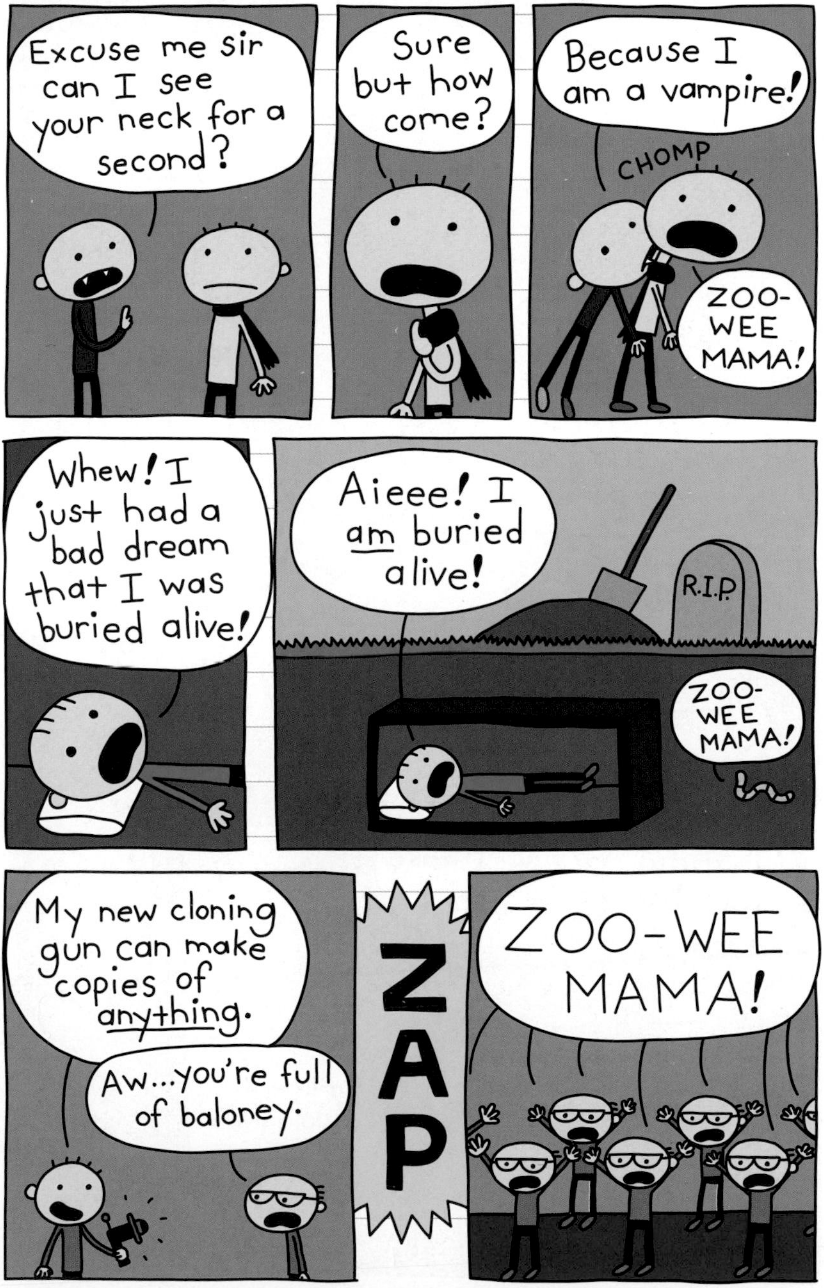
Excuse me sir can I see your neck for a second?
Sure but how come?
Because I am a vampire!
CHOMP
ZOO-WEE MAMA!
Whew! I just had a bad dream that I was buried alive!
Aieee! I am buried alive!
R.I.P.
ZOO-WEE MAMA!
My new cloning gun can make copies of anything.
Aw...you're full of baloney.
ZAP
ZOO-WEE MAMA!

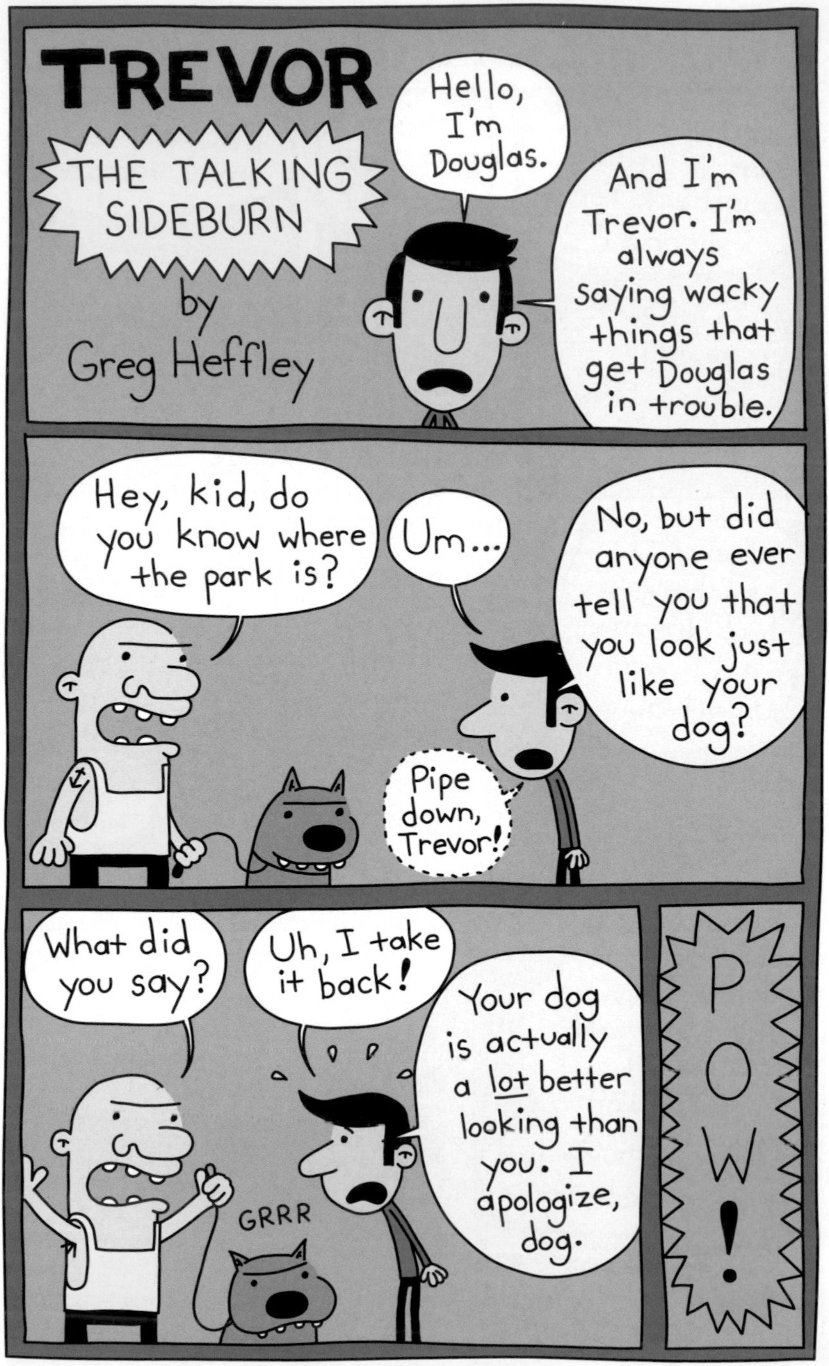
TREVOR
THE TALKING SIDEBURN
by Greg Heffley
Hello, I'm Douglas.
And I'm Trevor. I'm always saying wacky things that get Douglas in trouble.
Hey, kid, do you know where the park is?
Um...
No, but did anyone ever tell you that you look just like your dog?
Pipe down, Trevor!
What did you say?
Uh, I take it back!
Your dog is actually a lot better looking than you. I apologize, dog.
GRRR
POW!

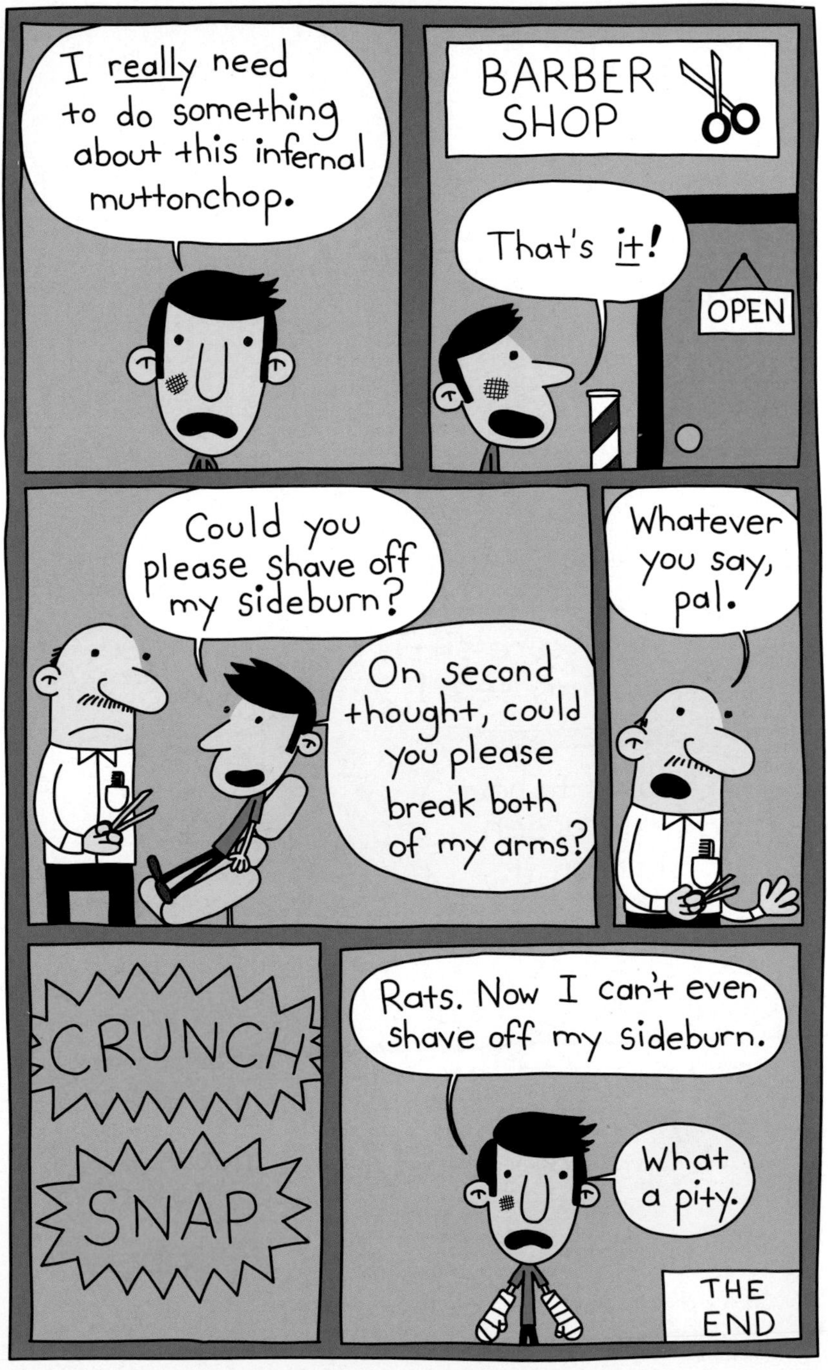
I really need to do something about this infernal muttonchop.
BARBER SHOP
That's it!
OPEN
Could you please shave off my sideburn?
On second thought, could you please break both of my arms?
Whatever you say, pal.
CRUNCH
SNAP
Rats. Now I can't even shave off my sideburn.
What a pity.
THE END

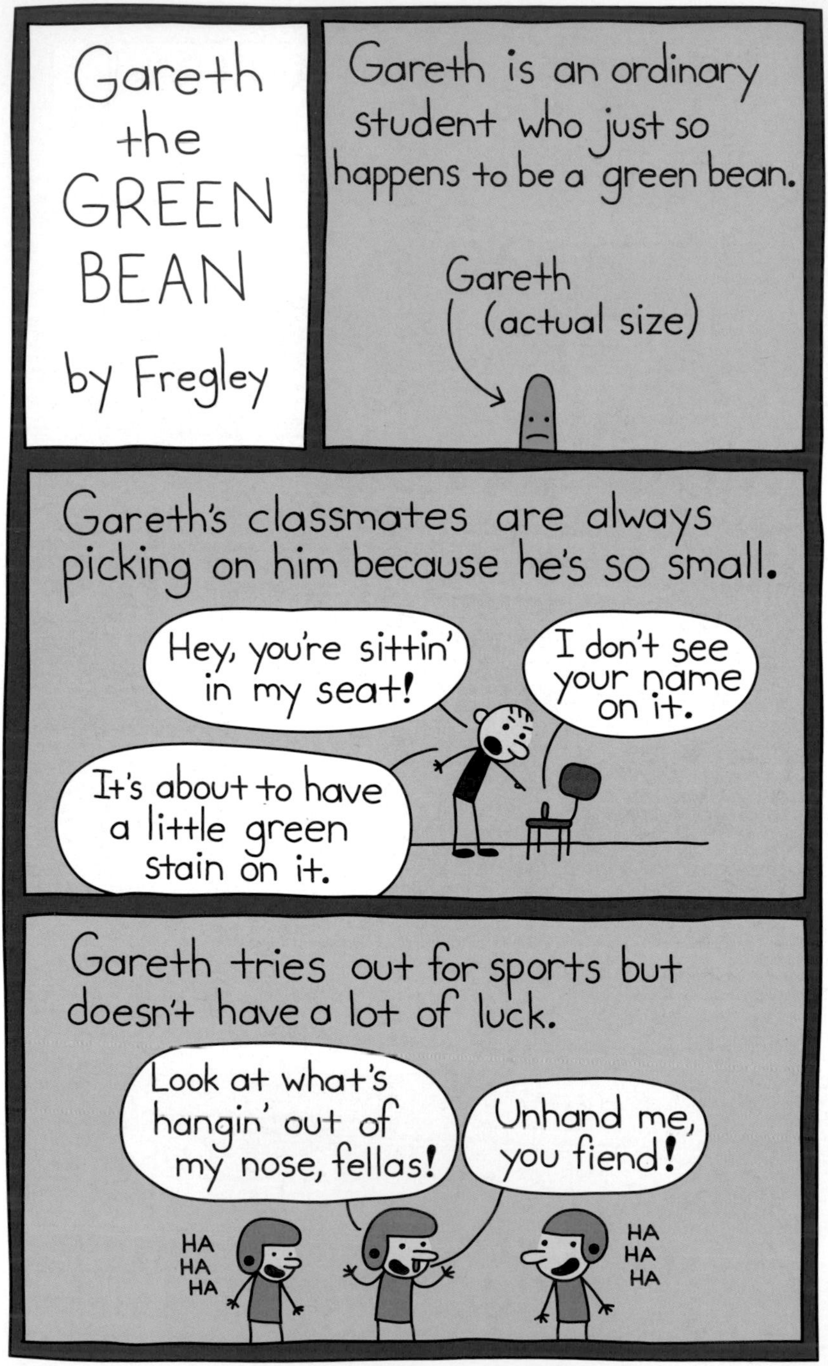
Gareth the GREEN BEAN
by Fregley
Gareth is an ordinary student who just so happens to be a green bean.
Gareth (actual size)
Gareth's classmates are always picking on him because he's so small.
Hey, you're sittin' in my seat!
I don't see your name on it.
It's about to have a little green stain on it.
Gareth tries out for sports but doesn't have a lot of luck.
Look at what's hangin' out of my nose, fellas!
Unhand me, you fiend!
HA HA HA
HA HA HA

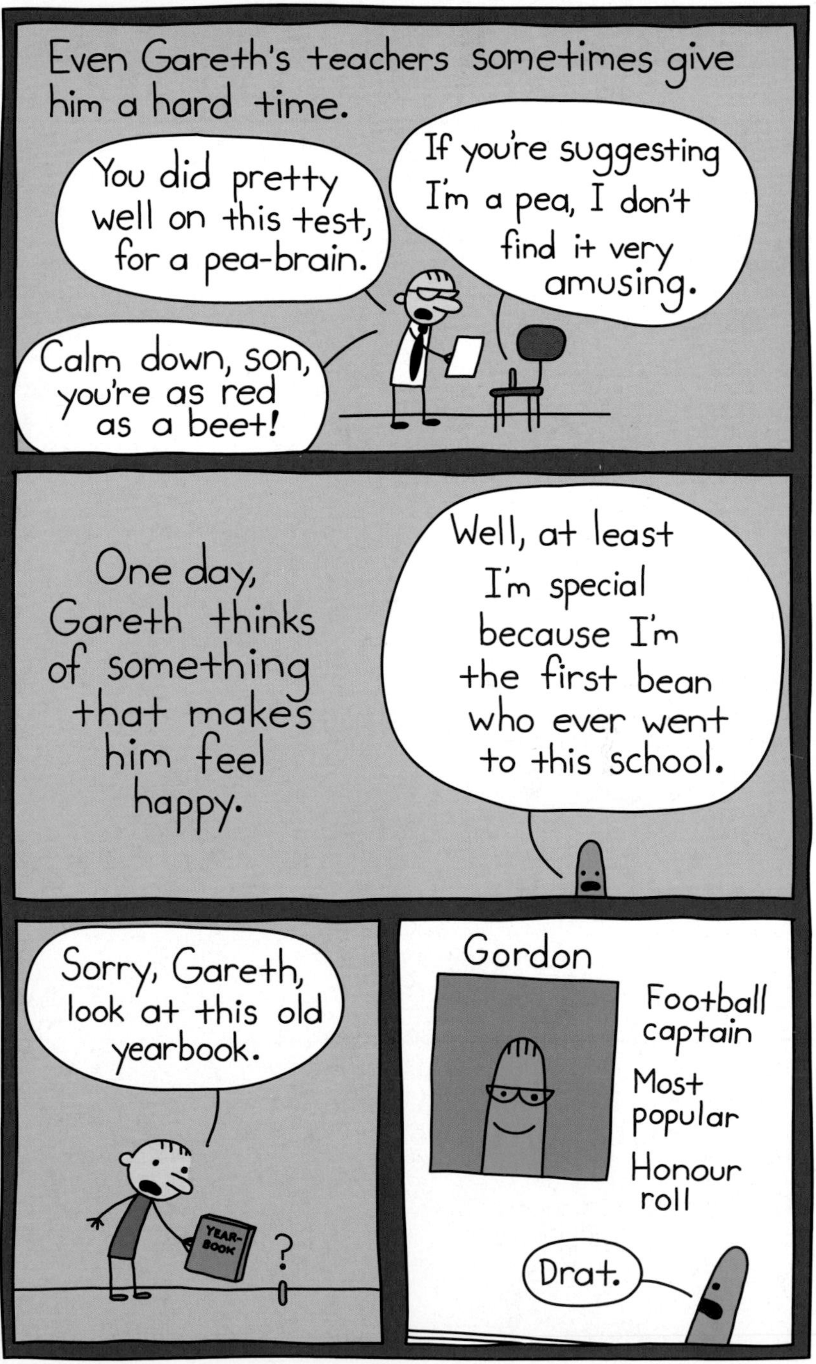
Even Gareth's teachers sometimes give him a hard time.
You did pretty well on this test, for a pea-brain.
If you're suggesting I'm a pea, I don't find it very amusing.
Calm down, son, you're as red as a beet!
One day, Gareth thinks of something that makes him feel happy.
Well, at least I'm special because I'm the first bean who ever went to this school.
Sorry, Gareth, look at this old yearbook.
YEAR-BOOK
?
Gordon
Football captain
Most popular
Honour roll
Drat.

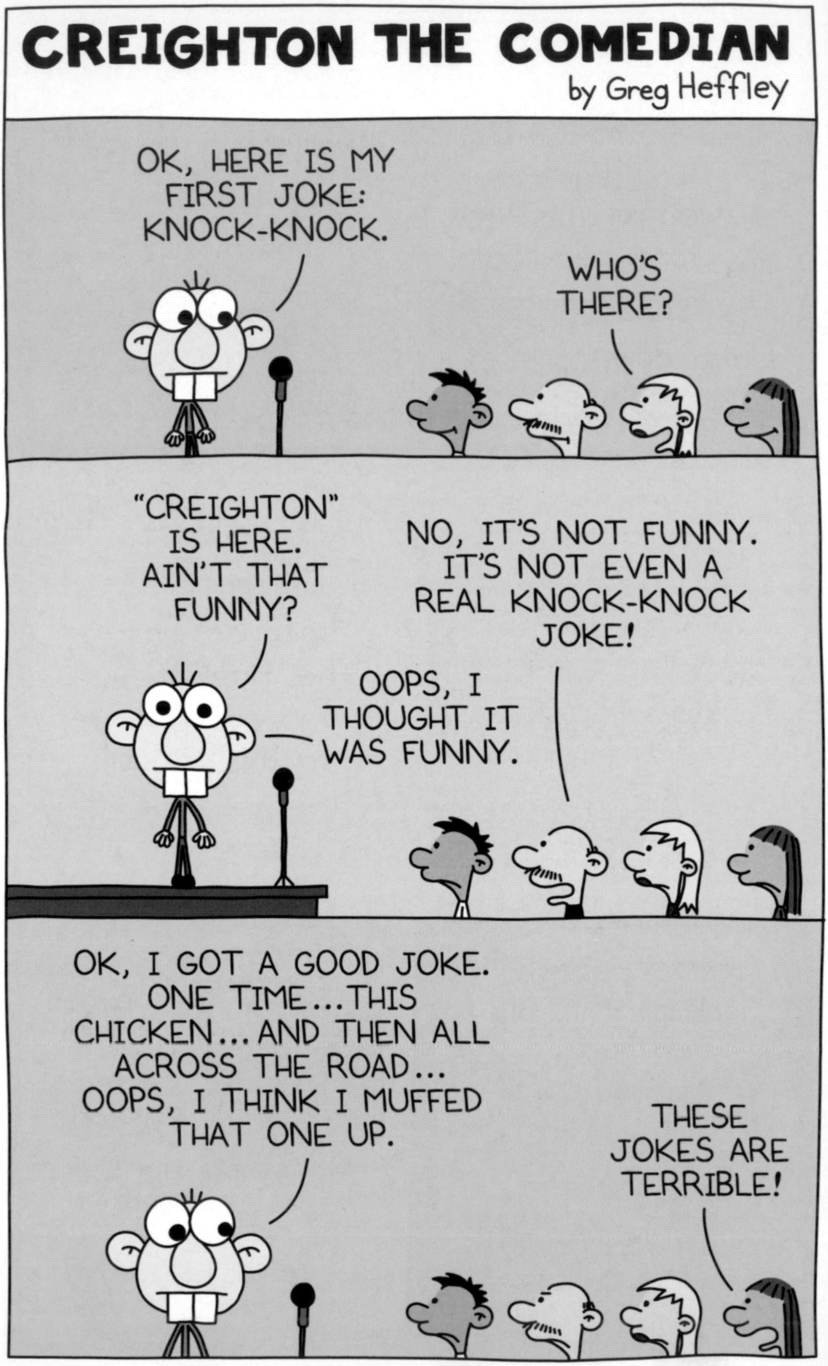
CREIGHTON THE COMEDIAN
by Greg Heffley
OK, HERE IS MY FIRST JOKE: KNOCK-KNOCK.
WHO'S THERE?
"CREIGHTON" IS HERE. AIN'T THAT FUNNY?
NO, IT'S NOT FUNNY. IT'S NOT EVEN A REAL KNOCK-KNOCK JOKE!
OOPS, I THOUGHT IT WAS FUNNY.
OK, I GOT A GOOD JOKE. ONE TIME...THIS CHICKEN... AND THEN ALL ACROSS THE ROAD... OOPS, I THINK I MUFFED THAT ONE UP.
THESE JOKES ARE TERRIBLE!

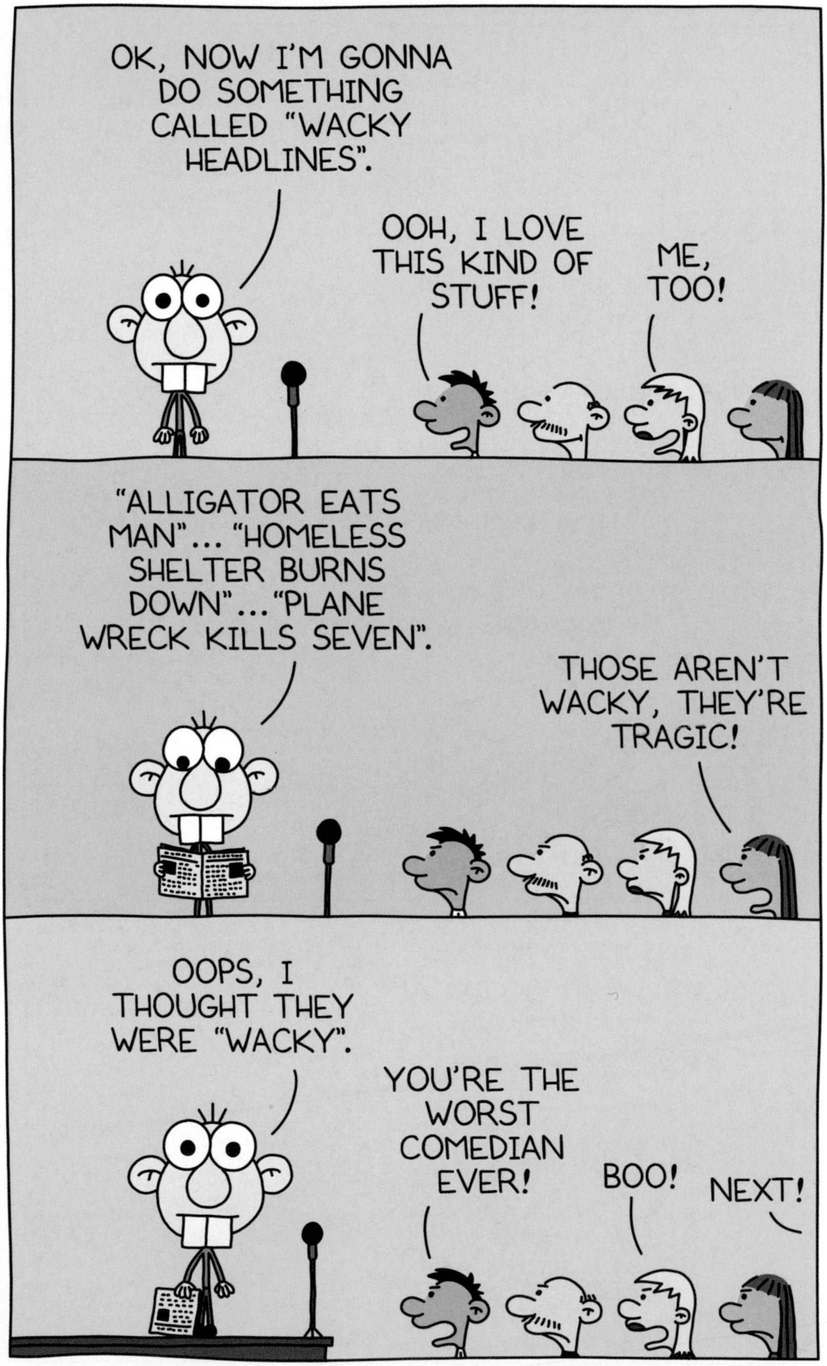
OK, NOW I'M GONNA DO SOMETHING CALLED "WACKY HEADLINES".
OOH, I LOVE THIS KIND OF STUFF!
ME, TOO!
"ALLIGATOR EATS MAN"... "HOMELESS SHELTER BURNS DOWN"..."PLANE WRECK KILLS SEVEN".
THOSE AREN'T WACKY, THEY'RE TRAGIC!
OOPS, I THOUGHT THEY WERE "WACKY".
YOU'RE THE WORST COMEDIAN EVER!
BOO!
NEXT!

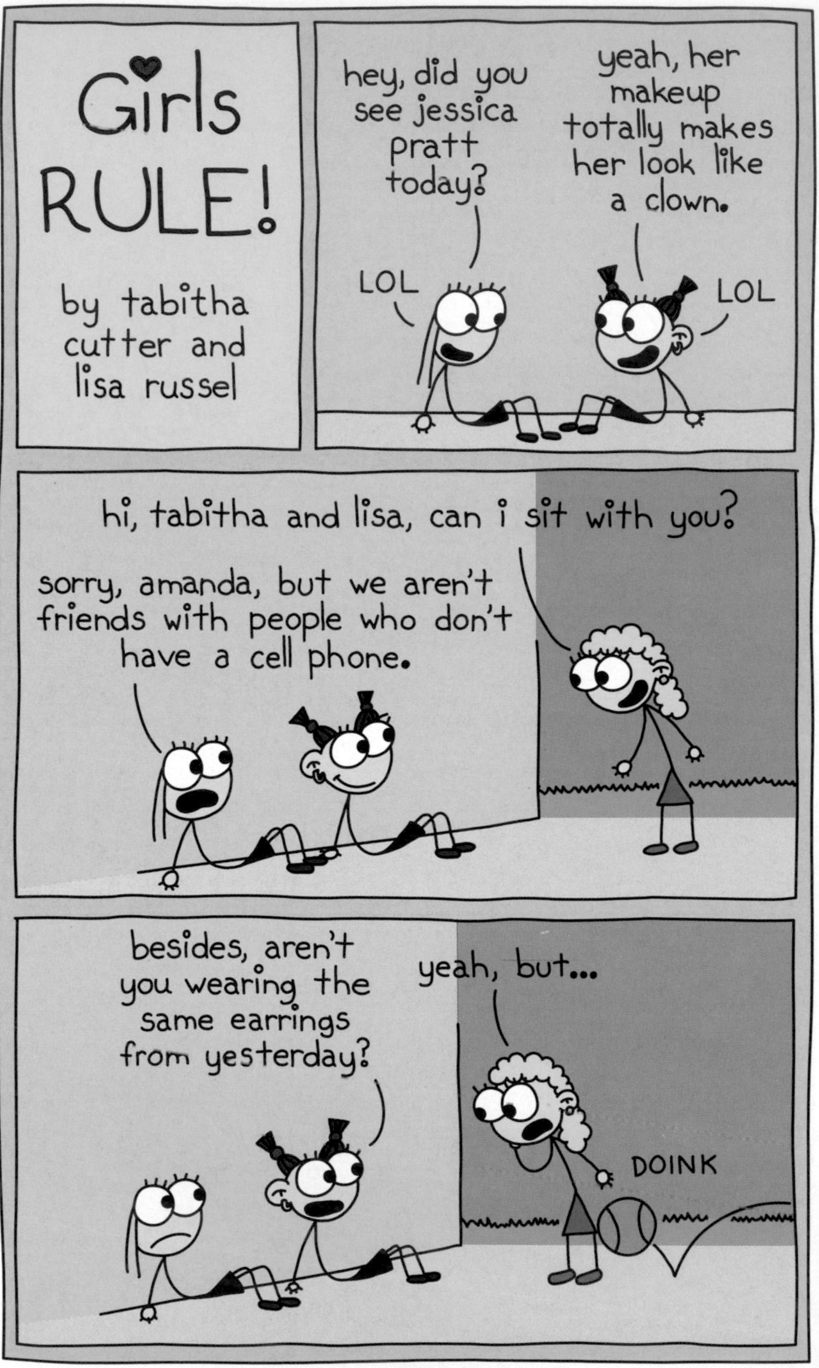
Girls RULE!
by tabitha cutter and lisa russel
hey, did you see jessica pratt today?
yeah, her makeup totally makes her look like a clown.
LOL
LOL
hi, tabitha and lisa, can i sit with you?
sorry, amanda, but we aren't friends with people who don't have a cell phone.
besides, aren't you wearing the same earrings from yesterday?
yeah, but...
DOINK

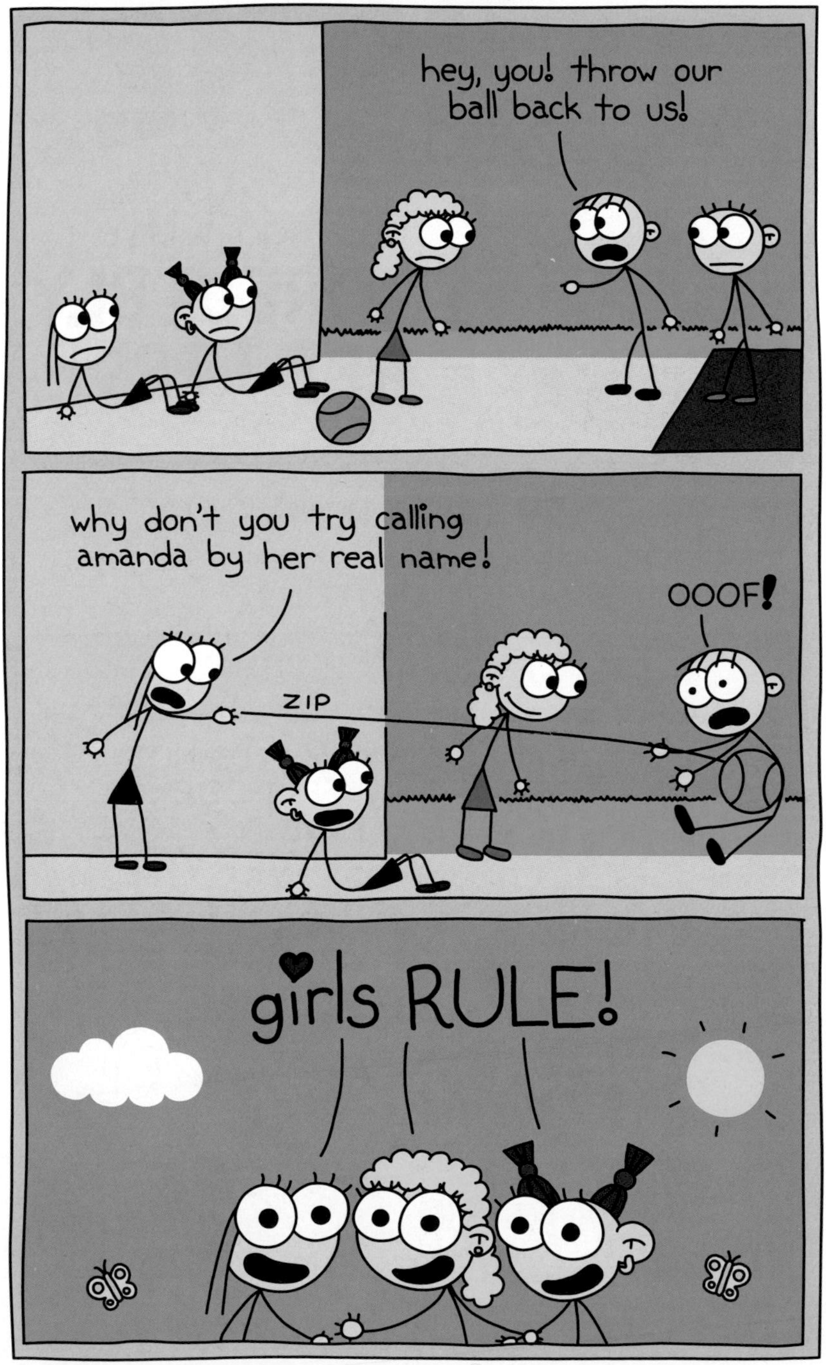

hey, you! throw our ball back to us!
why don't you try calling amanda by her real name!
ZIP
OOOF!
girls RULE!

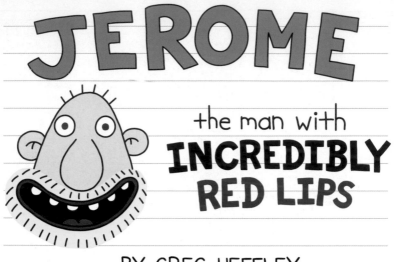

# JEROME

## the man with **INCREDIBLY RED LIPS**

BY GREG HEFFLEY

JEROME AT THE GYM
HEY, WHAT'RE YOU DOIN' WEARIN' LIPSTICK IN HERE?
IT'S NOT LIPSTICK... I JUST HAVE VERY RED LIPS!
ARE YOU SASSIN' ME, PUNK?
GULP.

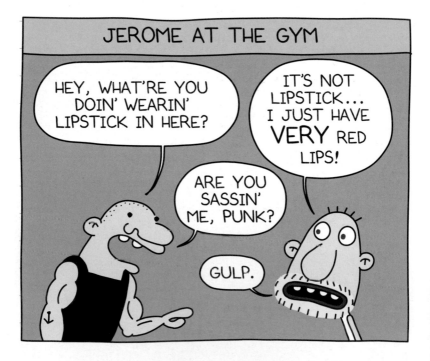

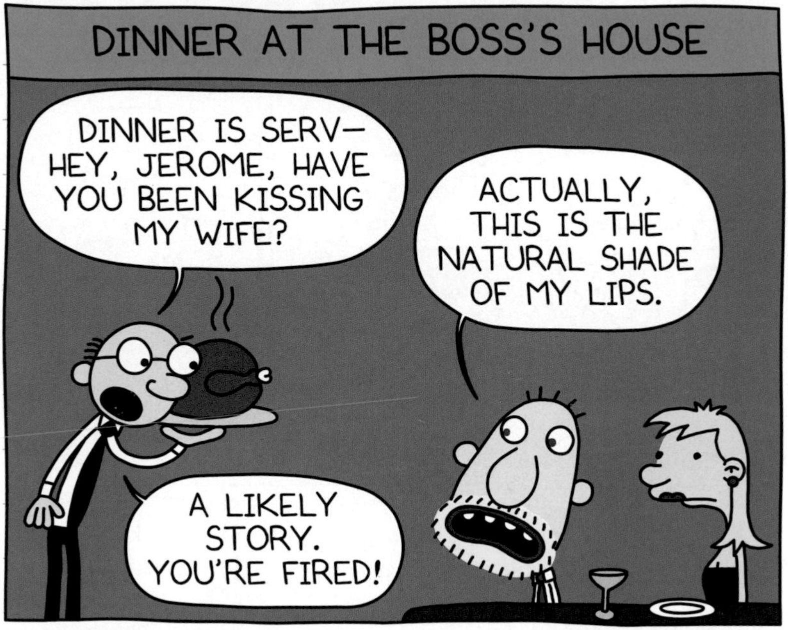
DINNER AT THE BOSS'S HOUSE
DINNER IS SERV— HEY, JEROME, HAVE YOU BEEN KISSING MY WIFE?
ACTUALLY, THIS IS THE NATURAL SHADE OF MY LIPS.
A LIKELY STORY. YOU'RE FIRED!

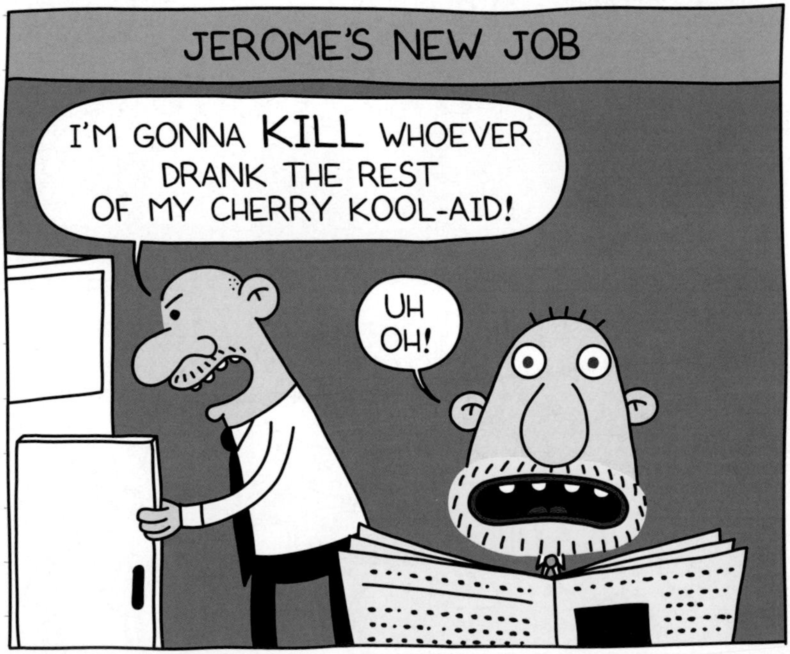
JEROME'S NEW JOB
I'M GONNA KILL WHOEVER DRANK THE REST OF MY CHERRY KOOL-AID!
UH OH!

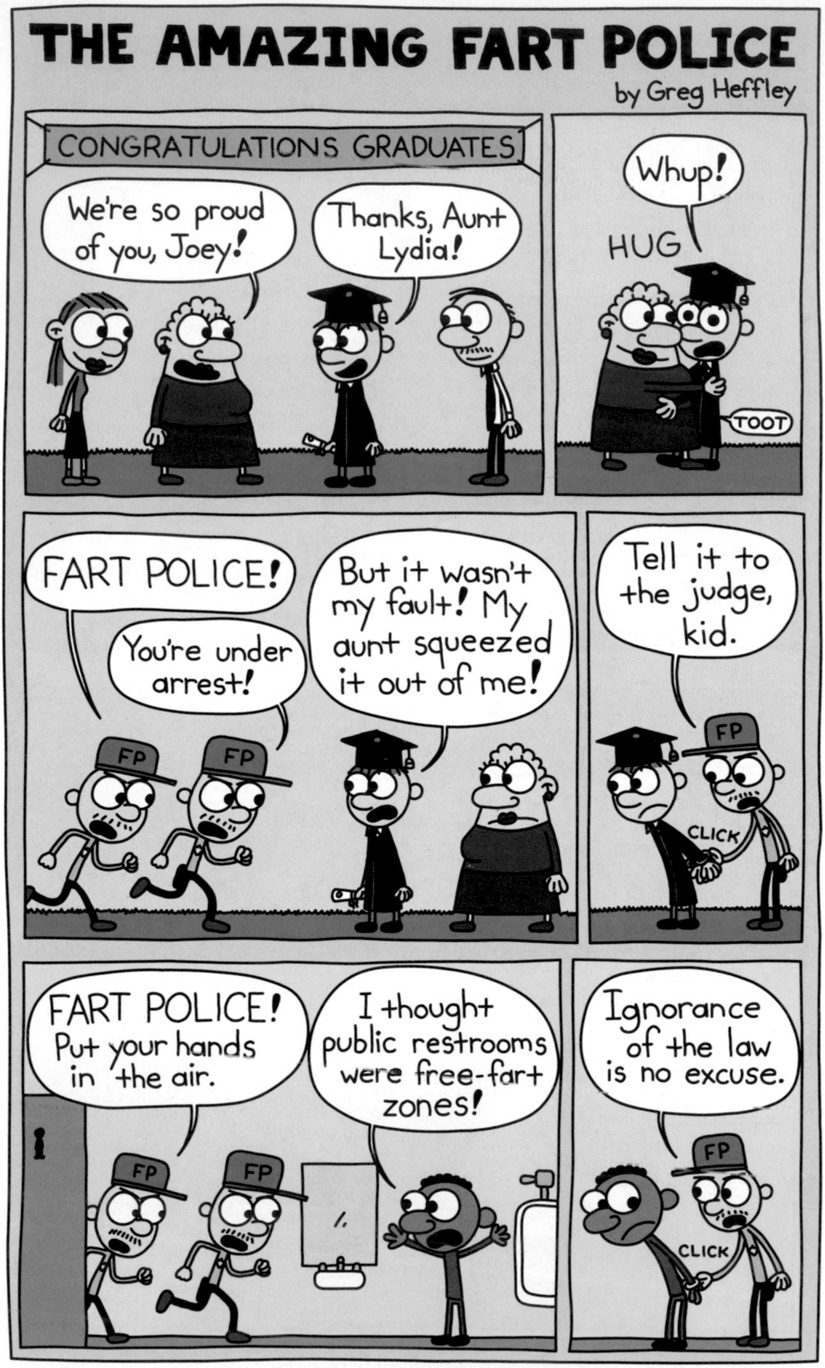
THE AMAZING FART POLICE
by Greg Heffley
CONGRATULATIONS GRADUATES
We're so proud of you, Joey!
Thanks, Aunt Lydia!
Whup!
HUG
TOOT
FART POLICE!
You're under arrest!
But it wasn't my fault! My aunt squeezed it out of me!
Tell it to the judge, kid.
FP
CLICK
FART POLICE! Put your hands in the air.
I thought public restrooms were free-fart zones!
Ignorance of the law is no excuse.
CLICK

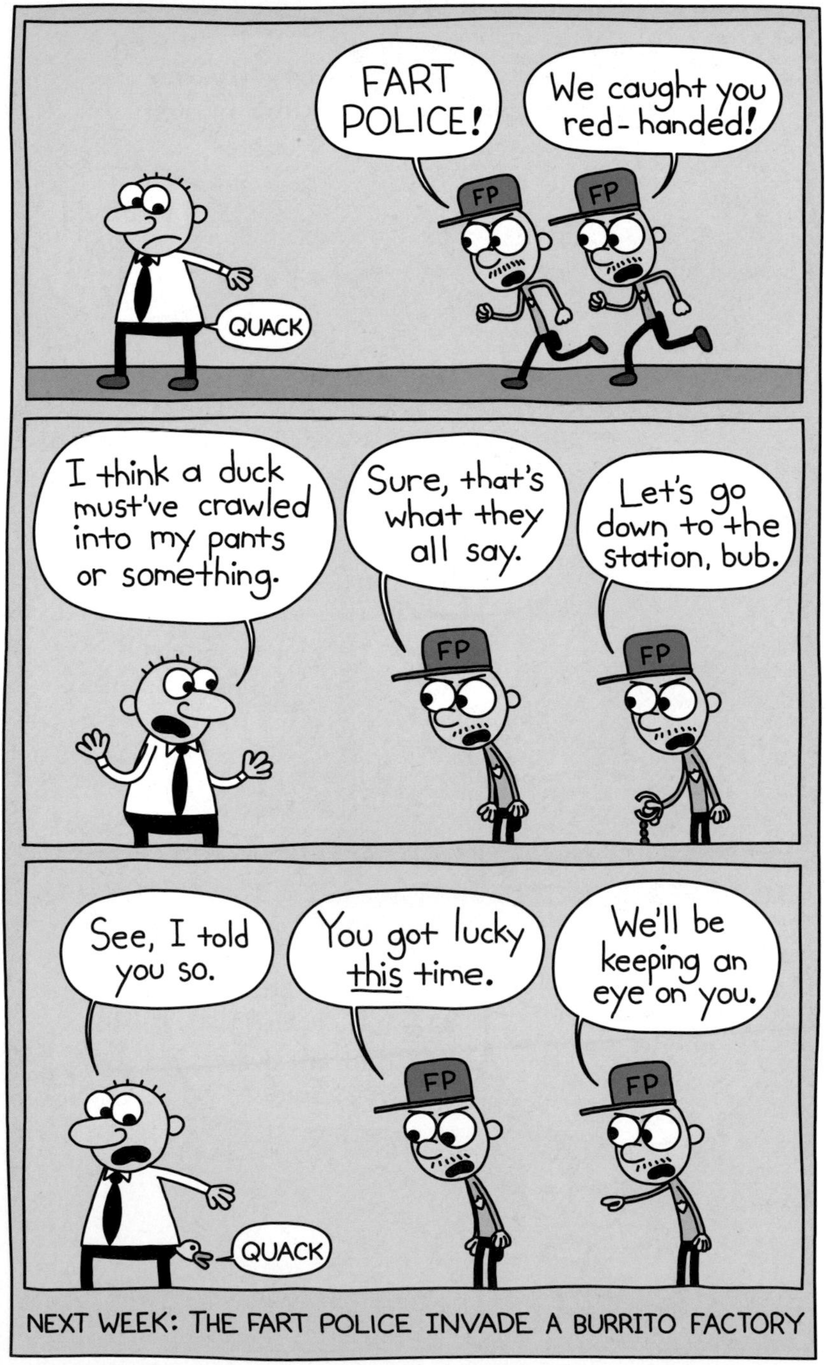
QUACK
FART POLICE!
We caught you red-handed!
I think a duck must've crawled into my pants or something.
Sure, that's what they all say.
Let's go down to the station, bub.
See, I told you so.
You got lucky this time.
We'll be keeping an eye on you.
QUACK
NEXT WEEK: THE FART POLICE INVADE A BURRITO FACTORY

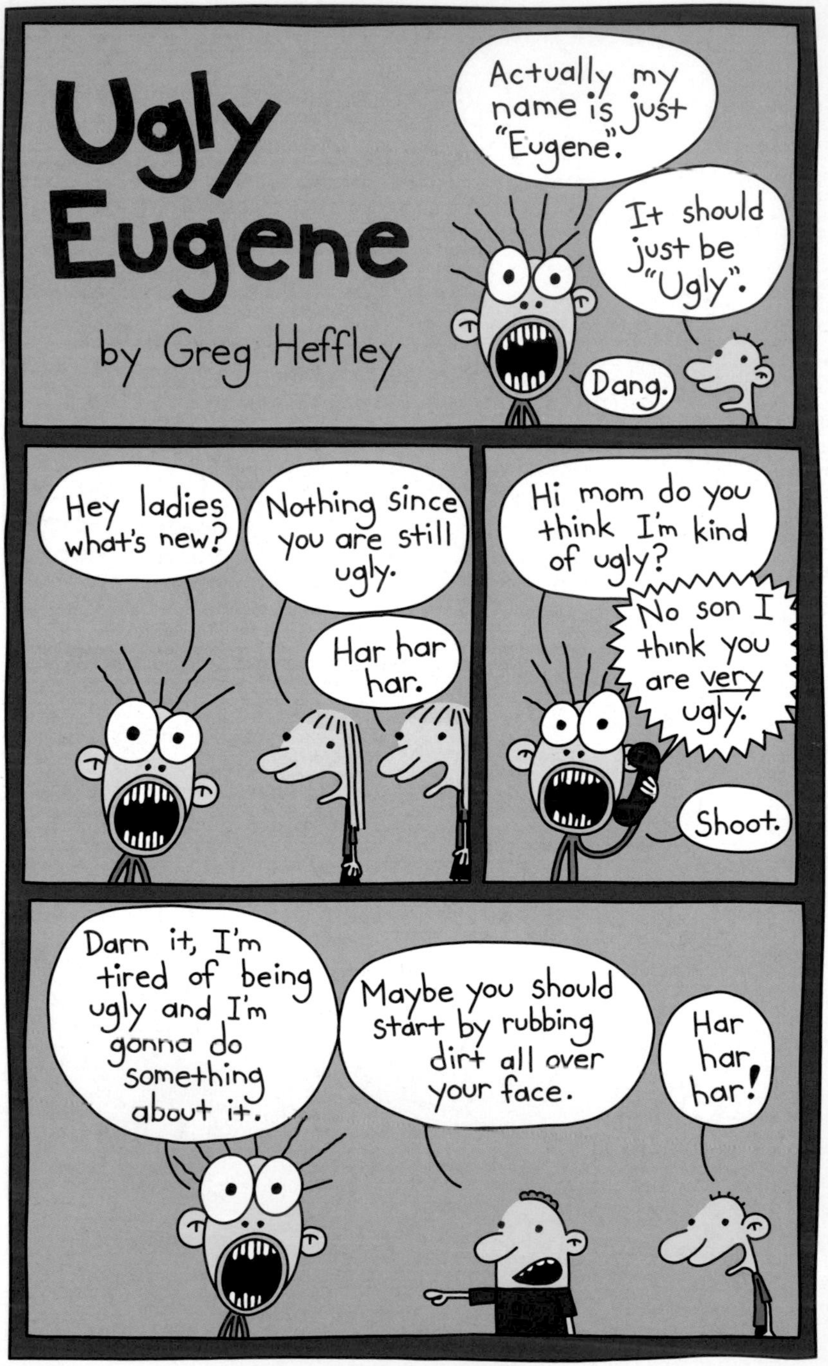
Ugly Eugene
by Greg Heffley
Actually my name is just "Eugene".
It should just be "Ugly".
Dang.
Hey ladies what's new?
Nothing since you are still ugly.
Har har har.
Hi mom do you think I'm kind of ugly?
No son I think you are very ugly.
Shoot.
Darn it, I'm tired of being ugly and I'm gonna do something about it.
Maybe you should start by rubbing dirt all over your face.
Har har har!

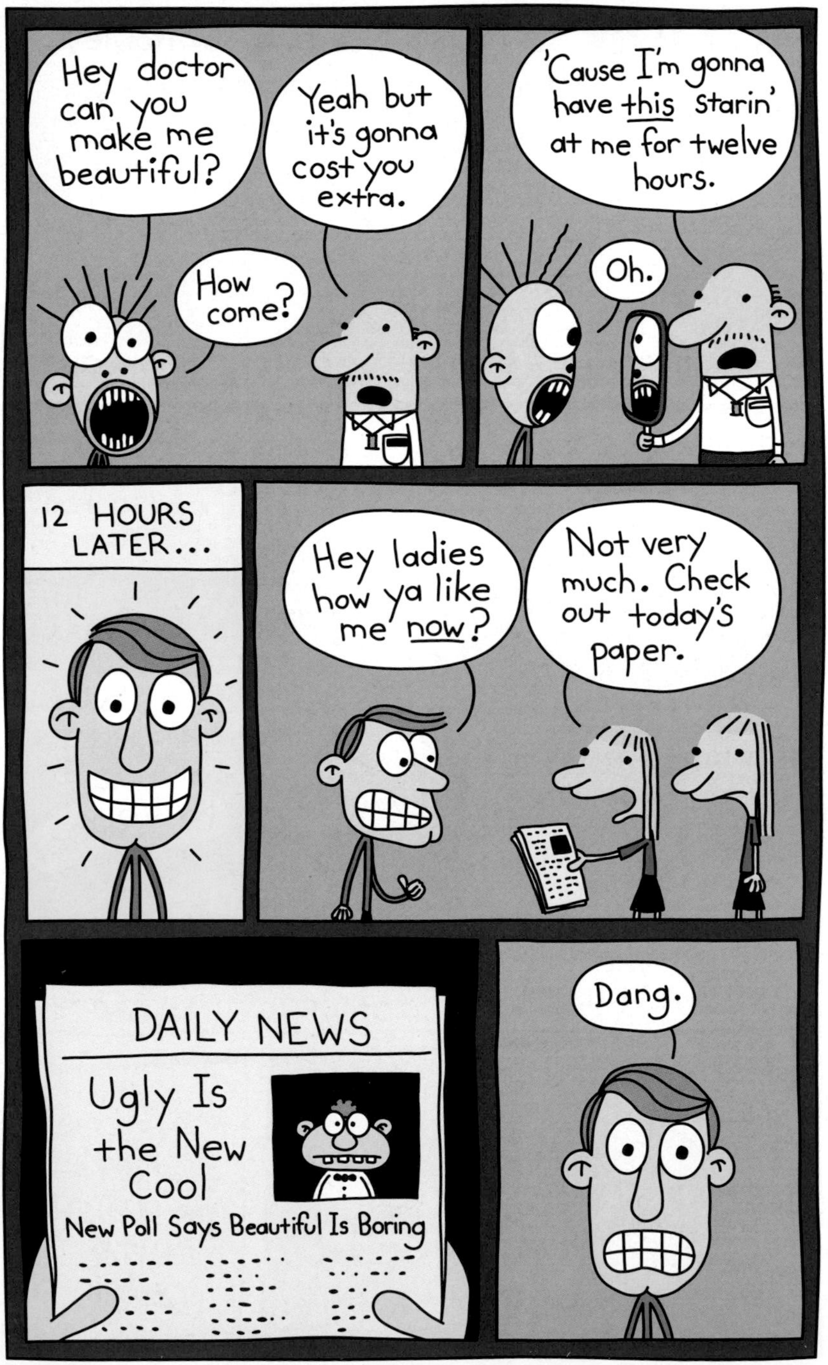
Hey doctor can you make me beautiful?
Yeah but it's gonna cost you extra.
How come?
'Cause I'm gonna have this starin' at me for twelve hours.
Oh.
12 HOURS LATER...
Hey ladies how ya like me now?
Not very much. Check out today's paper.
DAILY NEWS
Ugly Is the New Cool
New Poll Says Beautiful Is Boring
Dang.

# ACTION FIGHTERZ by Rowley

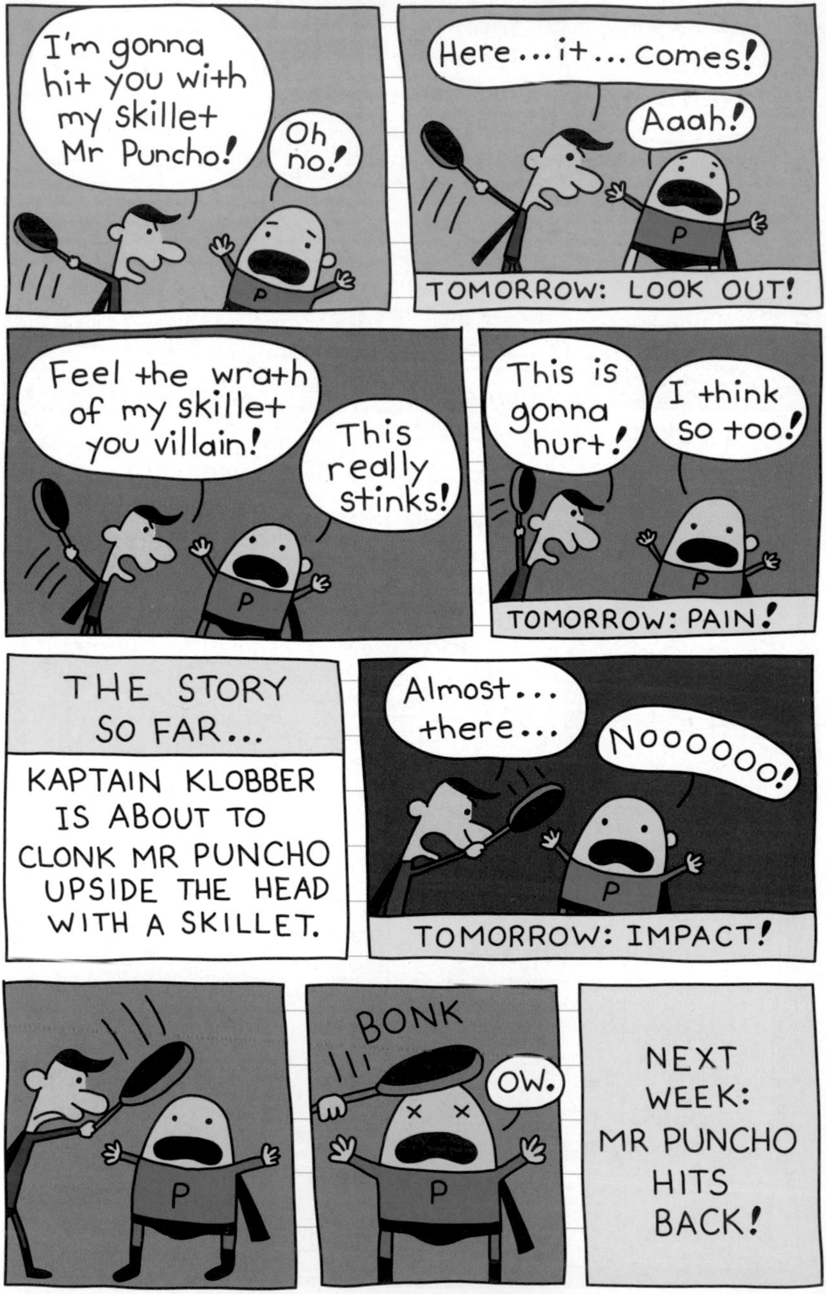
I'm gonna hit you with my skillet Mr Puncho!
Oh no!
Here... it... comes!
Aaah!
TOMORROW: LOOK OUT!
Feel the wrath of my skillet you villain!
This really stinks!
This is gonna hurt!
I think so too!
TOMORROW: PAIN!
THE STORY SO FAR...
KAPTAIN KLOBBER IS ABOUT TO CLONK MR PUNCHO UPSIDE THE HEAD WITH A SKILLET.
Almost... there...
Noooooo!
TOMORROW: IMPACT!
BONK
OW.
NEXT WEEK: MR PUNCHO HITS BACK!

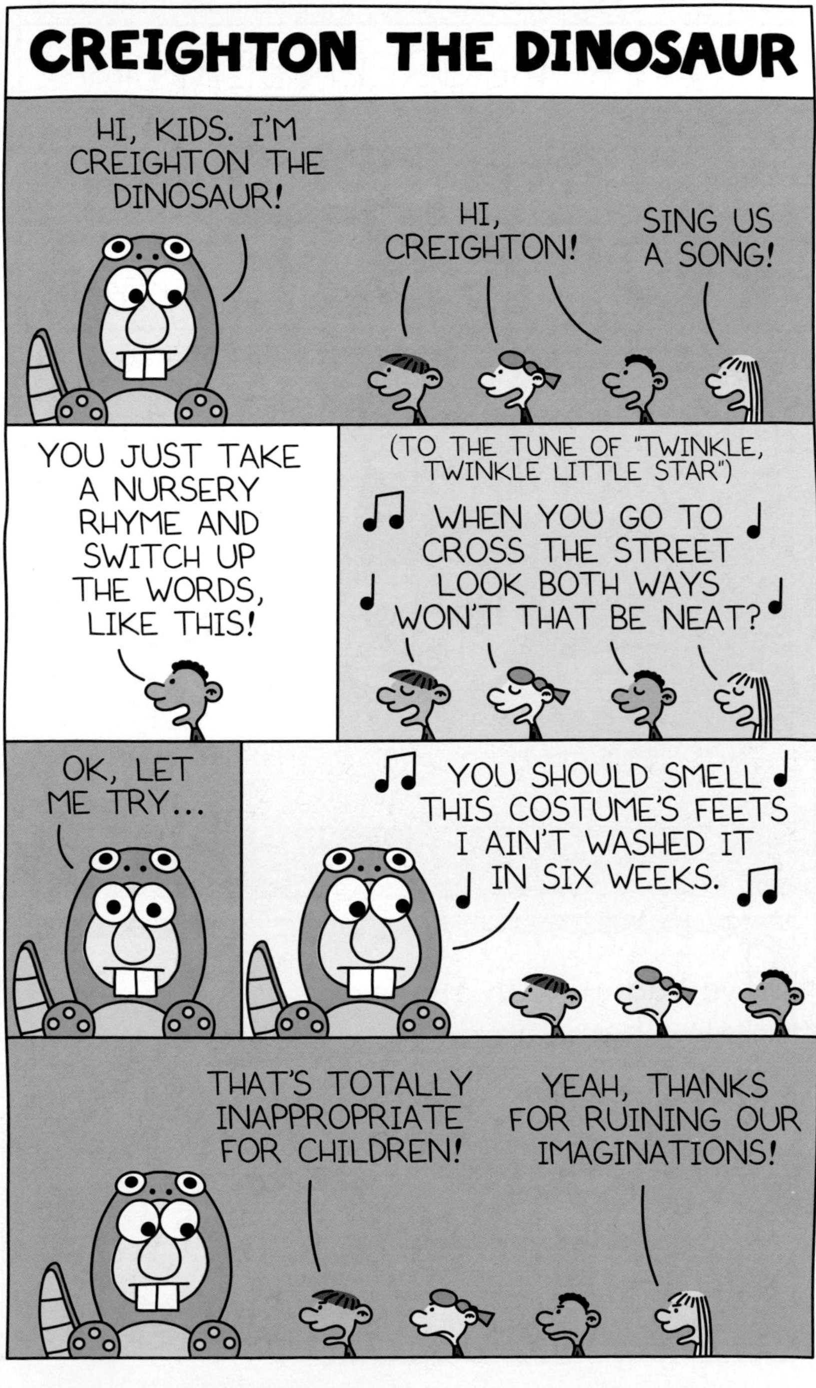
CREIGHTON THE DINOSAUR
HI, KIDS. I'M CREIGHTON THE DINOSAUR!
HI, CREIGHTON!
SING US A SONG!
YOU JUST TAKE A NURSERY RHYME AND SWITCH UP THE WORDS, LIKE THIS!
(TO THE TUNE OF "TWINKLE, TWINKLE LITTLE STAR")
WHEN YOU GO TO CROSS THE STREET LOOK BOTH WAYS WON'T THAT BE NEAT?
OK, LET ME TRY...
YOU SHOULD SMELL THIS COSTUME'S FEETS I AIN'T WASHED IT IN SIX WEEKS.
THAT'S TOTALLY INAPPROPRIATE FOR CHILDREN!
YEAH, THANKS FOR RUINING OUR IMAGINATIONS!

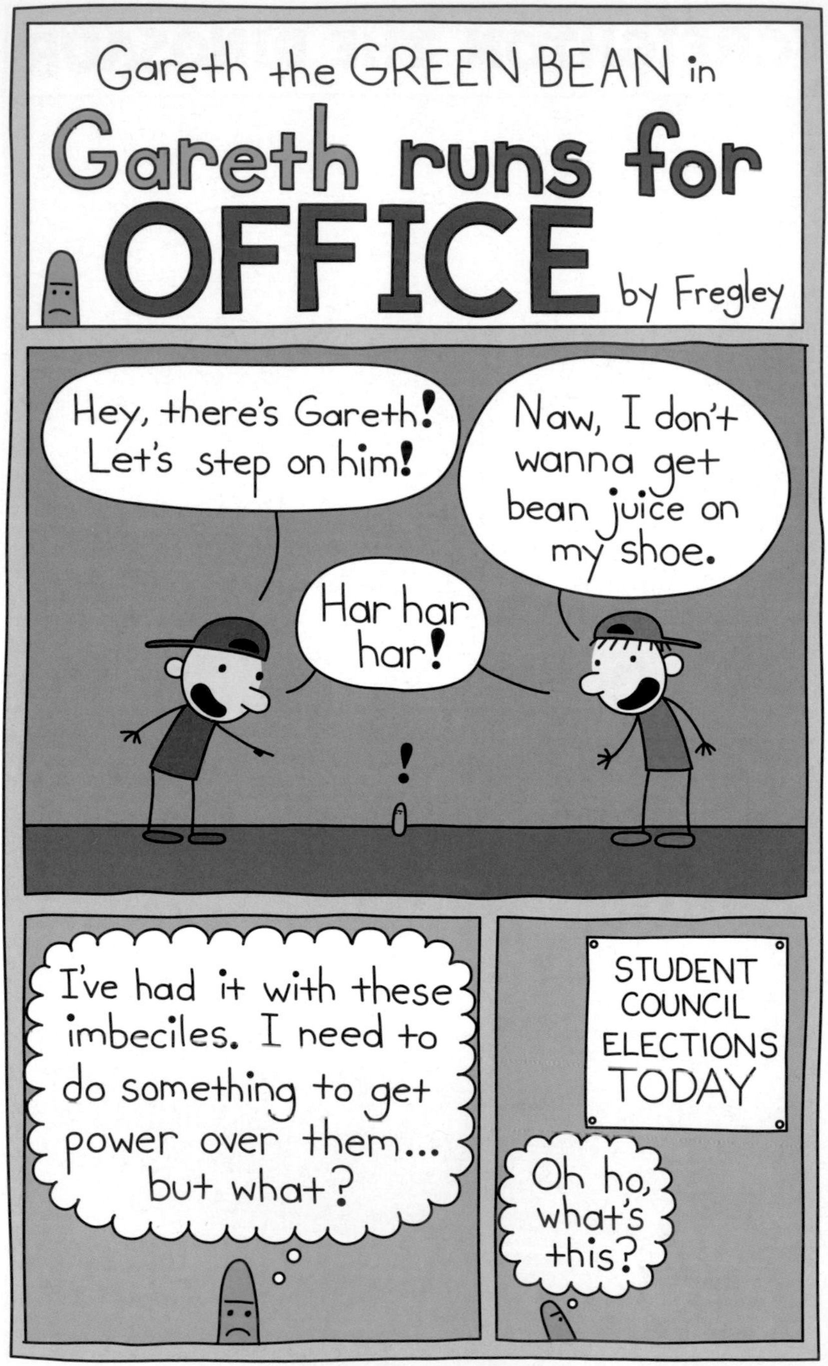
Gareth the GREEN BEAN in
Gareth runs for OFFICE
by Fregley
Hey, there's Gareth! Let's step on him!
Naw, I don't wanna get bean juice on my shoe.
Har har har!
!
I've had it with these imbeciles. I need to do something to get power over them... but what?
STUDENT COUNCIL ELECTIONS TODAY
Oh ho, what's this?

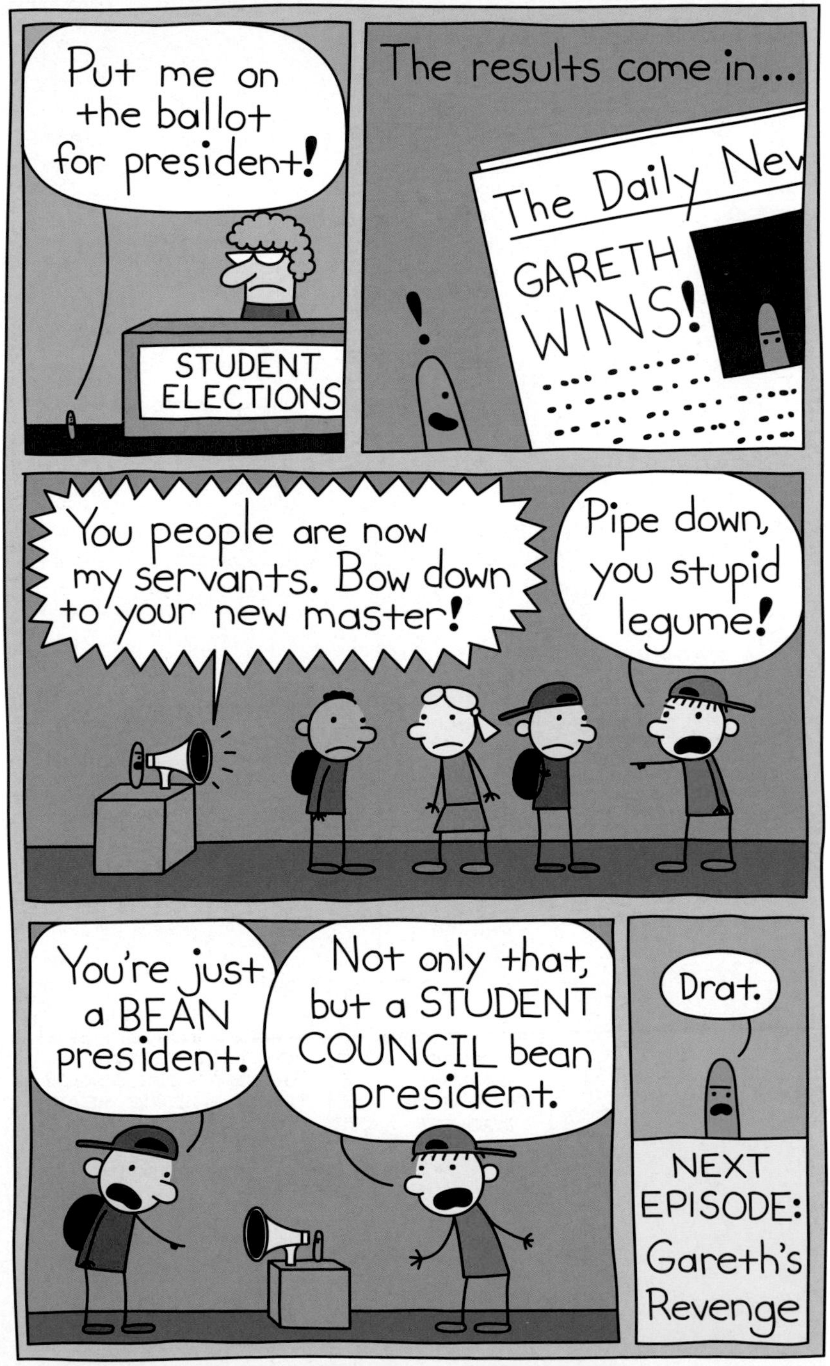
Put me on the ballot for president!
STUDENT ELECTIONS
The results come in...
The Daily New
GARETH WINS!
You people are now my servants. Bow down to your new master!
Pipe down, you stupid legume!
You're just a BEAN president.
Not only that, but a STUDENT COUNCIL bean president.
Drat.
NEXT EPISODE: Gareth's Revenge

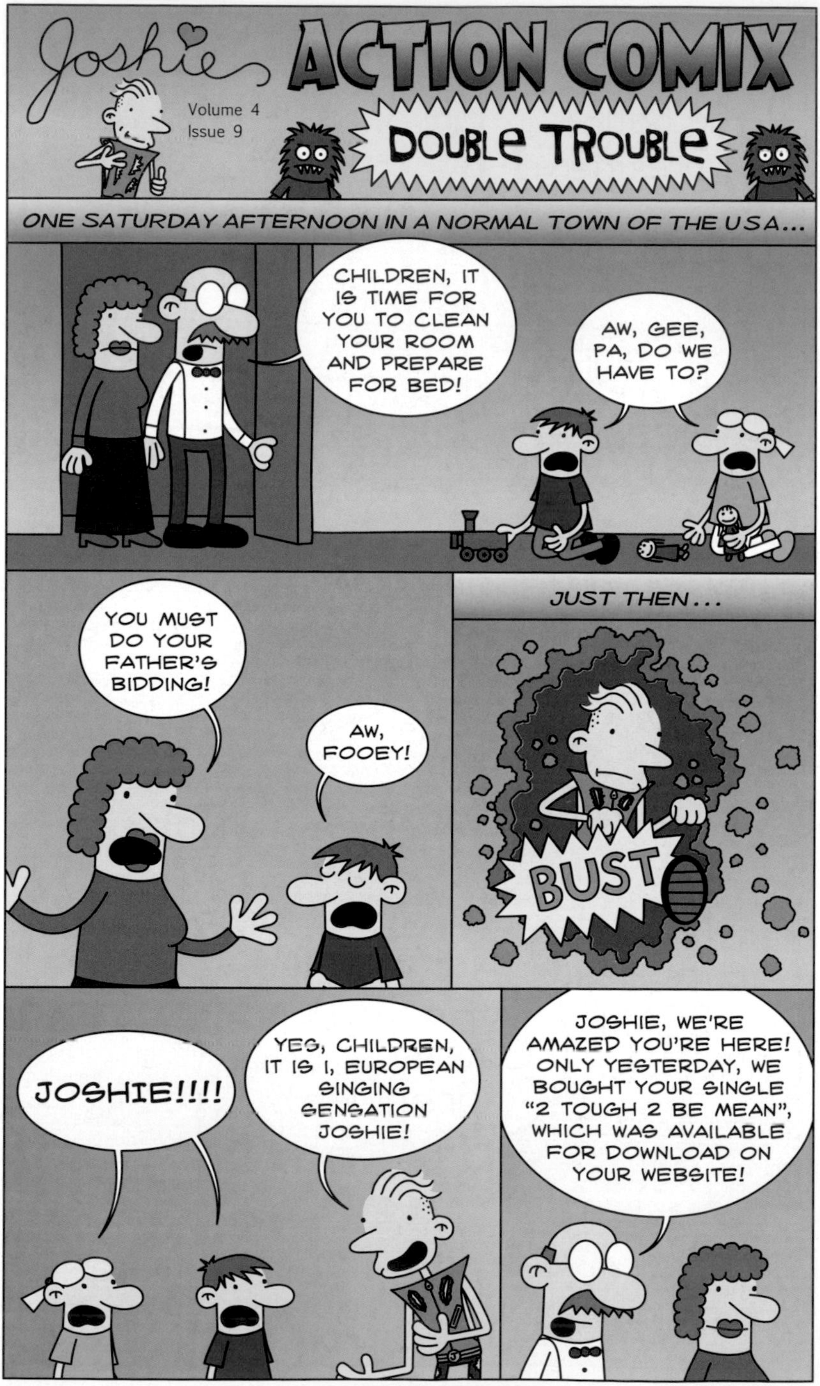
Joshie
ACTION COMIX
Volume 4
Issue 9
DOUBLE TROUBLE
ONE SATURDAY AFTERNOON IN A NORMAL TOWN OF THE USA...
CHILDREN, IT IS TIME FOR YOU TO CLEAN YOUR ROOM AND PREPARE FOR BED!
AW, GEE, PA, DO WE HAVE TO?
YOU MUST DO YOUR FATHER'S BIDDING!
AW, FOOEY!
JUST THEN...
BUST
JOSHIE!!!!
YES, CHILDREN, IT IS I, EUROPEAN SINGING SENSATION JOSHIE!
JOSHIE, WE'RE AMAZED YOU'RE HERE! ONLY YESTERDAY, WE BOUGHT YOUR SINGLE "2 TOUGH 2 BE MEAN", WHICH WAS AVAILABLE FOR DOWNLOAD ON YOUR WEBSITE!

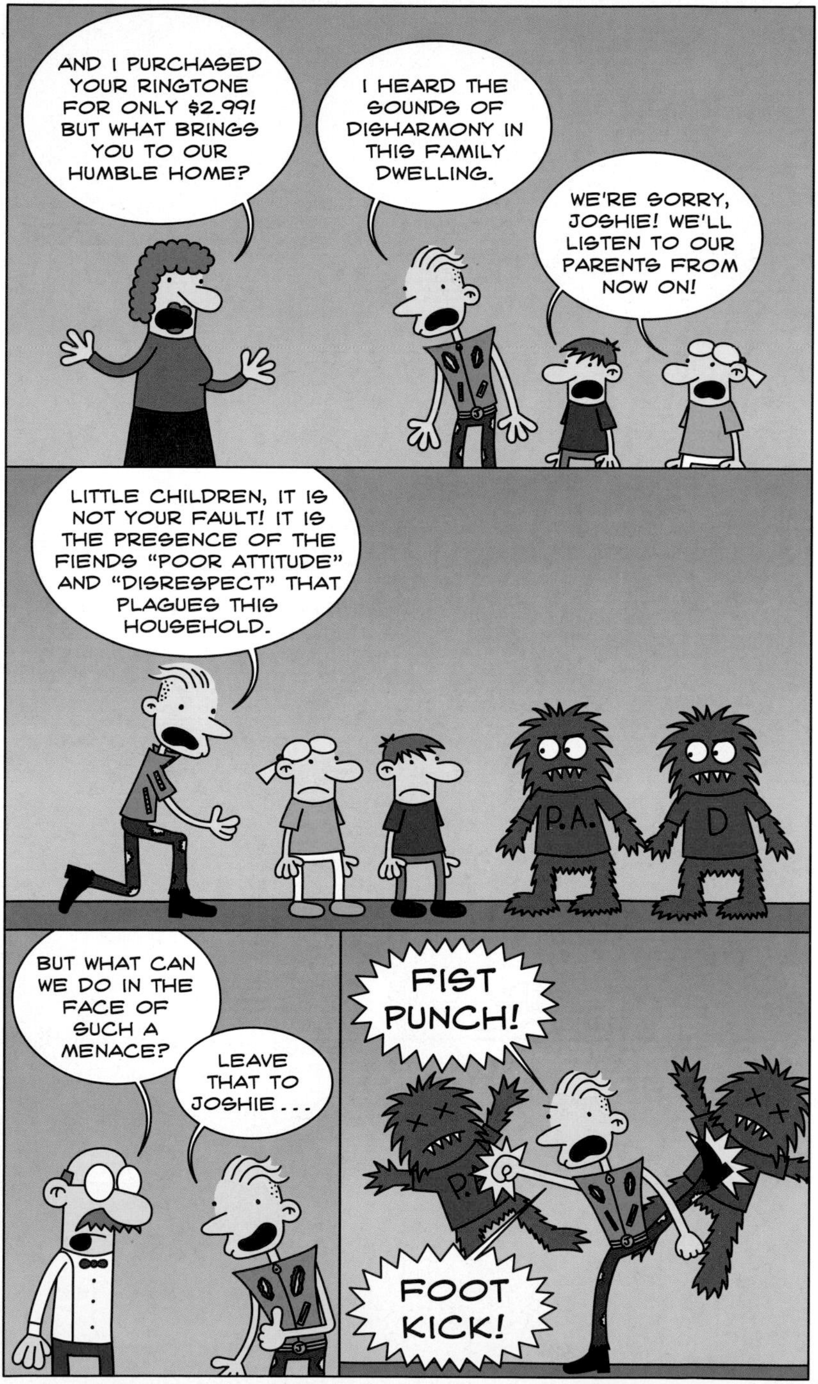
AND I PURCHASED YOUR RINGTONE FOR ONLY $2.99! BUT WHAT BRINGS YOU TO OUR HUMBLE HOME?
I HEARD THE SOUNDS OF DISHARMONY IN THIS FAMILY DWELLING.
WE'RE SORRY, JOSHIE! WE'LL LISTEN TO OUR PARENTS FROM NOW ON!
LITTLE CHILDREN, IT IS NOT YOUR FAULT! IT IS THE PRESENCE OF THE FIENDS "POOR ATTITUDE" AND "DISRESPECT" THAT PLAGUES THIS HOUSEHOLD.
P.A.
D
BUT WHAT CAN WE DO IN THE FACE OF SUCH A MENACE?
LEAVE THAT TO JOSHIE . . .
FIST PUNCH!
FOOT KICK!

TURN THE PAGE!

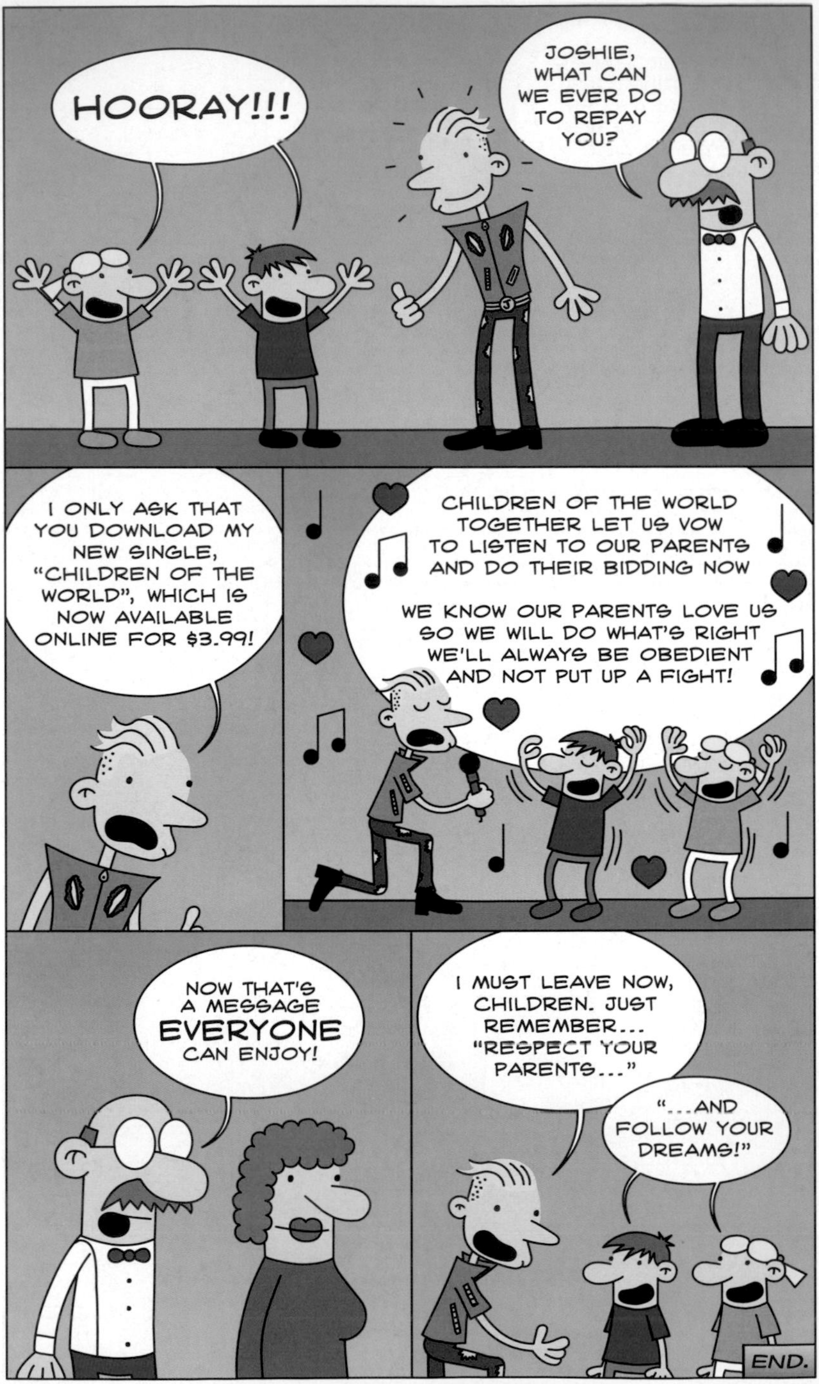
HOORAY!!!
JOSHIE, WHAT CAN WE EVER DO TO REPAY YOU?
I ONLY ASK THAT YOU DOWNLOAD MY NEW SINGLE, "CHILDREN OF THE WORLD", WHICH IS NOW AVAILABLE ONLINE FOR $3.99!
CHILDREN OF THE WORLD TOGETHER LET US VOW TO LISTEN TO OUR PARENTS AND DO THEIR BIDDING NOW
WE KNOW OUR PARENTS LOVE US SO WE WILL DO WHAT'S RIGHT WE'LL ALWAYS BE OBEDIENT AND NOT PUT UP A FIGHT!
NOW THAT'S A MESSAGE EVERYONE CAN ENJOY!
I MUST LEAVE NOW, CHILDREN. JUST REMEMBER... "RESPECT YOUR PARENTS..."
"...AND FOLLOW YOUR DREAMS!"
END.

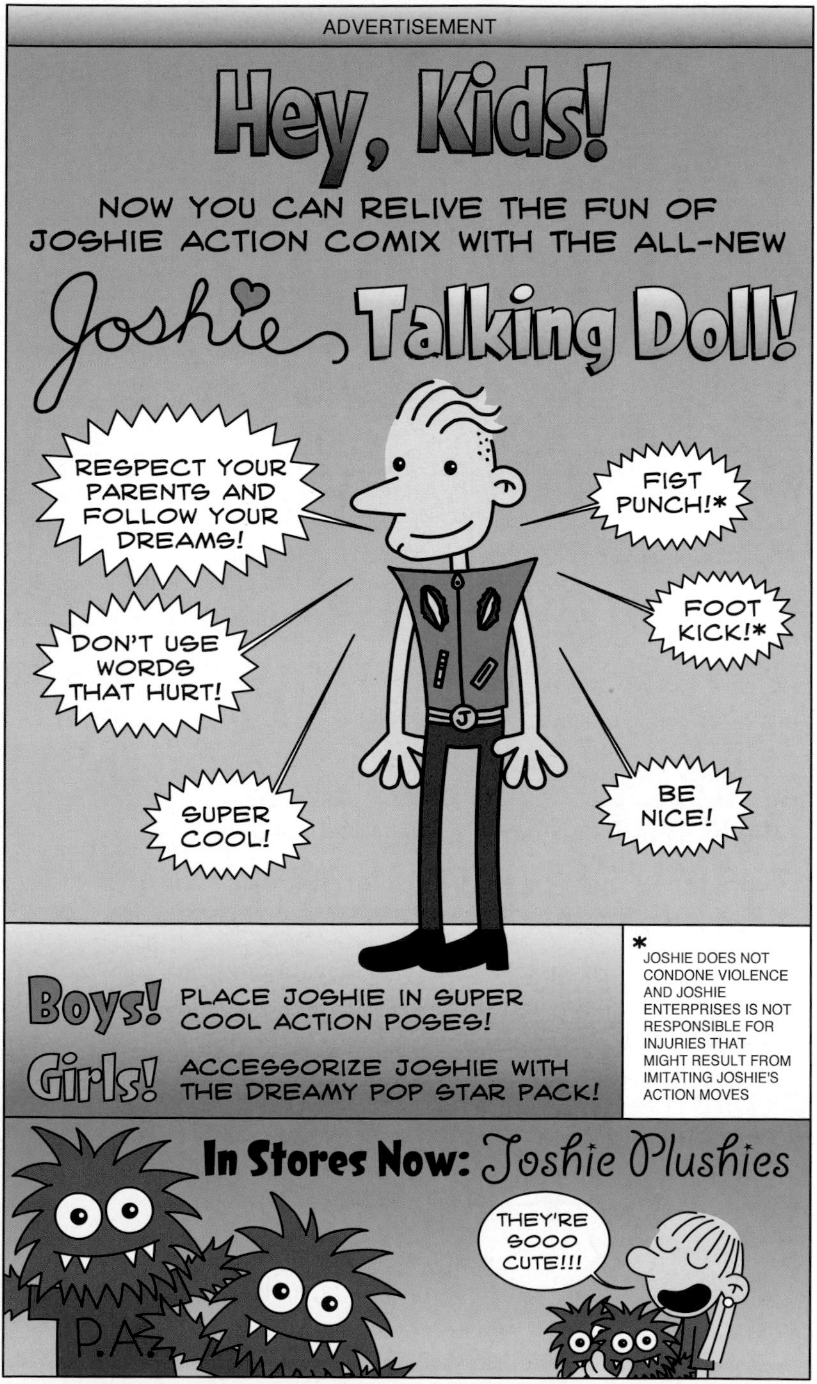
ADVERTISEMENT
Hey, Kids!
NOW YOU CAN RELIVE THE FUN OF JOSHIE ACTION COMIX WITH THE ALL-NEW
Joshie Talking Doll!
RESPECT YOUR PARENTS AND FOLLOW YOUR DREAMS!
FIST PUNCH!*
DON'T USE WORDS THAT HURT!
FOOT KICK!*
SUPER COOL!
BE NICE!
J
Boys! PLACE JOSHIE IN SUPER COOL ACTION POSES!
Girls! ACCESSORIZE JOSHIE WITH THE DREAMY POP STAR PACK!
* JOSHIE DOES NOT CONDONE VIOLENCE AND JOSHIE ENTERPRISES IS NOT RESPONSIBLE FOR INJURIES THAT MIGHT RESULT FROM IMITATING JOSHIE'S ACTION MOVES
In Stores Now: Joshie Plushies
THEY'RE SOOO CUTE!!!
P.A.

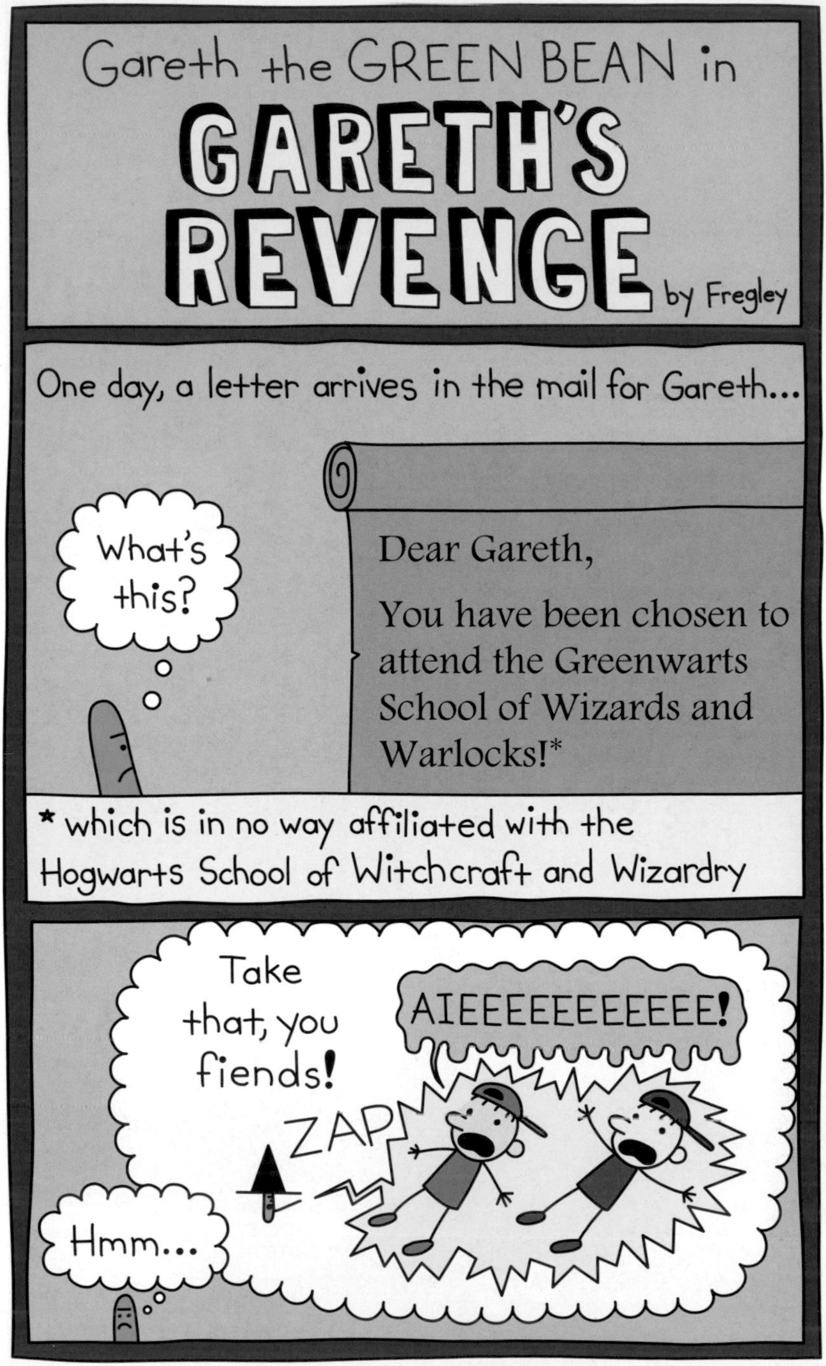
Gareth the GREEN BEAN in
GARETH'S REVENGE
by Fregley
One day, a letter arrives in the mail for Gareth...
What's this?
Dear Gareth,
You have been chosen to attend the Greenwarts School of Wizards and Warlocks!*
* which is in no way affiliated with the Hogwarts School of Witchcraft and Wizardry
Take that, you fiends!
AIEEEEEEEEEEEE!
ZAP
Hmm...

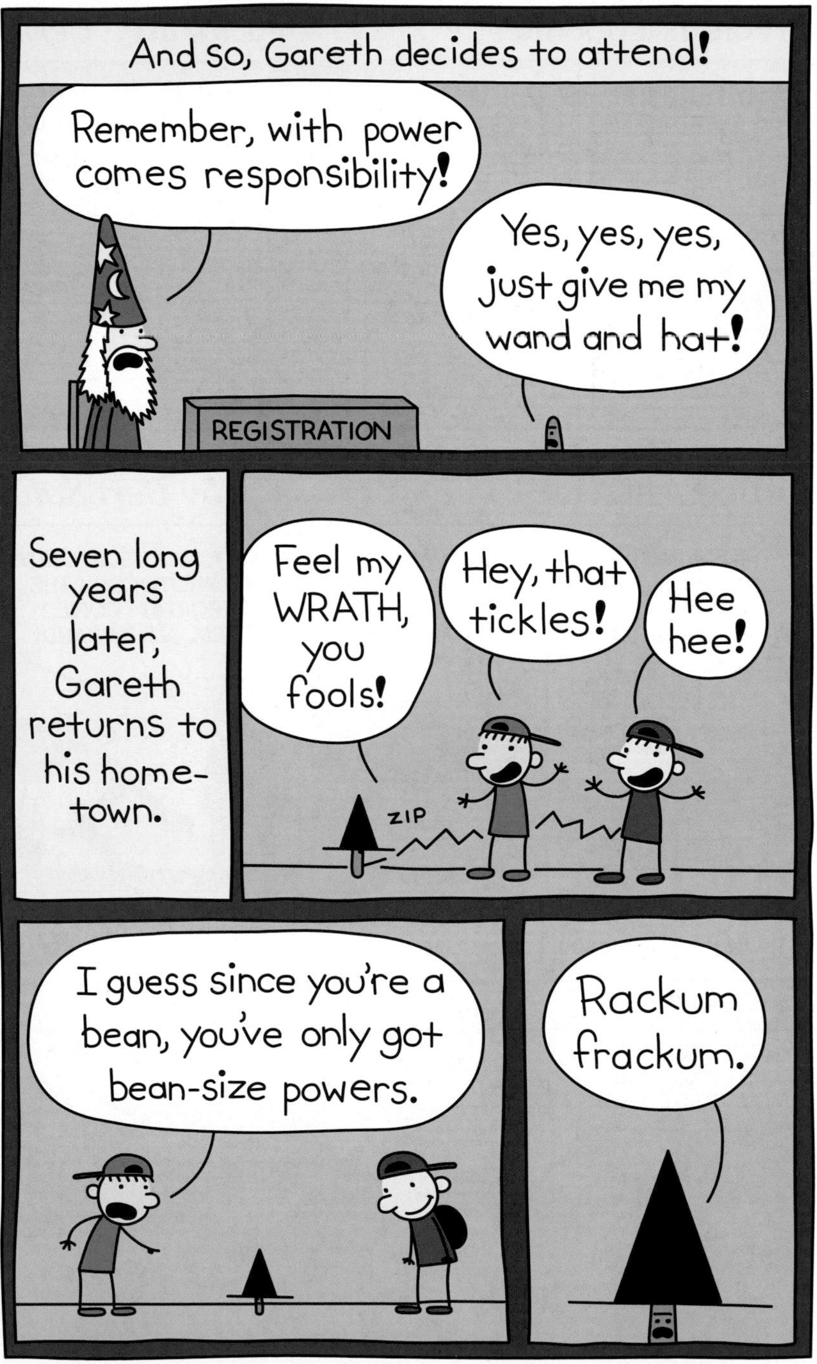
And so, Gareth decides to attend!
Remember, with power comes responsibility!
Yes, yes, yes, just give me my wand and hat!
REGISTRATION
Seven long years later, Gareth returns to his home-town.
Feel my WRATH, you fools!
ZIP
Hey, that tickles!
Hee hee!
I guess since you're a bean, you've only got bean-size powers.
Rackum frackum.

Precious Poochie *by Eldridge Perro*

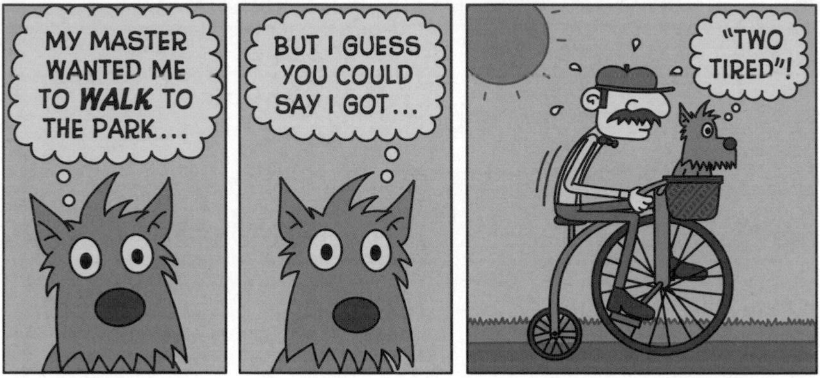
MY MASTER WANTED ME TO **WALK** TO THE PARK…
BUT I GUESS YOU COULD SAY I GOT…
"TWO TIRED"!

Office Antix *by Bert Salas*

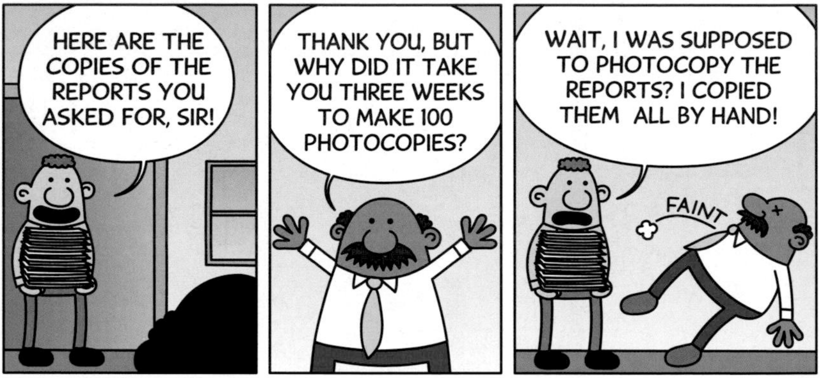
HERE ARE THE COPIES OF THE REPORTS YOU ASKED FOR, SIR!
THANK YOU, BUT WHY DID IT TAKE YOU THREE WEEKS TO MAKE 100 PHOTOCOPIES?
WAIT, I WAS SUPPOSED TO PHOTOCOPY THE REPORTS? I COPIED THEM ALL BY HAND!
FAINT

Oh, Grampsie! *by Beverly Bliss*

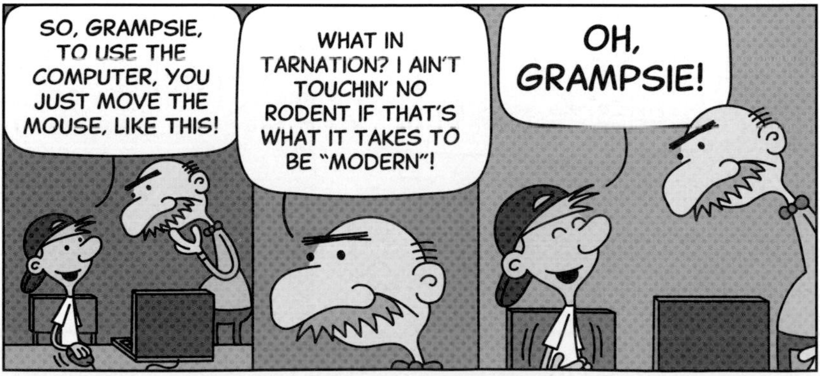
SO, GRAMPSIE, TO USE THE COMPUTER, YOU JUST MOVE THE MOUSE, LIKE THIS!
WHAT IN TARNATION? I AIN'T TOUCHIN' NO RODENT IF THAT'S WHAT IT TAKES TO BE "MODERN"!
OH, GRAMPSIE!

# DIARY of an Awesome, Friendly Kid

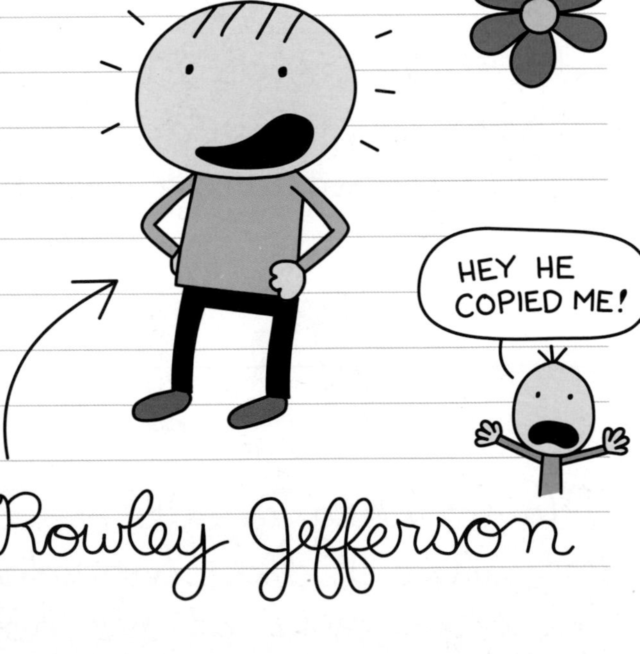
HEY HE COPIED ME!

by Rowley Jefferson

Dear Diary,
Today I spent my allowance money on a gift for Greg. He is my very best friend in the whole wide world so I got a locket we could both wear to make it official.

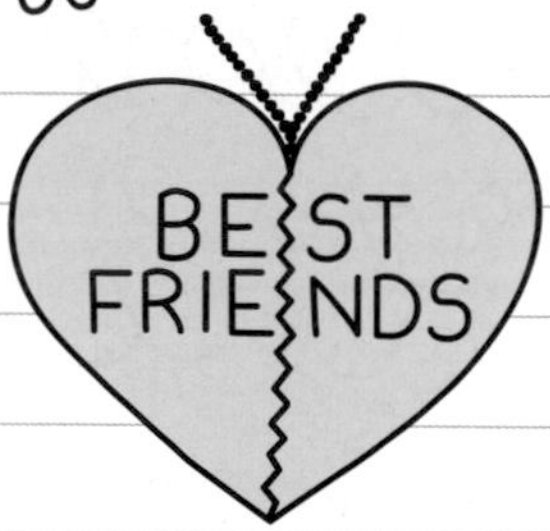
BEST
FRIENDS

It turns out Greg doesn't really like jewelry, but I'm still gonna wear my half.

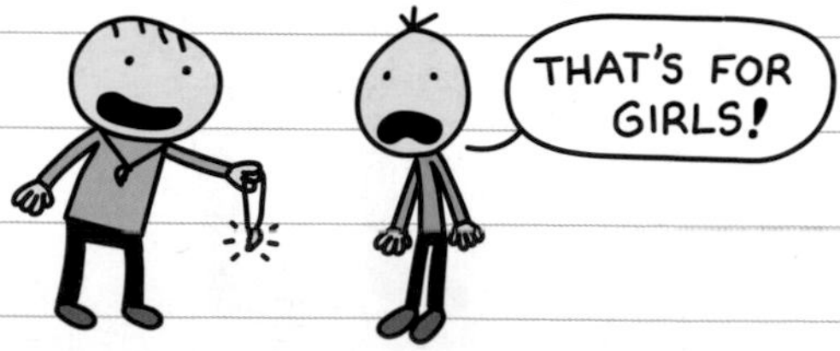
THAT'S FOR GIRLS!

Maybe Greg is still mad at me for what I did Saturday when I slept over at his house.

He caught me in the bathroom trying on his retainer, and he yelled at me for ten whole minutes.

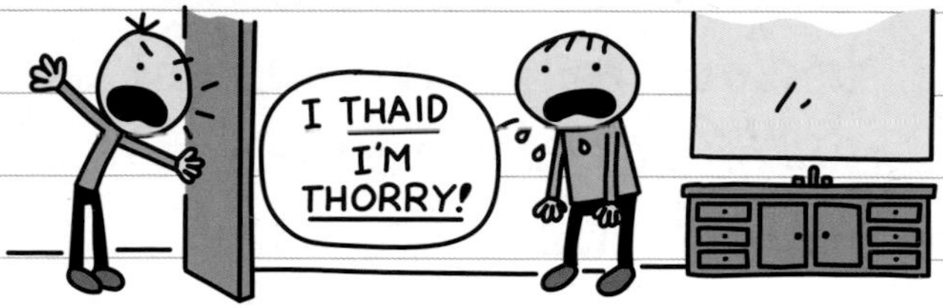
I THAID I'M THORRY!

Sometimes Greg gets frustrated with me and calls me bad names, but I don't mind too much. I still know I'm an awesome, friendly kid because my mom and dad are always telling me so.

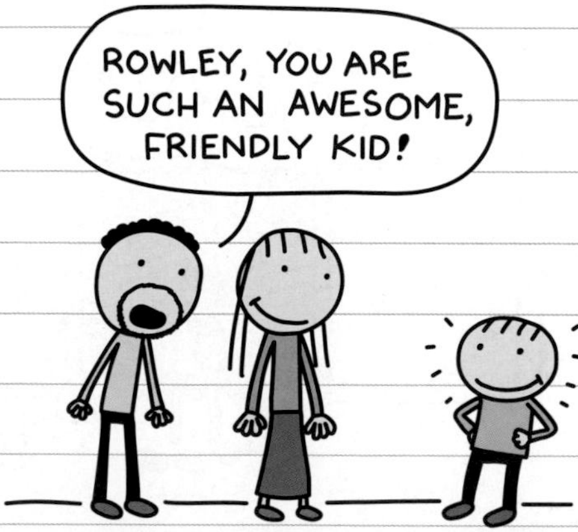
ROWLEY, YOU ARE SUCH AN AWESOME, FRIENDLY KID!

Dear Diary,
I sure am glad to have Greg as my best friend because he is always giving me tips about school. Like today he told me the boys' and girls' locker rooms in the gym were labeled wrong.

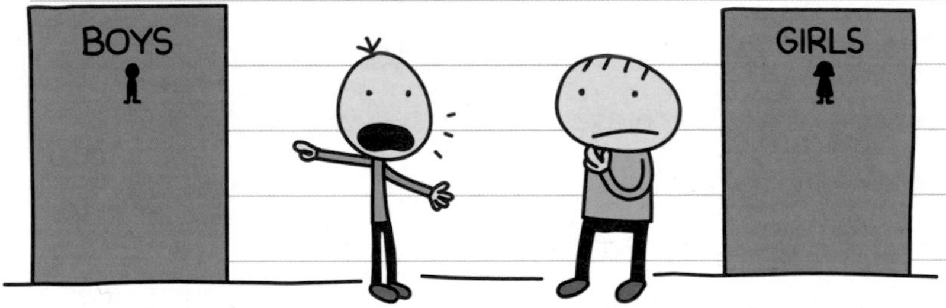
BOYS
GIRLS

Well, it turns out Greg got his facts mixed up on that one.

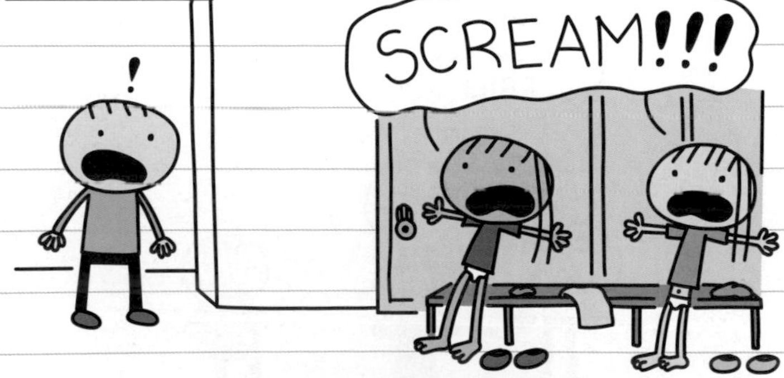
!
SCREAM!!!

I got sent to the principal's office and after that I found Greg to tell him the doors weren't labeled wrong after all.

Greg actually makes those kinds of mistakes a <u>lot</u>. Last year Greg told me the next day was pajama day at school, and it turns out he was wrong.

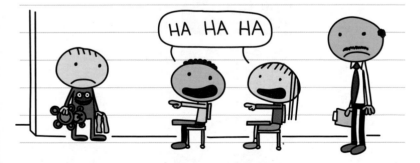

Luckily Greg forgot to wear his pajamas to school so he didn't get embarrassed too.

Sometimes Greg is a little grouchy, but I am always doing things to cheer him up.

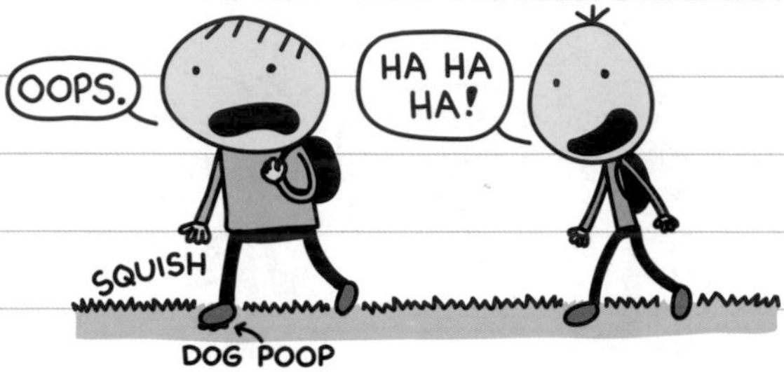
OOPS.
HA HA HA!
SQUISH
DOG POOP

So now you can see why me and Greg are such good pals and why we will always be

# BEST FRIENDS

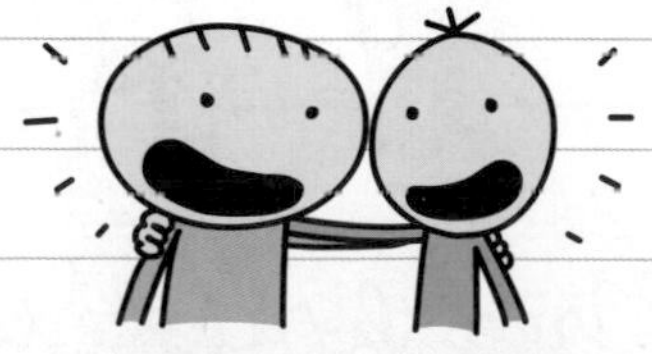

# 4-EVER

# Create your own COVER

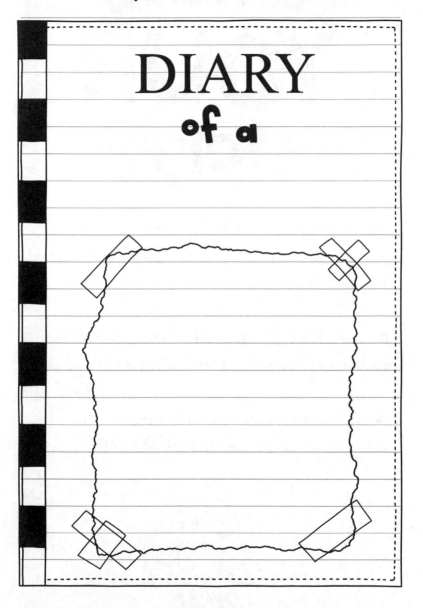

DIARY
of a

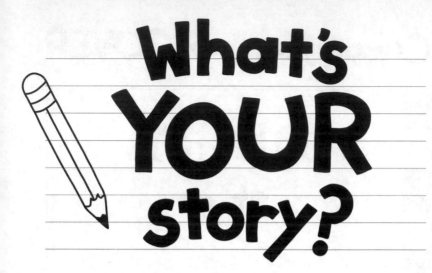

# What's YOUR story?

Use the rest of this book to keep a daily journal, write a novel, draw comic strips, or tell your life story.

But whatever you do, make sure you put this book someplace safe after you finish it.

Because when you're rich and famous, this thing is gonna be worth a FORTUNE.

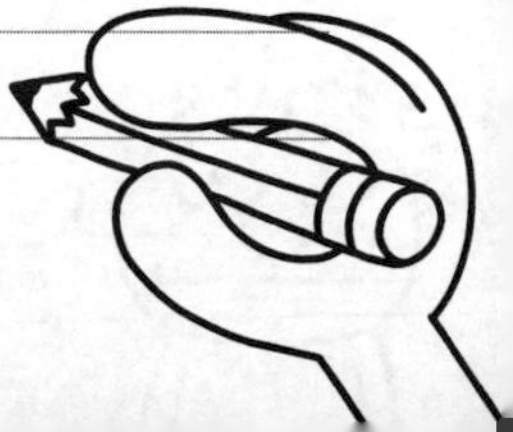

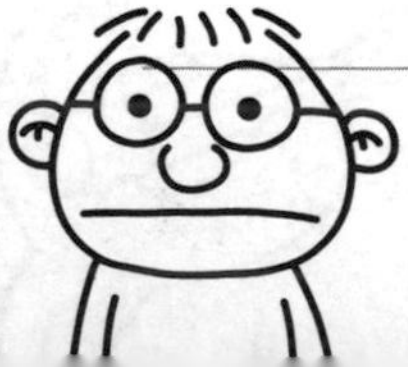

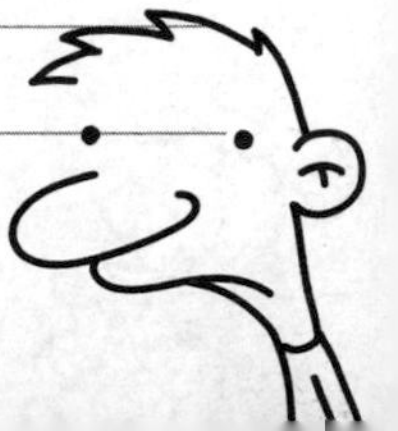

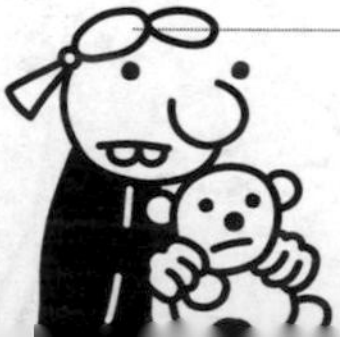

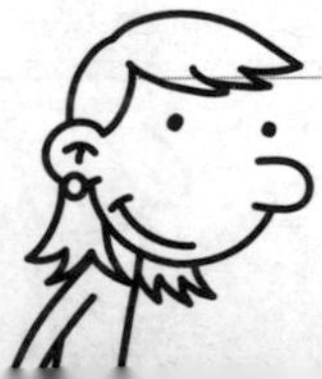

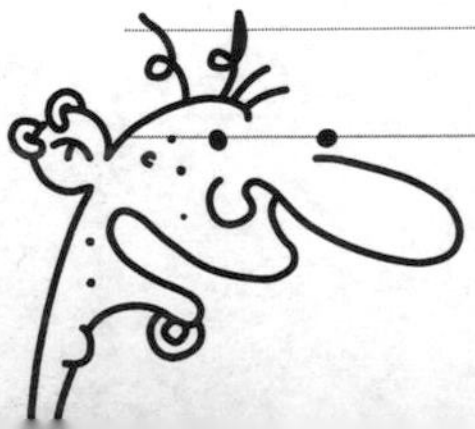

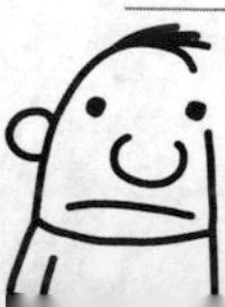

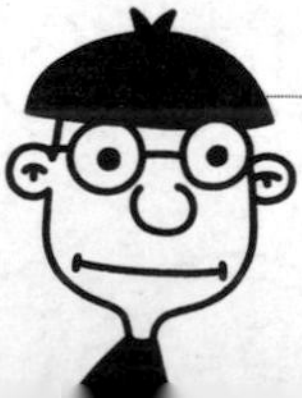

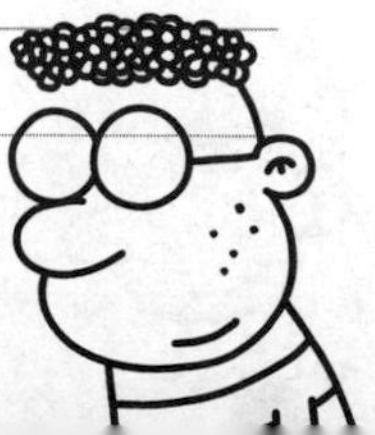

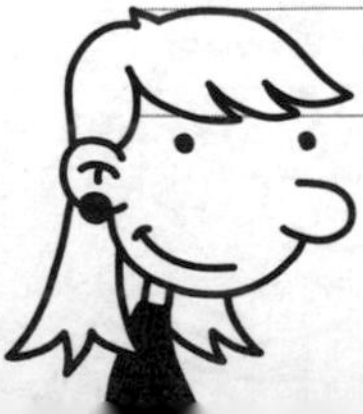

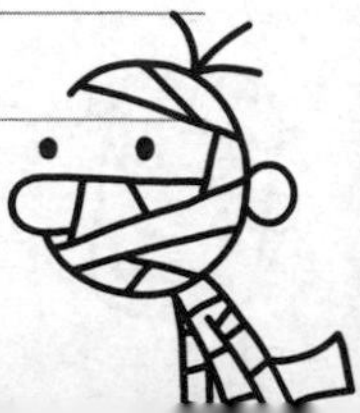

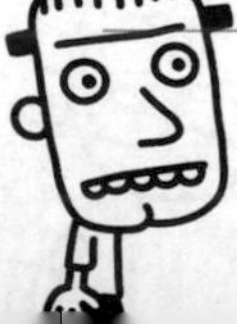

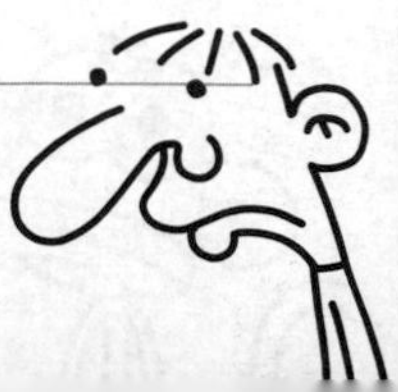

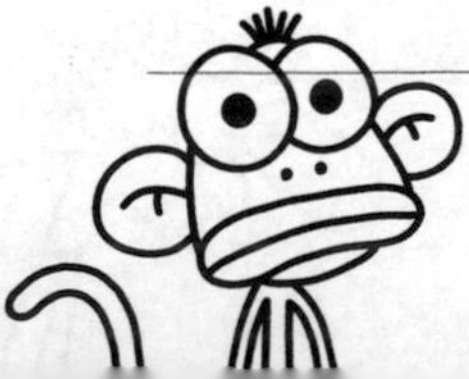

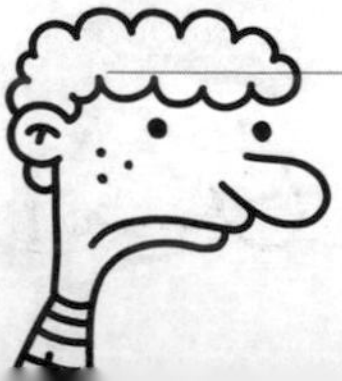

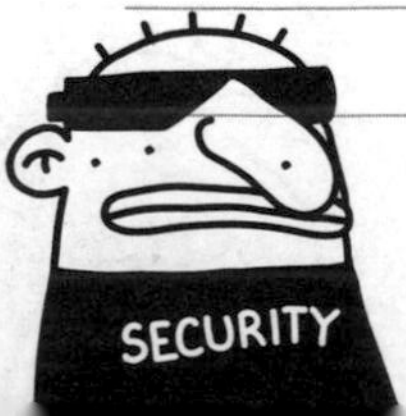
SECURITY

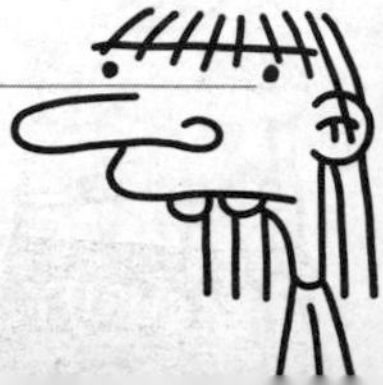

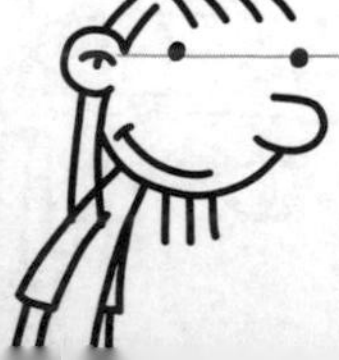

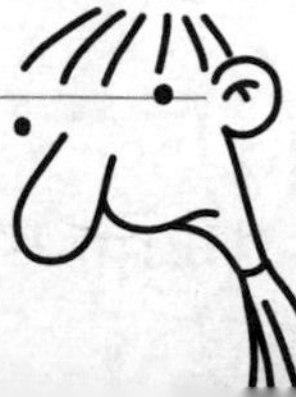

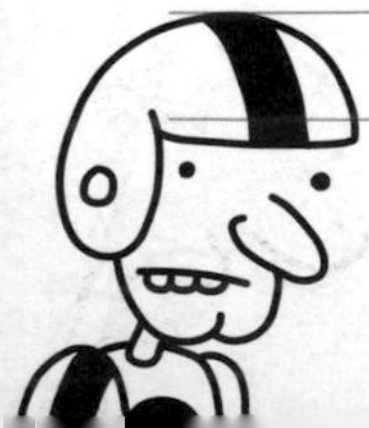

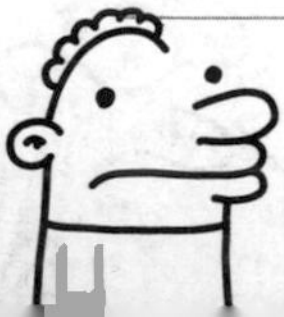

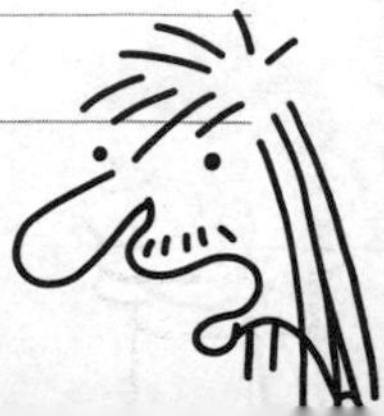

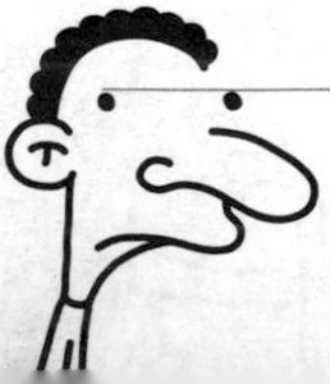

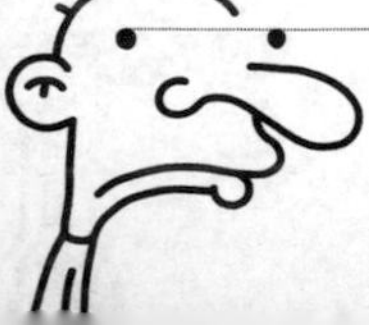

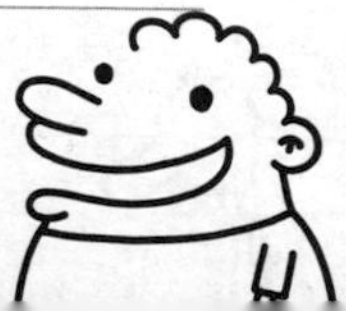

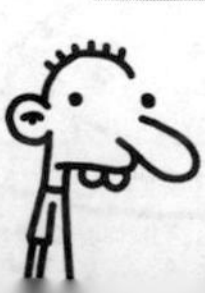

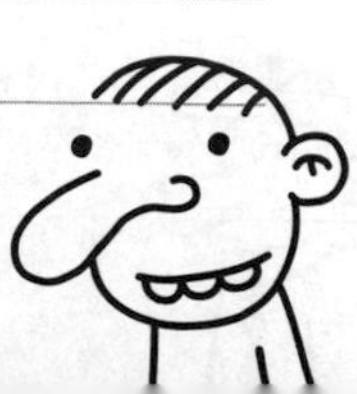

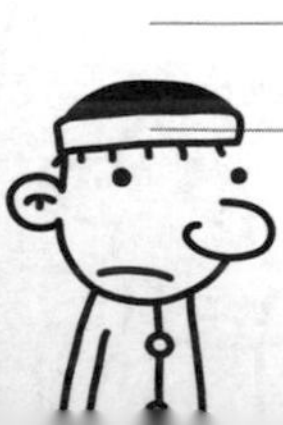

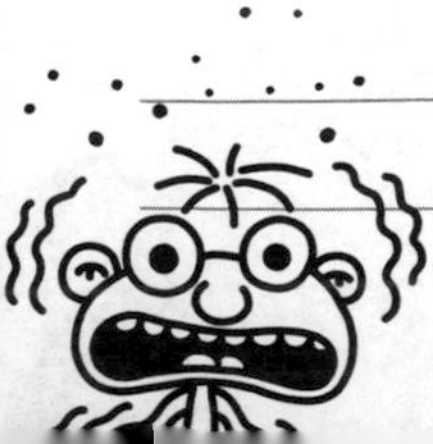

## ABOUT THE AUTHOR

(THAT'S YOU)

## ACKNOWLEDGEMENTS

(THE PEOPLE YOU WANT TO THANK)